Blood of Gansbaai

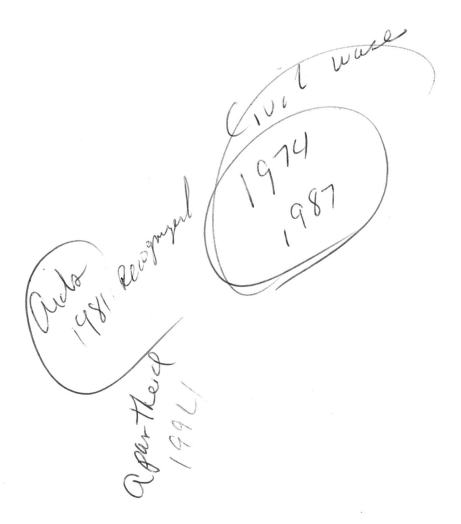

To order additional copies, please contact us.
BookSurge, LLC
www.booksurge.com
1-866-308-6235
orders@booksurge.com

FJ STURMAN

BLOOD OF
GANSBAAI

INSPIRED BY TRUE EVENTS

2006

Blood of Gansbaai

What an injustice it would be, not to hear the roar of a lion, the singing of a songbird in the early morning light, or not to climb a great chestnut tree on a warm summer's eve. What would it be like to exist no more, to never walk in green fields or swim in a turquoise-blue ocean? What would it be like to know that you are the last of your species, and no others will walk the paths you have walked?

F J Sturman

For My Son
Caden Joseph Sturman
Whom I'll Love Forever

PROLOGUE
South Africa, 1940

Ten-year-old Conrad Sinclair followed closely behind his father. The Afrikaans man and his son moved quickly around the rocks. Ahead of them was the mighty Cape Lion.

The lion moved with stealth amongst the rocks of the Drakensberge Mountain Range. Conrad looked ahead at the rock formations as he quickly followed his father. The sun's glare and the heat of the day were wearing on him. He brushed his dirty-blond hair from his eyes. There in the distance was the Cape Lion making his way up a steep incline of jagged rocks. And then, the lion was gone again.

"Come, Conrad. He is moving again." His father turned. "Let us meet this beast," he said with a wink and a smile.

Moments later, the lion stood upon the mountain cliff looking down onto his domain and the man and boy who hunted him. The Cape Lion, with his large, black mane and larger-than-life-presence, knew the great changing was upon him. The hot Cape wind blew on his black mane as he stood with pride, waiting for his pursuers. As the moon began to cross before the sun's path, the afternoon's scalding light began to dim. Conrad looked to the sun, and for the first time in his life, he saw the moon making its way across the heavens.

"Father! Father, look to the sun!" Conrad cried as they made their way along the rocky path before them.

"It's an omen, Conrad." His father squinted his eyes, looking at the beginning of the eclipse of the sun. "There he waits for us." Conrad looked ahead to the rocks, and there, no further than twenty feet away, was the Cape Lion, sitting on a large rock cliff, just above the path. Conrad followed his father as they made their way closer, his father silently wondering why the beast was waiting, thinking it an ambush. Conrad's heart began to race as he looked into the lion's gaze. His father surveyed the area and readied his musket.

As the lion looked into young Conrad's eyes, the boy felt the lion's spirit: They became locked, the lion and the boy, and before long, Conrad felt as if a change had happened. His heart wasn't racing anymore. His mind was calm and his thoughts were at peace. He knew the lion's thoughts as they watched each other.

The musket roared as thunder, knocking young Conrad from his feet. Falling to the ground, he saw the lion's body fall, dead. Conrad looked at the dead lion and was saddened, and began to cry. He was the last of his species.

***

As the sun darkened into eclipse, the Mamzibi warriors of Southern Africa looked to the sky of ill omen. With the killing of their spiritual protector, they knew troubled times were upon them: Famine, drought, sickness and death would now come to the land and its people. The great changing, as told by their forefathers, was upon them and Africa would never be the same.

CHAPTER 1

Fifty-two years later, the same Cape breeze blew from the Southern Atlantic swells, sweeping across the Cape of Good Hope and into the Drakensberge Mountain Range. It was hotter than most seasons in Africa and summer was ushering in more changes than the weather. Jessica Sinclair was far from her homeland of South Africa and even further still from the safety of her family. Angola was a diversified land made up of dry desert plains and green brush. She felt for the people who had undergone years of turmoil from greedy military leaders, hunger and drought. And it was this year's drought that had brought her team of relief workers to Angola. She felt the people's need and longed to help them; yet they smiled as if the sun itself was their father and the earth their mother. *They are the ancient people that still walk the land of their forefathers,* she thought. *The place where life is said to have begun, and death is forever in the air.*

The supply trucks rolled passed village after village, bumping and bouncing from side to side as they neared their destination. Jessica looked out over the passing landscape until the driver muttered the village name in broken English: "Cacolo, it is just up ahead, miss."

Jessica loved the African land and cherished its people, but, like the passing of the Cape Lion many years before, transformation was coming to the land once again and the great changing was upon the people of Africa.

As the supply truck stopped Jessica jumped to the dry and dusty ground, shielding her eyes from the grit and bright, unforgiving sunlight. She looked around, expecting more of the village. Tribal children ran to the trucks; like all curious children, their intrigue and curiosity played on their minds. From a distance, the elders sat quietly alongside their shaded mud and grass huts and kraals and watched. Scattered around the village center was a broken-down school building with no door and a broken entrance gate made of old trees that secured the village entrance.

"There's work to be done here." She glanced around the open expanse. "Let's unload!" she shouted in a commanding tone. Her team jumped into the backs of the trucks and began removing supplies: As the hours passed, food, water and medical boxes began piling up next to the trucks. The tribal villagers sat in the shade, quietly contemplating the presence of the team. Jessica rolled up her sleeves, jumped onto the food-supply truck, and helped pass equipment and boxes of food. It was hot, really hot, and the sun beat down on them, making the lifting hard on her hundred-and-fifteen-pound frame, but she loved the work and loved helping the people. The hours passed as sweat soaked her shirt and dust filled every pore of her tiring body. She brushed her hands through her short, dirty-blond hair and shook the dust from her clothing.

"Can I help you with that, young lady?" came a lively, English-accented voice from behind a group of tribesmen. A man of fifty or so, around her father's age, leaned his head over the shoulder of one of the elders. "Need some help there?" He smirked sarcastically.

"Yeah. We could use a hand." She studied the man as he walked to the truck.

"These people are nice, they smile a lot, but try and get them to work and they'll run away," he cracked. "I'm the resident doctor here, I'm John Hanson."

"I'm Jessica Sinclair, the resident supplies deliverer."

"Well, hello, Jess."

"Hi. I'm beginning to notice these people don't move too fast." She frowned. "Roll up your sleeves if you don't want them to get dirty," she said, grabbing a large sack of flour and tossing it to the end of the truck.

With a large thump, and a tearing sound, the sack broke open; flour whirled in the air and all over John Hanson. She raised her hands to her now open mouth. "Oh my God! I'm—-I'm, so sorry," she said as she began to laugh. John Hanson stood there in shock. Slowly opening his eyes, he raised one eyebrow, giving her a witty smirk.

"Roll up my sleeves, did you say?" he said jokingly. Jessica felt the warmth in the man. He seemed to have her father's ways about him, though he was not an Afrikaner.

"So, whitey"—her voice shook as she began laughing uncontrollably—"you look a little out of place amongst all these black people." The tribesmen and children were laughing and pointing their fingers at him. Some of the children ran up and touched him, laughing; they ran away and hid behind the laughing elders. She saw her father in him; he seemed genuine and good-natured. As her father would say, he had warmth.

"I don't suppose Halloween's here yet?" He frowned.

"Halloween? What's Halloween?" She shrugged her shoulders and slid another bag his way. He began to help unload the truck. The sun was hot and high in the African sky. There had been no rain for months and water was scarce.

He pondered her question. "I thought you were an American. Most of the caregivers are American university kids helping out while on their break from school." He knew that the supply trucks were coming to the camp and had anticipated their arrival, but had not considered seeing new faces. He wondered

2

what had happened to the other caregivers he knew. With a sweaty frown, she tossed another bag of flour at him. He saw the expression on her face had changed.

"I was hoping that bag would break as well." She smirked. "Do you always insult a person when you first meet them?" She tossed another bag toward the rear of the truck. "For one, I'm South African, not American, and...for the other, not a child." She stood upright, dusting the unrelenting grit from her hair, wiping the sweat from her brow with her sleeve, and dusting the dirt from her clothing. He saw pride in her eyes.

"I'm a Sinclair," she said with pride, again passing supplies to the back of the truck. "I'm from Gansbaai, South Africa." She looked at him. He was tall, around fifty years old, but he seemed younger. He had a receding hairline and was balding on the back of his head. *He seems comical*, she thought, and his black knee-high socks and long tan shorts made her giggle.

"I should have recognized your Afrikaner accent. Sorry, Ms. Sinclair," he said, hearing the change in her voice. "I didn't mean to insult you."

"You sound like an Australian and, for that matter, look like one, too," she snapped back quickly and grinned.

"Witty and beautiful is no way to go through life, young lady! You remind me of my daughter back home. God, I think she's in her late thirties now." Smiling, he grabbed the bag of flour and lowered it into one of the helpers' hands. "I'm from that other bloody island...the one in the Atlantic. I'm the medical genius in these parts. I'm on the Queen's budget and at your faithful and hungry service: So—the question is—should I cook tonight or should you?"

Jessica looked at the doctor. *What a character*, she thought to herself. He seemed honest and good-natured. She could tell they'd get along just fine. She perked up as she wiped the sweat from her eyes again. "Let's get this work done," and giggled. "You can cook."

The day drew on and the sun began lowering toward the distant horizon. The twilight slowly gave way to the African night and darkness crept from the eastern sky. Jessica and Dr. Hanson discussed the day's work and the long-awaited arrival of the supplies. They talked about everything and anything, helping pass the time as they continued to unload the four supply trucks. She quickly learned that he enjoyed good conversation and relished the company of a younger female.

After unloading the trucks and setting up camp, she welcomed the clean shower that followed. Though it was makeshift, a milk container and garden hose, it proved useful for washing away the day's grime. Jessica's thoughts settled and she began to relax as the water rinsed over her body. She thought of her life in South Africa, the journey she was on and her home in Gansbaai. She turned her neck from side to side, releasing the tension of the day, thinking of the turquoise-blue ocean, the seagulls and the migration of the whales. She and her father, Conrad, would always take long walks to the cliffs and caves of the De Kelders and look out over the rolling waves, searching every movement for the coming whales.

Her father was a good man who taught her the meaning of nature, helping the people of the land and being strong when needed. He was a commander in the South African Army and he knew the ways of Africa.

***

"Dinner is served!" Hanson shouted. Jessica could not help but smile every time the doctor said something. He had a way about him that made her feel at ease. She shook her head and smiled.

"Coming!" she yelled back, drying her hair with a towel. She thought about the water she had used while washing. It seemed such a waste but she knew she needed to clean the dirt from her aching body. She could smell the cooking meat and baked bread on the open fire. *Sweet smelling like my mother's stew*, she thought. "Is that fresh-baked bread?" she yelled to the doctor. Hanson slowly stirred the wildebeest stew and checked the bread. He prided himself on his cooking. Like most British people, he enjoyed a good stew when the meat was available.

"Anytime you're ready, Jess." He chuckled, "I'm bloody hungry. And yes, I made fresh bread."

"I'm already impressed," she called back to him.

Dinner was good. *The doctor could cook as well as eat,* she thought. *Still, nobody could cook like her mother,* she remembered, as she finished the wildebeest stew.

"That was good, Doctor." She sat and watched the last of the day's sun fall into the distant horizon as the workers cleared the tables.

"I wonder how my father and mother are doing? They're far away," she softly said to herself as she looked into the darkening sky. "The sunsets are too fast and the day's too long." She watched the night overcome the day with an enchanting array of orange, purples and reds. The African night came with pride and strength. The fire burned high and played upon the encampment, bringing images of primeval ancestors dancing under the star-filled sky. They seemed to summon the cosmic gods to bring the sun another day and make the night pass with calm.

"How long have you been away from home, Jess?" He'd been watching her stare at the fire, transfixed as if she were in another land; her gaze seemed to reflect her past. He'd been away from home too long and knew the look all too well. After his wife left him, he had decided to travel. Finding himself in

Angola, wishing he'd never set eyes on the place, for he knew he'd never leave. It was a harsh country of immense beauty. When it was green, it was dazzling; when it was dry, it was like straw; and when it was wet, it was steeping. With the green came life, with drought came death and with rain came both life and death. Uncertainty ruled the land and the land took and gave as the gods permitted.

"Three years now. Sometimes I think longer," she said, thinking back to the day she had left South Africa. "Three years and no relief in sight, it seems."

"No relief is right. This is Africa, my dear; there hasn't been relief here in a million years." Then Hanson grinned boyishly. "Speaking of relief, would you like a glass of wine, Jess?"

"Sure!" She smiled wryly. Nobody ever called her, Jess.

"I was saving it for a special occasion. With the arrival of the supplies and newfound friends, I'd say it was as good of a time as any to break out the good stuff."

"Are you trying to wine me out of my shoes? My, what would the tribal elders say about this *wine?*" she looked at him and winked.

Hanson giggled like a young boy getting into mischief. He had known the case of wine would come in handy as he watched it age. "Well, young lady, as *much* as I don't like saying this, I'm old enough to be your father. So I think I'll have to keep my shoes on tonight."

They both laughed and continued with their stories. Hanson, it seemed, had an eye for younger women in his older years. Married or not, he'd say, "There's nothing more satisfying than the touch of a woman's body." Jessica blushed at his abrasive, womanizing talk. She thought he must have been hard to handle in his younger years.

The night drifted on as they talked. As the wine began to take its effect on Jessica she retired to her tent for the night, anticipating another day in the African bush. The cot felt good under her weary body. *It's been three years of hard work with the Red Cross,* she thought as her head felt the comfort of the pillow. *American university student!* She muttered, thinking of what Hanson had said when they'd met. She looked around her tent. It was a nice tent, around ten feet by seven feet with a dresser and a night table near her bedside that held a small lantern. "Home." She softly smiled. She began to fade into a deep sleep, a much-needed sleep. The air was still and little noise could be heard outside her tent. It was a warm, quiet African night. Off in the distance a lion's roar could be heard. It commanded attention from those who were near. The night drew silent as the distant pride went on the hunt. The ancient dancers leaped with each flame of the fire. Their dance would end in the darkness of the night with the cooling embers and the impending first light of the new day.

Jessica rested well. She began a strange dream. She found herself walking along a white, sandy beach on a warm, sunny day. The sun felt good on her face. The blue sky was streaked with long, wind-blown clouds of white. The beach was deserted. She could smell the clean ocean air and hear the crashing of the waves.

"Gansbaai?" she questioned herself. "No, this isn't Gansbaai." She walked to the ocean's edge and turned toward to land. People were standing quietly on the dunes; they were holding candles. In the background was the Drakensberge Mountains.

"It's Gansbaai!" She looked around with excitement, and began to walk down the beach. She felt the warmth and love of her homeland as she walked. She was home. As she walked, a strong wind caught her and lifted her off the ground. She began to fly like a sea bird, circling above the beach, dancing upon the unseen forces that held her with love and care. She felt the sun's warmth intensify. *So many people*, she thought, as she looked down upon them standing on the dunes.

"They're the people of the world," a soft voice spoke from around her. It was a voice familiar to her heart.

"Why are they here?" she questioned as her body soared above the beach.

"They are here for you, Jessica. For you they have come from the world," the voice said. Just then Jessica's body began turning to ashes and began scattering with the warm wind as it lifted her higher into the air and toward the bright sunlight. The last thing she remembered before waking was the love she felt as her body became one with the earth, sky and universe. On the dunes the African people sang and the last thing she heard was the voice asking her to come home.

***

She woke to a beautiful morning. Sitting on the edge of the bed, brushing her hair from her blue eyes, thinking of the dream, she glanced down. On her night table was a single flower, a King Protea, the national flower of South Africa. She picked it up, wondering who'd brought it, and smelled its beautiful scent. One of the tribal children must have put it there. She glanced around. "But it's not easily found in this part of Africa," she murmured.

The commotion from outside her tent began to build as she washed her face and hands in a water bowl. The sound of pots and pans, people and trucks created a normal morning, but, she distinctly heard more English speaking voices amongst the, too-common Africa dialect that had played upon her ears over the last few years. She pushed open the flaps of her tent and sniffed the sweet-smelling King Protea.

Then, looking up from the flower, she yelled excitedly, "Daddy!" running to her father's open arms. He lifted her off the ground.

"Hey! Hey! You're going to break my back." Conrad Sinclair smiled. "How's my little girl?"

"Oh, Daddy! It's so good to see you!" Jessica hugged her father with a love that only fathers and daughters can understand, a special love and bond, a heart-warming love that every father remembers through the years and every daughter cherishes.

"When did you get here?" she asked, wiping the tears from her eyes. "I cannot believe it! I didn't hear any trucks come in during the night."

"We arrived yesterday around noon," Conrad said proudly. "We flew in, trucked it up from the border and camped down the road near the waterhole... or what's left of the waterhole."

"What do you mean, 'we'?" She turned, looking around the encampment. There sat her brothers, Ian and Duncan, stuffing their faces at the breakfast table. With them sat Doctor Hanson, filling his belly.

"Howzit?" Duncan grinned. "Howzit" was a familiar South African greeting that she had not heard for quite some time. Duncan was her oldest brother and was cheerful and outgoing. He stood six foot two and weighed around two hundred pounds. He looked big but had a gentle fun-loving heart.

"Hey, Jessica," Ian said with a warm smile, "we brought breakfast with us." He gave a wink and continued eating. She felt warmth in her heart. Ian seldom ventured away from home after his army duty up in the Northern Transvaal years back. He also was a well-built man who stood six feet tall. He'd seen a lot of fighting during his army duty and had since become quiet and introverted. An explosion had caused him to lose most of his hearing and now he used sign language as well as the spoken word to communicate. After his return from the war, she'd find him sitting in the dark by himself on many nights. She loved both her brothers deeply but she had a certain place in her heart for Ian. She knew he had seen some bad fighting, from what her father had told her, and she knew he would never kill again. Even during the safaris and hunts, he would not kill.

She signed, "I love you," to Ian as he ate. He winked at her.

"I thought we taught you to sleep lightly?" Duncan said around a mouthful of boerewors and egg. "Dad said you were sound asleep when he walked in your tent."

"Thanks for the flower, Daddy!"

"Flower. What flower?"

"Oh...come on, the King Protea." Jessica raised the flower to her father.

"Sorry, sweetheart," he said, turning to his sons. They both shrugged their shoulders and continued eating. "Being given a King Protea means someone's watching over you, little one." Conrad grinned warmly. Jessica pondered the flower and her dream, smelling the flower's sweet scent. She looked at Hanson with a humorous interrogating stare, scrunching her eyes as they bore into him. Hanson continued his conversation with Ian and Duncan as they ate.

"Good sausage. What do you call it again?" Hanson said, his mouth full of food.

"Boerewors," Duncan said. "We brought it from South Africa. It's our banger, as you English call it."

"Tasty!"

***

It was an exciting morning at the Cacolo Red Cross camp. Conrad Sinclair and his sons talked about their trip north through Angola. They had not been out hunting for some time and thought they'd kill two birds with one stone. Seeing Jessica made Conrad feel good. His little one, so far from home, was safe and looking well. She was a little older and tougher, but doing fine. Her safety was always a concern for her parents. She was their only daughter and they loved her so. Mary, back home at the estate in South Africa, had asked Conrad to take the trip north after hearing of troubles in the region. In that summer of 1994 it seemed new powers were trying to take control in Angola and Mary and Conrad Sinclair were concerned for their daughter. South Africa, too, was being transformed by the ending of Apartheid, but civil unrest seemed to linger in both lands. The warm winds began to blow across the African landscape and the night sky revealed the coming change. An omen from the black sky roared across the darkness for all to see, and the Khoikhoi tribesmen looked to their gods for answers. The dances of the ancients were seen in the flames of the night fires for the first time in a hundred years.

"So how do you like Angola?" Hanson asked Conrad and the boys. He was about the same age as Conrad and Jessica's brothers were still boys in his eyes. He also wondered why the trio had come to Angola. Was it to check on Jessica or some higher purpose or both? Could be he was just over-thinking, for he had been known to do that from time to time.

"I've been here before," Conrad said, "years back on a military mission. It's a hard place." He stared into the distance, remembering back to harder times. He knew the country all too well, all the killings and all its troubles. "It's Africa," he said, turning toward the group.

"That's for sure," said Hanson.

"We didn't only come for the hunt." Conrad's voice began to change. His English-Afrikaner accent was hard for Hanson to follow. Conrad considered his words carefully as he looked into Jessica's eyes. She looked at her father, respecting and admiring him greatly.

"I've heard there's instability in the region." Conrad's appearance seemed to shift from loving father to protector and military man. "I heard that a new government, a military faction is trying to take control here. It usually means trouble. Have you heard anything, Doctor?"

Hanson, as well as Jessica and her brothers, seemed surprised by Conrad's statement. Looking concerned the doctor stopped eating, put down his fork, and wiped his mouth. He knew what was being asked. "When are you leaving?" was Conrad's hidden message. Conrad was not a man for beating around the bush; he would come directly to the point. He was a South African, an Afrikaner who knew Africa, its people and war. This was a land of great diversity, of life and death, of joy and sadness. He had seen it and lived it from his birth. He was born in Africa and understood its soul.

"I've heard of some troubles to the northeast near Luanda." Hanson's nonchalance seemed to fall by the wayside. He was concerned, knowing what this meant for the people—the poor people who cared for neither government nor military rulers but hungered for what little they had in life.

"We haven't received any word from the Red Cross that we should leave yet," Hanson said.

Conrad cleared his throat and looked at Jessica. He knew what this meant to people who cared for the hungry and poor. Maybe he was hardened from years of fighting and protecting his family; South Africa had its own problems with the coming end of the Apartheid years and the new government powers taking shape. He saw the concern in his daughter's eyes. It was concern for the people.

"Jessica," he said softly, "I'm concerned for you. It may become dangerous in the coming weeks or months. Things like this have a way of making people suffer."

"Look at these people, Daddy." Jessica's face became hard and her smile faded with Conrad's hidden meaning. "They have nothing, nobody but us to help them." Her mouth began to quiver as her eyes filled.

He interrupted. "These people have survived in these lands for hundreds of thousands of years. They know how to survive. They know what war means. War or no war, they'll take care of their own."

"What are you saying, Daddy? We should leave...just get up and leave?" A tear trickled down her cheek. "Dad! You know we have to help these people; it's our job, our obligation. We're not animals. We don't just run away when our own kind is attacked...we help."

"Jessica!" Conrad barked in frustration. "Our own kind fought and died... *died,* trying to help people like these. I know what it means to help in time of need." He was angry now. Resting his boot on the corner of the bench, he stared directly at Jessica, who looked her father in the eye. "When push comes to shove," he went on, "it's people like you and me who suffer along with them. I know what this means to you, but think of the future...not the present...think of helping them in the future."

He walked a few feet away for a moment, frustrated and concerned. He knew that what he had to say would not go over well. He was a concerned father. He was a loving father who always protected his little girl, his family and his country. He turned toward the table. "Jessica. I'm concerned for your safety. There are some things I don't want you to see. There's a lot of evil in these countries. Not everyone is like you."

"I know, Dad. I also know that this time I need to make my own decision. I'm no longer a little girl. I've experienced pain, suffering, hunger and have seen death. These are the things that make us who we are; you taught me that, remember? Hey! I'm a South African, right? I'm tough!"

"Yes. You are, but you will always be my daughter first," Conrad said as he gazed at her, contemplating what to say next. He knew what he should do. He should tell her she must leave. She'd hate him for it, but it would probably save her heartache. He thought about the troubles he'd known, the way he had raised her to be strong. He was proud of her, of the person she had become. He remembered the little girl who once walked by his side, eating ice cream.

"You sure have your mother's way about you." He grinned. "You promise me you'll be careful and watch yourself?"

"First sign of trouble and I'm gone." She wiped away the tears on her face.

"Jessica, I mean it! First sign of any trouble and I want you to leave. You've seen a lot of things since you left home, but war is something I want you to stay away from."

"You're the best, Daddy." She threw her arms around Conrad's neck and crushed him, swaying from side to side. "I love you, Dad."

Conrad hugged his daughter, knowing what he had said was wrong. He looked over her shoulder at Hanson, Ian and Duncan. Hanson knew the look: Take care of my little girl.

The time spent with her father and brothers was wonderful. Jessica was in her glory. Conrad moved his camp nearer to the Red Cross camp and spent a few weeks in Angola, hunting what he could and watching, watching for signs of trouble. He woke every morning knowing that every day was closer to their departure and, reluctantly, he wanted to have one more conversation about her leaving but knew he'd just anger her and ruin the bond they had. He relinquished any thought of asking her to leave and tried to cherish the time they spent together.

Jessica introduced her father to everyone she met and taught him the things she had learned in the Red Cross. He was proud of his girl, no longer little but becoming a woman. He knew one day he would be walking her down a wedding aisle.

The night before their departure, Jessica walked with Conrad across the endless grasslands of Angola. The setting sun brought hues of every color across the endless African sky: red and orange mixed with purple and blue brought an end to every evening. Rifle slung over his shoulder, Conrad walked beside his little girl.

"It's a beautiful sunset." She held his arm as they walked. "I remember all the good times of my childhood. You were always a good father to us." She smiled. Conrad smiled, too, remembering the child he once knew and the now young lady he walked with. He placed his arm around her shoulder.

"Do you remember the time we camped in the Great Karoo, Jessica?"

"Yes. It's one of my fondest memories."

Conrad looked into the array of colors that blended in the distant sky. The setting sun was still hot, an unforgiving heat. "You kept saying you saw a native boy on one of the rocks. Nobody believed you."

"Yes. I was around nine years old. Mommy, Duncan, Ian and Uncle Pete never believed me. The boys kept teasing me and saying I was seeing things."

"I have a confession to make," he said calmly. "I saw him too."

"You did! Why didn't you say something?"

"I think he was a boy from one of the nomadic tribes, Hottentots or Khoikhoi, as they call themselves. We call them the Mamzibi; they're a secret and secluded tribe, different from the other Khoikhoi. He was covered with certain marks, a custom that distinguishes his tribe from other tribes in the area. I didn't say anything because he was no harm to you, and lore has it that anyone who saw a Mamzibi would capture some of their magic. They are known as the Mosquito people."

"So he was a Bushman?"

"No, not a Bushman. A Hottentot. They're similar but different in that they are more spiritual in nature than the Bushmen. The Hottentots fear Bushmen and are less warrior and more nomadic. It's said that at one time, long ago, they were one people. After the great flood, one chose to farm and hunt and the other chose to wander and hunt. The Khoikhoi believe that the Supreme Being, called TsuiGoab, is the sun and that the red dawn brings the light to mankind's heart. You had a look in your eyes; it seemed magical. I didn't want to take that away from you."

"But you saw him too?"

"Yes. I saw him, too, but he was watching *you*. His eyes seemed transfixed on you, and that's different. I wanted you to feel the magic, the mystery of

Africa. Now, looking back, I know you captured that magic. No matter where you travel in the world, the magic of Africa and the Mamzibi will always be in your soul."

Jessica, reflecting on what her father had said, squeezed him close to her. She saw Africa in him too. He was a man of Africa, hardened by the land and spiritual in its ways. Conrad cared for his family and was wise to the changing times. He knew that the days of mighty hunters, the hundreds of miles of open land, and the nature and freedom of Africa were ending. Peace was never a constant in Africa, he knew that, but Africa was changing, times were changing, and he could feel it in the air.

"Smell that? In the air?" Conrad looked to the horizon. "It's rain." He squinted his eyes, looking into the distance. "Somewhere out there, storms are rolling across the dry land. They're bringing life to some and death to others. That's the beauty of Africa, Jessica. Some die because of the storms and some live because of it and become stronger, but everything that happens, good or bad, happens for some divine reason. You were born on a rainy day in Gansbaai."

"I'm going to miss you, Dad," Jessica said sadly.

"I'm going to miss you too. You're our little treasure. Your mother's first words when you were born were, 'She's a treasure.' She misses you dearly."

"I miss her too. I'll be home soon. I promise. Tell Mom I was asking about her."

Seeing her father and brothers depart brought sadness to her heart. Jessica would miss them greatly. Before leaving the camp, Conrad handed Hanson a .45-caliber pistol.

"Use this if you need to," he said sternly. Hanson placed the pistol and box of ammunition in his night table. *I don't even know how to use one of these things,* he thought nervously. Some time after her fathers and brothers' departure, Jessica began to smell the coming rains. "Damn!" she giggled. "He smelled them coming weeks ago."

One morning she went for a long walk into the bush. The gazelles and springbok played in the distance. The day seemed calm. She was content and happiness filled her heart. The trees were scattered across the plain and stretched toward the blue sky. A true African sky, high and expansive, it captured her soul. She walked far, thinking. She feared nothing and was concerned for nothing as she walked. Even the animals seemed at peace as they roamed and played. She watched the Thomson's gazelles chase each other. A great bird flew high, in search of its breakfast. The landscape orchestrated a harmony of vibrant colors—green, red, orange and brown played on her mind—colors that would be even more vibrant as the rainy season commenced.

When she returned to camp, Hanson, concerned about her absence, could not help but ask her where she had been all morning. In fear of sounding like her father, he gently questioned whether or not she had eaten breakfast.

Jessica took a deep breath and said wittily, "Do you smell that? Rains coming soon—I was walking in the bush, just in case you were wondering—you should just ask next time."

"I'm not concerned!" Hanson stuttered. "I'm not! Really!"

"*Really?*" She laughed.

"Okay.... okay, well, it's dangerous walking by yourself in the bush. Happy now?"

"You're just so cute...old, but cute." She giggled, calmly looking at the clear blue sky. "You know how I know it's going to rain?"

"No, tell me, young lady, how *do* you know it's going to rain?"

"The Khoikhoi believe that when a person who was born on a rainy day walks into the bush alone, and places two stones on top of each other, it will bring rain. I was born on a rainy day and I placed two stones on top of each other."

Hanson looked up. Raising his eyebrow. "You kids think you know everything. Who the bloody hell are the Khoikhoi?"

Jessica patted him on the shoulder. "It's okay, John; your senses are dulled from old age. Senility is setting in just fine." She laughed again.

"Oh...you wait, you wait, young lady. One day it's going to happen to you too."

"Nope! Not me." She walked away still laughing. "I'm never growing old."

"Hey! What the bloody hell is a Khoikhoi?"

***

That evening, in a quiet night sky, the first rains of the season began to fall. Hanson lay in his bed, thinking. "How the bloody hell did she know it was going to rain? Damn kids...think they know everything...Khoikhoi, probably made that up."

The night became alive with celebration. The first rains had come to the dry land. Life came with every drop as the children laughed and the animals played in the open fields. The elders watched as the rain filled their buckets. They had seen this many times before. It was life to them, and with it came the "great changing," as they called it. The sky would be different, the stars would be different and the land would transform before their eyes. However, with life came death. Somewhere, ancient riverbeds were renewed with rushing water. Homes would be flooded; people and animals would die and become life for others. This time, the great bird in the sky would find its breakfast with ease.

***

A few weeks after the reunion with her father and brothers, Jessica and Hanson sat by the evening fire enjoying each other's conversation, bringing an end to their day's work. The sunset was a fantastic array of colors, a gift to their eyes; the array filled their minds with the wonder of Africa and the gift of life. The setting sun left with a fiery red glow as stars began to appear by the multitudes in the east. Like angelic beings, the stars watched and protected the cosmos, bringing the night to unfold over the day. The deities conspired as the ancients prayed for the living. The fire felt good and Hanson's stock of red wine had not run dry. They enjoyed a glass and toasted to another magnificent African sunset.

Some of the tribal elders sang songs in a distant hut. It was a beautiful rhythm of humming and clicking sounds that played upon an ancient spirit. Out of the darkness a lion's roar stilled the night. Even the crickets silenced their songs of love at the threat in the air. The fire crackled, bringing a dance of shadow before their eyes, mystical and primitive. They felt helpless as a springbok in the dark African night. Their eyes widened in search of the predator that lurked in the shadow.

"Did you hear that? Sounds near!" Hanson softly whispered to Jessica.

"Yes." Whispering, she leaned toward Hanson. "I think he is close."

"I don't know. It could be." He placed more wood on the fire, making the flames leap into the night. He remembered the pistol in his night-table drawer. Would it be able to kill a lion, a full-grown lion? Fear filled his mind. Hesitating, he wanted to retrieve the handgun from his tent. But it was darker near the tents and he now feared the darkness of the night.

"You know, lions have been known to attack people around fires?" Jessica whispered, handing the doctor a piece of wood.

"Really?" Hanson squirmed.

"Yes. I heard of hunters being eaten alive. The larger Cape Lion would watch them by the campfire eating and drinking, and attack as soon as they went for a pee. The Cape Lions have been known to jump over walls and run straight through fires to kill their prey. They are very alert to the ways of humans."

"Oh my God!" Hanson's voice began to quiver to a higher pitch. "Are you serious? I thought lions feared fire?" He felt a need to pee.

"Nope," Jessica said quickly. "What's that?" She became alarmed as she stood up, looking over the fire and into the darkness.

"What! What is it...the lion?" Hanson said, eyes probing the night. "Do you see something?"

"Yes...I think so...it's moving...there's something just over to the right."

"What? What is it?" He began to shake.

"I don't know yet."

"Is it the lion?" Hanson shrank into his seat. Thoughts of his gun rushed through his head; his eyes darted back and forth from the darkness to the tent. "Jessica, you shouldn't stand up like that. He'll see you."

Jessica began to giggle softly as she sat down and drank her wine. Hanson's face became confused.

"What?" he said, frightened. "Aren't you worried?"

"That lion's about two miles away," she said gleefully. "And besides, lions don't like fires."

"But he sounded so close. And you said they've been known to jump through fires."

"I made that up...I was just kidding you, old man."

"You bloody arse! You scared the bloody shit out of me! I almost pissed my pants." She began laughing at him.

"What are to trying to do, give me a heart attack?"

Rocking with laughter, Jessica dropped her glass of wine to the ground.

"You crack me up. You should have seen your face. God! How long have you been in this country?"

"Too long indeed! Well, would you want to be eaten alive?"

"They'd go after your big ass, or should I say *arse*, before little old me. Oh man, if my brothers and father were here they'd be rolling on the ground." She poured more wine for herself. She loved a good practical joke and knew he could take it.

"I have to pee. You're a bloody *arse*." He laughed nervously, softly pushing her arm. "My big *arse*! What about your big *ass*?"

"I have a nice curvy ass." She smiled broadly. "It's not a carving arse like yours."

"No lion's taking a bite out of this arse," he replied.

"Sorry. I couldn't help myself. My brothers pulled that one on me years ago in the Karoo. We were camping near the Drakensberge Mountains."

"God, Jessica...you're something. If I were younger I'd sweep you off your feet and give you the paddle. I have to go pee now."

"Knowing you...you would carry me to your tent." She yelled after him, "don't let the lions eat you while you're peeing."

After a quick relief and a quick walk in the dark, Hanson returned for another glass of red wine. The night was moving on and the fire felt good on their faces. The nights were becoming cooler with the changing of the season and fall would soon usher in heavier rains and, the coming winter.

"What am I going to do with you, Jess? You know, all kidding aside, you've made me laugh over these past months many times. I really want to thank you for that." Hanson became emotional with thoughts of his past and his family. "It's been many years since I've seen my daughter. You're something. I've enjoyed having you around."

"You make it sound like I'm leaving."

He looked into the fire and sipped his wine. Heavy-hearted, he sighed. "It's a beautiful night."

"What?" Jessica poked his arm with her finger. "What's the matter, John?" She turned in her seat and faced him, lightly placing her hand on his wrist. She always called him by his first name when she was serious. "What's wrong?"

Hanson's eyes started to fill as his mind raced for an answer. She could see he was sad, troubled and worried.

"Jessica, you're like a daughter to me now. I mean that with all my heart. But I was thinking what your father said was right."

"What do you mean, right?"

"That you should leave, Jess."

"What! Why? Is there something wrong? I haven't heard anything." She became alarmed. Thoughts of leaving raced through her mind.

"I've received word, a letter from the Red Cross headquarters in Zaire. They're asking that all personnel leave Angola."

"No! Why? What's happening? Is it bad?"

"Calm down, Jess."

"Calm down nothing, what's happening, John? *Tell* me!"

"The fighting is spreading to the outlying regions and things are becoming unsafe."

"Who are they?"

"They're calling themselves freedom fighters but they're just terrorists"

"But they wouldn't dare touch us, we're only here to help."

"These people don't care about you and me, Jess. They care about control, money and power...life means nothing to them."

"How soon is the Red Cross asking us to leave?" Jessica squirmed, overwhelmed by the news.

"By week's end."

"But you said I was leaving, what about you?"

Hanson stood up, and walked to the edge of the fire, and looked out into the darkness. "I'm going to hang on a while and see everyone off."

"Then I'll stay with you until everything is done."

"No, Jess. You have to go with the others. It can become unsafe very fast. I don't want to see you get hurt...and I promised your father I'd watch out for signs of trouble and see you off if any came about. Plus, your father would kill me if you got hurt under my watch."

"Oh...be serious, John. I'll leave when you leave. We'll go together. You know, the 'last airplane out' thing."

"I made a promise to your father, Jessica. First sign of trouble and you're on a plane out of here."

"Is that an order, Doctor?" Jessica stood and walked to Hanson's side. "Are you ordering me out? It seems I can't get away from people ordering me around. I love my family but I had enough of being ordered around. When I was a child, it was do this and do that—watch yourself—be careful. Nobody ever asked me what I liked. Nobody listened to me!"

"Jessica, please calm down. They were just looking out for you."

"Maybe so, but I needed to grow and be myself. Be who I wanted to be. That's why I left to work with the Red Cross, to grow and learn who I really am."

"But that's what helped you to be strong. You come from a good family. They just cared a little too much, maybe. All in all, this is Africa, my dear; better safe than sorry. The lion could have been just over the hill. Just the same, a group of terrorists could be just over the hill. I fear them more."

"I know, maybe I'm being too harsh. I just want to take care of myself. Be myself and make my own decisions. I'm a grown person. Not a child."

"I know you're not a child." Hanson turned toward her and held her hands. "See your hands, Jess? They're proud hands. African hands. You made these hands help people and you are the life in these hands. I know you're strong. I see it in you. I know you want to take care of these people. I once thought the same way. But there are many times that I wanted somebody to take care of me. Look after me. I made a decision to take care of myself a long time ago. It's a lonely life; caring for yourself and having nobody else care for you. Just remember that you are part of a family who loves you. They're not perfect and neither are you, so don't go giving up on what family does and doesn't do. Just remember the life and love they've given you. All the watching and caring they did for you when you were younger is what helped make you who you are today."

"I know. I guess I just don't want anyone treating me like a child. I've come a long way and don't want to be told what to do."

"Yes. Well, we all are told what to do, even when we get older, from time to time. So, it's an order." Hanson turned and walked away. He sat down next to the fire and stared into the burning yellow flames. "Come on, Jess, we can make base camp in Mozambique or Kenya. We'll come back after its safe. So what do you say? We agree?"

"Yes, Doctor." Smiling warmly she gave him a sassy look. She knew she'd hang on for a while longer. The doctor was older and needed help with packing. She worried for the people, for the children. She had become friends with the tribal villagers and loved watching over them, helping them and feeding them. She would make sure they were secure, that Hanson was secure. They needed her.

The night closed in on them with the distant sounds of a lion's roar. Off in the darkness, the pride was on the hunt. Life was ending and Africa was being renewed once again. The firelight flickered and danced to the sounds of the African song of life and death. The ancients sat in silence, awaiting the coming daylight.

CHAPTER 2

Over the following weeks, Jessica helped Hanson and the team break down the camp and ship off the extra supplies. One morning, as dawn broke to a cloudy gray sky, Jessica heard thunder rolling across the distant valleys. The birds sang their songs of joy as a new day ushered in the coming rains. She walked from her tent, yawning, stretching her arms to the gray light. It was early fall and soon heavier rain would be rolling moisture across the dry plains. Springbok and gazelles could be seen running across the grassy bush as the wildebeest commenced their early ritual of eating.

It was a time of uncertainty for everyone. There was excitement in the air. The smell of freshly fallen rain, the breakdown of the camp and the change of the seasons were upon them. It had been three weeks since her talk with Doctor Hanson, and the last letter from her father and mother. The day seemed unusually quiet, she thought, looking around the camp. She wondered why there were no tribal people strolling about the camp as they usually did. The sun broke through the clouds for a time and in the distance, she saw a tribal boy standing on a rock formation. *Unusual*, she thought, *such a young boy alone.* A ray broke through the gray clouds, shining directly on the boy. As she looked closer, she realized that it wasn't a boy, but a man, a Hottentot. *What is he doing this far north?* She thought as she watched him. The Hottentot was watching her as well, raising his hand to the sky, gesturing acknowledgement. She felt his spiritual presence fill the air and she raised her hand in return. The sun began to drift behind the rolling clouds again as they stood there watching each other, two people born of a harsh land. Distance separated them in this life, one primordial and the other modern, but their spirits met in this time in space.

The roar of a distant truck engine prompted Jessica to turn and look toward the road. When she looked back toward the Hottentot, the man had vanished into the landscape, vanished as quickly as the rains began to fall from the darkening sky.

Hanson's jeep roared passed the clay homes and up the road toward the compound. He swung around the broken entrance gate, and came to a sudden halt, then frantically jumped from the truck and ran toward Jessica.

"Jessica!" his voice rang out with alarm. "Get whatever you need and fast!

We have to go!" He was scared and breathing heavily. Panic filled the air. "We have to leave immediately! Hurry!"

"Why? What's the matter?" Jessica had never seen him so panicked. Her thoughts raced as she watched him fumble and drop the keys to the ground.

"They're coming! The soldiers are attacking the villagers. They're in the village at the edge of the valley," Hanson said, running toward his tent to gather his things.

"No!" Jessica cried. "No! The children...we have to help the children." She grabbed the keys from the ground and ran for the jeep. Slamming her foot on the accelerator pedal, the jeep jumped forward as she threw it in gear, and headed for the village.

"No! Jessica, no!" Hanson turned and ran after the jeep, then watched it career down the road, his arm stretched out into the rain. He looked on in despair, his head lowered as the rain ran down his face.

Carelessly Jessica swerved the truck around the gates and sped across the grassy plain toward the village. She didn't care about anything but helping the people. "They better not hurt the children," she cried aloud. Neither fear nor death would deter her from helping the children. Tears ran from her eyes, making it hard for her to see the muddy road in front of her. The rain fell from the slate-dark sky, and the wind began to blow harder. A storm had arrived, bringing an end to a beautiful morning.

"Damn it! Damn it!" She hit the wheel as she saw smoke rising from the village. The truck darted passed the village gate, a smashed array of large branches and tree fragments. It was meant to keep out lions and other predators, not trucks and soldiers. Slamming on the brakes, she jumped from the still-moving truck and ran toward the schoolhouse. She could hear the chaos from within. People and animals lay unconscious or dead in the mud. The village smelled of burning skin, smoke and blood. It was lifeless and cold. Danger and evil were in the air.

She raced into the schoolhouse, only to be stopped by a black uniformed soldier with an AK-47 rifle. He smashed her in the chest with his rifle butt, grabbed her hair, and forced her to the dry dirt floor.

The schoolteachers and children sat crying on one side of the room. Some men in uniform were striking an elderly tribesman, whose eyes filled with fear as a soldier placed a handgun to his head. The tribal women cried out for them to stop, but the soldiers kept them crammed in the corner of the room. Jessica forced the soldier's thumb back toward his wrist and twisted it. At the excruciating pain, the soldier released her. She scrambled to her feet, enraged.

"Who do you think you are?" She faced the soldier's AK-47 in defiance, pointing to the insignia on her uniform. "I'm with the Red Cross. I demand you leave these people alone." Turning, she pushed the soldier aside, and walked toward what seemed to be the leader of the group. "This is an outrage. I demand you leave these people alone. Immediately!" She stood in front of the elderly tribesman, shielding him from the soldiers' guns. "What gives you the right to hurt these people?" she yelled, pointing her finger at the soldier. The soldiers became nervous and confused by her arrogance and strength, and began to back off, lowering their weapons, until a strong, English-speaking voice barked commands to them from behind her. She turned to see a well-dressed, uniformed black man standing in the doorway, sunglasses hiding his eyes. He walked toward her.

"You ask what we do here? We are bringing fear to these people. There are traitors here."

"Traitors? There are no traitors here. These people are poor tribesmen. They know nothing of you and your war. Who are you to hurt these people?"

"I'm General Mobutu." His tone was arrogant. "These people are mine."

"Well, General, I demand you, *and* your troops, leave this place immediately! I'm with the Red Cross; *these* people are under *my* care."

"You are on our land, woman," the General barked. "These people belong to my government."

"Your government? What government is that, General? This is how you treat your people? Are you even a General? You people put on a uniform and call yourself generals every time there's a war. What did you pay for that costume?" Jessica raised her voice, trying to make him feel inadequate. She hoped he would back down, knowing she was right, that she knew the game he played. The medals he wore were nothing of his accomplishments. They were nothing but bird droppings on pins stuck to the chest of an egotistical man, a man who had little care for life, and would take life to gain power if he had to. She was playing a dangerous game.

"You talk too much, woman," he yelled. "You are nothing but a white whore. This is not your land, settler. You don't belong here."

"Who are you calling a whore? Let me tell you something, you fat slob, you don't belong here either. You take your little soldiers and get out!" Angrily, she walked to the door and held it open with her arm. "Get out!" she yelled. The General began to laugh, a deep laugh, a toying laugh. She could see his gold-capped teeth in the dimly lit room. The rain and thunder increased and the wind blew the shredded curtains at the schoolroom window. A storm had come to the land. The predator knew the game and contemplated the diminishing fear in the eyes of the tribesmen. He knew he would have to take control of this situation or leave. He had the upper hand, and knew he would not lose.

"You should be like these women. They know their place." He laughed, looking at the tribal women huddled in the corner of the room. Then Mobutu's face turned angry. His teeth began to grind. He would not be made fun of in front of his men. He walked over to Jessica and stood in the doorway.

His hand struck her face with crushing force. Like a lion, he felled his prey with one powerful swoop of his claw. Jessica fell to the ground, in pain; blood began trickling from her nose and mouth. The soldiers began laughing and she felt anger deep in her soul. As she began to stand, Mobutu kicked her in the ribs and she fell once more to the floor. She lay limp holding her side as the pain rushed through her body. The pain kept her from moving. She could see Mobutu walking away from her, toward the kneeling elderly tribesman. He pulled out his pistol.

"No," Jessica cried. "No, no."

The shot rang out as the tribal women wept and shrieked in horror. Children screamed as the blood splattered into the air.

The tribesman's body fell lifeless to the schoolhouse floor, blood forming a puddle around his head; she felt a great sadness in her heart. *Such little regard for life,* she thought. The tribesman was a grandfather, and an elder who was much loved. Mobutu walked over to the crying children, and fired above their heads. Dirt and rock from the school walls spattered into the air, and into their weeping eyes. Jessica tried to regain her strength and raise herself from the floor. A large boot smashed her head back into the dirt as if it was putting out a cigarette. In an angry voice, Mobutu ordered his soldiers to take her outside into the courtyard. They grabbed Jessica by her hair and belt, and dragged her from the schoolhouse, hitting her with the butts of their guns, tossing her into the mud. Mobutu walked from the schoolhouse, pistol in hand, went to Jessica, placing the gun to her head. Her eyes were filled with fear, but she looked at him defiantly. She thought of the children. He could see the anger in her eyes. Mobutu fired the gun. The bullet lodged in the mud next to her body and he walked away, laughing.

"Take her to the truck," he ordered his men.

The soldiers dragged her limp, wet, bloodied body to an army truck loaded with waiting soldiers, and threw her onto the truck floor. She could hear the soldiers screaming at the tribal people in their native language. She could hear the children crying and people screaming as shot after shot rang out. With each shot her body twitched. She prayed and envisioned an intervention from God overpowering the soldiers. That rain would burn the soldiers' eyes like acid. She now knew the sounds of death. She now knew the sounds of evil her father had warned her about. The rain and wind, the screaming and sounds of death, filled her heart with great sadness. She tried to move again, but had little strength. She was hurt and bleeding badly.

"Please help the children, please," she pleaded with the soldiers who looked down at her. They sat motionless, looking on with little care, smoking their cigarettes. She could smell the smoke, the death, and the horror in the air. She could see some of the frenzy through the cracks in the truck wall. She could see that John Hanson had arrived, and was talking with Mobutu. The rain, and the impact of the gunshot so close to her head, made it hard for her to make out what was being said. "John," she muttered. "Run, John...run." She tried to scream but only coughed up blood. She lay there looking through the cracks, helpless and broken. "John, run." She heard his voice yelling at Mobutu.

Shots filled her mind with horror. With each shot her body twitched once more. Once again she looked through the cracks in the wall, this time to reveal John Hanson's body lying on the muddy ground, lifeless, blood running from his head. The .45-caliber revolver in his hand revealed the desperate measure of a once-kind man. She lay, broken and filled with sorrow as the truck began to drive off down the muddy road. Her tears mixed with her blood, and her grief and broken heart overwhelmed her as darkness descended. She slowly closed her eyes, waiting to die.

***

She awoke to a darkened cell. The floor she lay on was cold and damp and she could feel pain throughout her body. Her head throbbed and her side and face ached. She was in an old cell from the past Portuguese colonial era, its walls chipped and cracked from years of neglect. The door was ajar, and men were sitting around a table, smoking, laughing and talking. In the corner she could see the General smoking a cigar and grinning. His evil laugh made her sick to her stomach. She coughed softly, regaining consciousness.

"The whore is awake." Mobutu walked to the cell door grinning. "You going to have a big mouth now, whore?" He ridiculed her as his soldiers laughed, smoking their cigarettes. "You've been good for my men these last two days, whore."

Laughing, he called over one of his men, saying to Jessica, "Now that you're awake, you'll get a chance to know what pleasure you have been to us."

He gestured to the soldier to undress. The man began loosening his belt buckle and removing his uniform. With barely any strength and pain rushing through her body, Jessica began checking her body, only to realize she was naked. She began to cry softly as she reached down her body, examining her vaginal area. "No. No. Please no," she begged. "No." She cried, thinking this wasn't happening, that they were testing her, testing her will—she brought her hand to her face and saw her blood on her fingertips. "No," was the only thing she could say. No to the horror she saw, no to the cruelty against her body and the atrocities against the people and their souls, no to the injustice that was yet to come. "No," was the only sound that issued from her deepest being. The soldier grabbed her broken frame and turned her over. Her face pressed against the cold, hard cell floor as the concrete scratched her face with every jerk of his body, as he forced himself on her. She began to lose consciousness, feeling the man's body on her back. The last thing she remembered was the darkness that overwhelmed her spirit and the horror of being raped.

Days later she opened her eyes and saw a single guardsman watching her. He said nothing to her as she began regaining her strength. She could smell the rain and dampness in the air and the cigarette smoke. *How long*, she thought, *have I been in this cell?* She tried to sit upright, only to feel a sharp pain shoot across her ribcage as if someone was jabbing a knife through her heart. The pain made her instantly check her body for other signs of damage, and she came to know the truth of her nightmare. She had been beaten and repeatedly raped. She closed her eyes to hide the shame and anger that overwhelmed her. Thoughts of her childhood began to fill her mind. The times she had walked the fields and hills of Gansbaai, the deserted beaches and long, rolling dunes she had escaped to as a child. It was a place she always felt held a great secret and treasure and safety. It was once again a time to visit the sands of Gansbaai. She needed the healing and magic of her childhood home. She envisioned walking the white sandy beaches and picking flowers from the rolling fields. It was her way to heal her spirit. It was her way to regain herself. She remembered her sister's grave and how she would place flowers next to her stone. The sister she never knew but always felt. As she lay dreaming and envisioning, she could still hear the wind of the Cape and the rustling of the grass around her. It was a magical place for little Jessica and a time of spiritual growing. She began to drift into sleep and dream of her childhood home, Gansbaai.

She dreamt she was walking along a worn path. It was a summer's day, hot, with soft Cape breezes blowing off the ocean. Behind her she saw her father, standing in the distance, arms folded as if watching her and protecting her from harm's way. She waved to him but he just stood there and let her walk farther and farther. She wondered why he didn't stop her. She walked across the field and continued passed the deserted beaches till she reached the edge of the Drakensberge Mountains near her home. She looked around to see how far she had walked but could not tell the distance. She became worried and began walking back along the path. The sun began to set as orange, purple, blue and red filled the sky. She walked faster and faster but the trail didn't look the same. She heard a buzzing and humming sound above her as she ran down the trail. As she looked up she saw a swarm of mosquitoes just above her head. She raised her hands to swat and swipe at them and fell to the ground and curled into a ball. The sound of swarming mosquitoes stopped and she opened her eyes to see a tribal boy standing above her body. The boy's body was covered with what seemed like mosquito bites or prick marks. The boy said nothing. He helped her to her feet and walked off into the field and into the distance. She turned to find her father walking toward her; he hugged her and told her everything would be fine. "You're a special child Jessica, God has plans for you, little one. Remember what I'm saying, be strong and remember you're the secret of Gansbaai." She turned to find the boy had gone off into the mountains. He stood on a rocky ledge overlooking the rolling hills. Above him, carved into the rock cliff was a giant mosquito.

***

The cell door slammed, waking Jessica from her dream. The guard had put bread and water on the table next to her bed. Jessica rolled over, pain shooting up her side. She began to eat the meager rations provided her for the day. Sitting in the distant corner of the room, the guard watched her quietly as cigarette smoke filtered the sun's rays that slanted through the barred window above her head. *Sun,* she thought. It seemed it had been raining through the night. Drops of water could still be heard dripping off a nearby roof. *Tick...tick...tick.* The day progressed into night and night into day with little commotion from outside the walled cell. It was days before Jessica heard sounds outside the walls, fear filling her heart at the thought of her captor's return. The guard had vanished behind the door and silence filled the room. The smell of dampness was in the air as Jessica lay on her makeshift bed of wood and rope. She watched and listened for information, dissecting each sound, imagining the worst was yet to come. After some time, footsteps could be heard in the distance, becoming louder and louder, the sound direct and commanding. She knew whose steps they were and why he approached. She watched the wooden door and prayed she was wrong. The footsteps stopped at the door and then there was the sound of dangling keys. The lock began to click as if a key was being used to open it. A distant yell could be heard, a soldier calling out, "General...General." Silence followed. The person still stood outside the door. She listened, eyeing the doorknob. It began to turn slowly. "General!" The voice rang out once more, closer this time. The doorknob turned, the lock clicked and the footsteps began to recede. Jessica closed her eyes and began to cry. "Thank you God, thank you." She curled into a ball again, hands between her legs; tears ran down her cheeks and onto the floor.

***

"What is it, Captain?" General Mobutu yelled as he walked across the courtyard.

"General. Our scouts report there are trucks approaching from the south."

"Trucks! What trucks? What else did they say? How many?"

"Before we lost contact—"

"Lost contact!" interrupted Mobutu. "What do you mean, lost contact?"

"Well...lost contact, sir. They stopped transmitting."

"What did you hear, Captain?"

"They said three jeeps and two trucks were heading up from the southern road; military trucks, General."

"Military! What military trucks would be coming this way? We control this sector."

"Well, sir, before they stopped transmitting, we thought we heard them say that the trucks were flying the South African flag."

"South Africans! Why would South Africans be coming here?" the General questioned, looking around the courtyard. He turned and faced the old cell house. Looking at the front door, he asked, "How much time till they arrive?"

"By nightfall, General."

"Put some men at the front entrance, some down the road, and some behind the rear building. We'll have a surprise for them. Whoever they are, we'll kill them." General Mobutu looked concerned, wondering what South Africans were doing in Angola. He looked around the compound and walked toward his office. He would not wait for the attack. He would watch from a distance.

***

Jessica sat quietly in her cell as the sound of men, trucks and equipment moved outside the walls. She wondered idly what was happening outside but caring little. As night began embracing the land, she once again heard footsteps approaching the door, this time more than one person, she feared. Her heart beat faster with the nearing steps. The door swung open, revealing Mobutu and two soldiers.

"Well, look what we have here," Mobutu barked. "So, you happy now, whore?" Jessica sat, with her head lowered. "Unlock the gate," Mobutu ordered his men. Walking into the cell, he grabbed her hair and lifted her head. Fixing his glare on her, he yelled, "Look into my eyes when I talk to you, whore."

Jessica looked into his eyes but hate filled her heart and mind.

"I just want you to know that I am going to kill you in a little while." Mobutu glared at her. "I don't like you and you are no use to my men anymore. I don't know where you are from but whoever is coming will find you dead."

Jessica's eyes filled with tears. She would not beg for her life from this monster. She would not give him the satisfaction. Mobutu shoved her head to one side and walked out of the cell.

"Kill her," he ordered the guard. "Before it gets too dark. Kill her before these invaders arrive."

The last sound Jessica heard was the General's laughter as he walked down the corridor and into the courtyard. The guard played with his .45 caliber handgun, watching Jessica in her cell. Minute after minute passed as darkness folded over the land. The guard walked toward her cell door, pointed the gun at her head, laughed and walked back to his seat. Each time, she lowered her head and closed her eyes, waiting for the shot. In the darkness, trucks could be heard driving off into the distance. Mobutu was smart; he would watch his men fight from afar, safe from defeat. Silence filled the night as Jessica's heart sank. Hyenas could be heard chattering in the bush, *a mocking sound,* she thought. She thought of her mother and father, family and friends, remembering her dream. "Be strong," her father had said.

Outside, Mobutu's soldiers watched closely and listened to the bush around them. They heard no sound of approaching trucks, just the African night around them and the hyenas' laugh. The guard walked toward the cell door once again, his dark glasses hiding his eyes as he opened the cell door and lifted his gun; he pointed it at Jessica's head. This time she did not lower her head but looked angrily at his face.

"Fuck you!" she yelled. "You fuckin' bastard." She waited for the shot. The guard's finger tightened on the trigger. She watched his hand tighten around the grip, and wondered if she would feel the pain. Her head lowered and her eyes tightened. The guard grinned, knowing he had broken her spirit. There was a shot. She heard his body hit the floor.

She was alive! The room fell silent once more. She opened her eyes to find the guard lying dead on the cell floor, blood dripping from his back. *Someone must have shot through the cell window, over my head,* she thought. She worked her way toward the back of the bed, listening. Outside the night was still. The hyenas' laugh had stopped. Death had come to the night. Her eyes began to close and everything became darker. She was beginning to lose consciousness once again, but knew she wasn't shot, and help had finally come.

***

Mobutu's sentry watched the bush, his AK-47 ready to fire. The night silence was unusual, but silence was better than trucks and gunfire. A sudden sound came from behind him. Quickly turning, he was face-to-face with a large South African soldier. The soldier's camouflage hid him well in the night. His grinning white teeth were the last things the sentry saw as a sharp blackened knife jammed and twisted into his chest. He fell limply to the ground. Eyes staring, filled with fear, he lay dead on the ground.

The silence of the African night abruptly erupted into gunfire and explosions. Jessica became alert to the sound of AK-47s and M16s. She slid to the corner of the wall and waited for what might come next. Seeing the guard's gun on the floor, she reached for it and secured it near her side. Fear filled her heart as the sounds of war filled her ears. As she listened to the fighting about her, she watched the door. Whoever walked through it, would die. She knew how to use a handgun and would use it if she had too. These were evil men, murderers who lived by bringing fear and hatred to the people.

The South African soldiers quickly secured the grounds and began inspecting the village. They were indeed on a mission and would stop at nothing in accomplishing their goal. The remaining trucks rolled into the courtyard like a thunderous storm. Faces painted with camouflage, they moved as lions in the dark. Jessica sat in the dimly lit cell, waiting for death. Her mind raced with thoughts of death as the darkness increased. She was weakened from the hardship and began to fade. The gun slipped from her hand to the floor. Before she heard any footsteps, the cell room door crashed open with great force. Metal and wood scattered across the floor. Her body twitched with the burst. She raised her head but could not make out who had entered the room. Her vision was blurred and her body ached as she lay on her bed. She fumbled for the gun but didn't have the strength to grab it. A dark figure carefully entered the room: a large camouflaged man with weapon in hand. Jessica's body curled; fear filled her mind; she closed her eyes, believing she was dead. The man's strength could be felt in the air. Death had arrived in the African night. The lion was roaring and animals feared for their lives.

"Jessica. Is that you?" came a familiar voice.

"Duncan." Her eyes closed as darkness worked its way over her at last.

Her brother lowered his weapon and ran to Jessica's side. After a close inspection he picked her up in his arms and moved toward the door. Her eyes glazed and distant, tears trickled down her dirty cheeks as her limp, broken body hung in his arms. "Duncan," she whispered as she fell unconscious. Duncan stepped over the guard's dead body, turned and looked at the sentry's chest, wondering who had killed the man. He glanced around the room once more before proceeding down the hall. Tears ran from his eyes as he approached the waiting trucks. Standing at the truck was Conrad Sinclair, in the full military uniform of a South African commander. He walked to Duncan as they approached the trucks.

"Is she alive?"

"Yes." Duncan's voice shook with anger. "But she's badly beaten, and… and other things have happened, I think." Duncan placed Jessica in the truck as medics began attending her battered body. Conrad looked at his little girl lying on the cot. He brushed his hand across her face, wiping away her tears. Ian came to the truck as Conrad and Duncan watched the medics attend Jessica.

"Is she going to be okay, Dad?" Ian said.

"I don't know, Ian. We have to get her to a hospital. I hope she makes it." Conrad turned to Ian. A calm anger could be seen on Ian's face, it was distant and cold, haunting and sad. He had seen war before and knew what killing was. He stared into a distant part of his mind remembering the horrors he once knew. Coldness could be seen in his eyes as he looked into the darkness. "There are trucks up on that hill over there." He pointed.

"I know," Conrad said. "Is anyone left alive here?"

"No! We've stabilized the grounds," Duncan said. "Anyone who was left to fight is dead. Seems they knew we were coming. Nobody over the rank of captain is among the dead. The men are searching the remaining grounds now."

Conrad glanced around the village compound and turned to his boys. Ian was now holding Jessica's hand as the medics cleaned her wounds. Tears could be seen building up in his eyes. His anger could be felt in the air. He rubbed his little sister's hand, crying and silently vowing that he'd kill the man who did this to her. He softly placed her hand on the floor and looked to the trucks that sat in the dark on the distant hill.

"Burn it!" Conrad ordered. "Burn it all." Looking around the nearby hillside and outlying area, he could see trucks driving off into the distance. "Let's get her home." He climbed into the jeep, looking into the night. The lions had come and death followed. The hunter became the prey. The lights of burning buildings filled the sky.

Mobutu drove off into the distance knowing that he lived another day; that he would find out who it was who killed his men. "They will pay." He laughed. "They have not seen the last of me."

CHAPTER 3

The cool Cape wind brought the scent of wild flowers and ocean mist through the open window. Noon sunshine began removing the chill from the air as sea birds circled above the deserted shoreline. Nearby crashing waves told of the coming winter and the seawater darkened with each approaching day as fall ended its hold on the land. The sea brought life to the African coast as days turned into weeks and the weeks passed. Jessica lay unconscious at her childhood home of Gansbaai. The doctors were uncertain of her recovery. They said she'd have to be strong in order to recover from such trauma. In time, they said; she was weak from the hardship she endured and her body broken. She needed to rest and regain her strength and time would determine her fate. It would have to be her inner strength, her willpower and others' prayers to heal her. Mary and Conrad prayed and watched her closely and tended her silent, resting body with hope for her recovery. The nights and days came with questions. Her scars began healing and her face seemed to glow with more color as the days transformed the season. Her first realization was the familiar smell of her childhood home and the smell of her mother's cooking. Opening her eyes, she blinked, hesitating for a moment because of the bright sun that lit the room. Was she dreaming, or was she really home in Gansbaai? Her mind raced with thoughts of being home as she slowly moved to the edge of the bed. She was still weak but determined to try to stand. On the table next to her bed lay a little straw doll, a makeshift medicine and good-luck charm, and next to that was a vase of King Protea in full bloom. She looked at the doll, assuming Jara, her maid since childhood, had made it for her. The flowers, she knew were from her father and mother.

She began to stand, bracing her hand against the bedpost for support. Her strength soon began to fade, bringing her body to the floor with a heavy thump. The door quickly swung open.

"Jessica! You awake!" Jara exclaimed. "Miss Sinclair! Mama, Jessica awake!" She began helping Jessica to the bed as Mary ran into the room. Mary's eyes filled with tears, seeing her daughter conscious and moving. She quickly helped Jara support Jessica, moving her to the bed.

"Sorry, Mom," Jessica said, feeling weak and embarrassed.

"Sorry, nothing." Mary hugged her daughter in return. "Oh, Jessica, I'm so glad you're here." Her tears increased. "Now I know everything will be okay."

"I'm feeling better."

"Good. Good, thank God."

"Where's Daddy?"

"Your father and brothers are out. They're going to be home shortly. They're going to be very happy you're awake. Everyone's been worried."

"How long have I been here?"

"A while, dear. We'll talk about that later. You almost toppled the intravenous bags." To her surprise, Jessica, did not even know she was hooked up to intravenous.

"We looking over you for some time, Jessica," Jara said, poking her head out from behind Mary's shoulder.

Jessica closed her eyes. "Jara, did you put that straw doll on my table?"

"Oh yes, little one. It good for you...magic stuff make you better; protect you from evil."

"Well, thanks, Jara. I need a little magic." Jessica sighed and Jara's eyes widened in delight. She had helped heal the "little one." Mary held Jessica's hand and wiped the tears from her own cheeks.

"Jara. Get some water for Jessica," she said. "And get some soup from the stove, please. She may be hungry."

"Yes, Mama."

"I'm not hungry, Mom."

"Still should eat something, honey." Mary brushed her hand over Jessica's head. "They've been putting medicine in you for weeks now and some home cooking will make you feel better. You need to build your strength. We can call Doctor Vieter and have these tubes removed from your arm."

"I'm just going to rest a little while longer," Jessica muttered, turning to her side. Mary again placed her hand on Jessica's head and brushed the hair from her forehead. Scars could still be seen on her face and neck.

"I love you, Mom," Jessica softly whispered, drifting into sleep.

Mary sat for some time with her daughter. The day waned as the tide changed and the sun began to set. In the distance could be heard the sounds of animals in the grasslands and near the beach. Mary looked at her little girl and wondered what trials she had been through and what lay ahead for her. As trucks approached, Mary once again, gently brushed her daughter's hair from her face. Jessica twitched and tossed from haunting dreams; she was recovering from the pain but would feel the hurt in her heart and mind for some time yet.

"I'm with you, Mom's with you, honey. Sleep sound," Mary said, looking at Jessica and wondering what it was she was dreaming about.

The next morning Jessica opened her eyes to find her father slumped in the chair next to her bed. Conrad had arrived in the night with the boys. He was well aware of the dark dreams Jessica was having. His little girl now knew death and destruction, pain and hurt, injustice and sorrow. He knew she would never be the same, that she would forever have this in her mind. Jessica lay watching her father sleeping in the chair. She knew he'd been there all night caring for her, holding her hand and wiping the sweat from her forehead.

Conrad opened his eyes to find his daughter awake.

"Hey. How long have you been watching me?" He beamed.

"Just a little while, Daddy."

He leaned over and kissed her forehead. "You had us worried. We had Doctor Vieter here every day. How you feeling?"

"Okay, I guess. Weak and...sad."

"Sad?"

"Yeah. I don't remember everything. I mean, I can't remember everything just yet. It's like I was in a bad dream but I know it happened." Jessica's eyes became distant and clouded. She knew the horror was real and knew the pain and sadness were real.

"The children!" She remembered as tears started from her eyes. "Daddy. They were hurting the children." She now sobbed uncontrollably. Conrad brushed the tears from her cheeks and knelt next to her bed, feeling her sadness too.

"Everything will be okay," he said.

Jessica covered her face. "My God!" she cried, remembering the horrors. "They've hurt the children! Daddy, they've hurt the children!"

Now tears could be seen building in Conrad's eyes. He was sad and angry; sad for what his daughter had seen and angry with the men who had hurt her.

The door opened, but he didn't turn. "Not now," he said softly as Mary stepped into the room. She turned and quietly closed the door behind her.

"We're here for you," Conrad whispered. "We'll take care of you, honey. You're home now."

Jessica cried herself to sleep. She dreamed of the beautiful beach of Gansbaai again; long and deserted, it called to her as if she knew its spirit and it knew her soul.

The days became weeks as she slowly regained her strength. She found herself taking long walks. She walked the old paths of her childhood. She remembered how she would search for hidden treasure. The secret treasure of Gansbaai, she imagined. It would save the world. The birds sang and waves crashed as she experienced the quiet solitude. She kept most of her thoughts to herself during this time of healing. The winter came to the land as the chilled wind increased. She often thought of the tribal people and John Hanson, imagining hearing their voices in the wind. Her tears mixed with the ocean tides more than once during this time. She walked along the rocky cliffs as the waves crashed far below. The wind seemed to call to her as she walked dangerously close to the edge, not caring about the danger.

Her arms outstretched as the wind blew, she believed that she was flying like a seagull, soaring high above the land, twisting and turning with the changing wind. High above the mountains she circled around and through the soft white clouds.

"Jessica!" Conrad's voice rang out from behind her. She suddenly turned to find her father approaching. "You're a little too close to that edge, honey."

"Sorry. The wind felt good on my face. What brings you out here, Daddy?"

"Just walking."

"Me too. I like the cliffs. It's peaceful here and the walking helps ease my mind. I come out here often. When I was younger I would come out here and make believe I was searching for treasure." She looked away from her father and into the distance, into the past.

"I used to come out here too." Conrad looked out at the violent sea as the waves crashed on the rocks below. "I would sit and think. It was before you were born. When I was a little boy, your grandfather would take me for long walks. He loved to walk. I think you take after him. I'll tell you what he told me back then…'Stay away from the cliff's edge.'"

"I will. I didn't realize how close I was, Dad."

"Your grandfather was a real Boer. They don't make Afrikaners like him anymore."

"Oh, I wouldn't say that. I think they made one more after him." She smiled.

"Thanks, Jess."

"You called me Jess. You never called me Jess. What made you do that, Dad?" She, remembered John Hanson calling her Jess.

"I don't know. It just sounded easier to say. Do you prefer Jessica?"

"No. I like it! It's nice. It reminds me of someone, someone kind." She walked to her father and hugged him lovingly.

"Come on, let's get you home, young lady." Conrad put his arm around her shoulders. "It's getting chilly out here and I'm hungry. Let's get some of your mother's fantastic cooking," He glanced back curiously at the cliff's edge. "Duncan and Ian are bringing fresh meat from town and will cook it up tonight as well. Those guys love to briaa meat over an open fire. They actually cook well, if I don't say so myself…I taught them how to briaa. "

They walked back to the house

The sun began to set, as supper was prepared. Wildebeest stew simmered on the stove filling the house with the sweet aroma of herbs and cooking meat. Freshly baked bread also filled the air. Duncan and Ian cooked the extra meat outside on the open fire; the fire working its magic on boerewors and spiced lamb chops. Jessica and Jara set the table and retrieved bottles from the wine cellar. Conrad sat quietly on the front porch, smoking his pipe as he watched the tree branches sway from side to side as the strong Cape wind blew from the ocean. Life was in the air and South Africa was evolving once again. He remembered hunting with his father in Botswana, Kenya and Zambia. Those were good times and Africa seemed a larger place then. The world was turning with the times and South Africa was no exception to the changes at hand. Apartheid and white rule in South Africa was ending and the world looked to Africa. Namibia was no longer a part of the Republic of South Africa, and civil war was in Angola and Liberia. It was time for the old guard to watch the fires glow and let destiny take its course.

"Hey guys!" Jessica glanced around as she walked from the house. "Smells real good. I'm as hungry as a lion,"

Duncan grinned as he hugged his little sister. "Almost done, ah."

Savoring the moment, Jessica sat down and watched her brothers cook the meats. She gazed around the estate, remembering all the fun times they'd had as children, the times they had playing at the estate, the times while on safari and the times on the game reserves. Her brothers were three and four years older than she; Duncan, the oldest, was also the wisest. Both he and Ian had served in the South African military for three years. She remembered seeing them off to fight and protect the borders near the Northern Transvaal from guerilla fighters and terrorists of other countries.

Duncan turned toward her, handing her a piece of cooked meat. "Where you been off to today?"

"Walking. Just walking along the dunes and cliffs."

"You've been doing a lot of that lately," he said with a smirk.

"Yeah. I know. I like taking walks. But it's starting to get colder." She rubbed her arms. "After being up in Angola, I'm not used to the cold, even though it's not *really* cold yet."

"Well, watch yourself out there, man. You know things are different now. There are a lot of people coming in from other countries these days and they have little regard for other people, if you know what I mean." He remembered his sister's body in his arms the night of the fighting.

"I'll be safe. Meat's good." She pondered his words while changing the subject. Jessica had heard that things were transforming in South Africa, that there was pressure on the South African officials to end Apartheid once and for all. The world and the United States wanted it to end. They wanted a democratic society to emerge in South Africa, end what they saw as white oppression. The old ways that kept their country safe were no longer good for the world. She just wanted everyone to be safe, black and white, for everyone to enjoy life and the pleasures of living. She knew that there was more to it all, that Africa wasn't the United States or one of the European countries. Africa was a hard land of life and death. But she still wanted to see all people enjoy the fruits of life and wished it so.

"We're ready!" Mary Sinclair shouted to the boys. "Food's done on this side."

"Yeah, Mom, we're done. We'll bring it in to the table." Ian grabbed the tongs and began loading the meat onto the dinner platter.

In thought, Duncan watched Jessica as he helped Ian with the meat. "Hey, Jessica, I meant what I said: you watch yourself," he said sternly as she headed into the house.

"I will, big brother."

"Keep an eye out for her, Ian," Duncan said. "After what she's been through, she's going to need to be watched for awhile."

"I know," Ian said as he finished loading the meat onto the tray. "I've seen her sitting alone at Sarah's grave a few times, crying."

"I know. Me too."

Dinner was like a party. Jessica laughed at her brothers' joking and jesting, and Conrad's remonstration, "We are at the table." Her mother giggled softly as the brothers made jokes and toyed with each other. Mary never talked much at the dinner table. She could not help thinking that the three were children again, still to learn and experience life. Conrad told stories of hunting with his brother and father in the days of his youth. The time his father hunted the Cape Lion many years ago.

"This lion was bigger than the ones we see today," he said, remembering back to his father's tales. "It was almost twice as big as the lions we have now." Jessica watched her mother's eyes light up as Conrad told his stories. From time to time, Mary, got a word or two in, but was mostly content seeing the family happy and listening to Conrad talk.

"So what happened to the Cape Lion?" Jessica exclaimed.

"The last one was hunted and killed in my father's time." He stared at the fireplace, seeming to gaze into a distant memory. "I guess the Cape Lion's life here on earth was done. Once he ruled these lands. No predators to fear. I fear we have to watch the skies now...I mean...sometimes things just end," he softly muttered as he returned from his thoughts. "I think South Africa and Africa as a whole are becoming a new place. We have seen both good and bad, but now I see change in the air. I guess, unlike the Cape Lion, we must learn to adapt or be replaced."

Mary looked at Conrad as she watched his face become hardened. The tough Afrikaner she knew and loved was getting older.

"We'll see." He turned his stare toward the table. "We need to be strong. We'll show the world what we are made of. We're Afrikaners. We were born here in Africa and Africa is part of our blood too."

"Dessert!" Jara yelled, swinging the kitchen door wide. "Why everyone so quiet?" she said, placing the pies and cheese on the table.

"Just some remembering-back talk," Mary said with a wink. Then turning to Jessica, she said, "So, I see you are reading books about America. Why don't you visit my sister? She's living in the States, your Aunt Sarah."

"Mary!" Conrad barked. "I don't think it's a good time for Jessica to travel."

"Well, it's the beginning of summer there now, isn't it?"

"Yes, but it's not a good time for travel, Mary." The room became tense.

"It's okay, guys," Jessica interrupted. "I was just looking at some pictures."

"Good!" Conrad looked angrily at Mary, disbelieving what she had said.

"I'm thinking of going there next summer." Jessica smiled nervously, looking at her father for approval. "That would be sometime in June, right. Then it will be getting cold here and warm there again."

"Jessica," Conrad said, frustrated, "it's a long way from here and I don't think you should go just yet."

"I'm not, Daddy. Its months away and I want to enjoy my time here, with all of you. Then I'll have enough saved to travel there."

Conrad looked into Jessica's eyes for some moments. Jessica sat, anticipating his next remark.

"We'll see what happens over the months."

"Thanks, Daddy." But she knew that, no matter what he said, she was going to America.

Conrad sulked, contemplating his daughter's request, not liking the idea. Mary hesitated, looking across the table at Conrad, fearing the coming disagreement that would take place that night. Everyone began eating the dessert as Jara proclaimed from the kitchen, "Jessica going to America, Jessica going to America..."

CHAPTER 4

Thomas Jennings pushed the rigging of the *Blue Heron*'s to the side and readied her for his sail. The summer heat was rising as the sun edged over the eastern horizon, and the smell of the salty sea was in the morning mist. The Shark River Inlet was calm and the warm summer breeze provided a soft southeasterly wind. Within minutes the sloop's canvases were filled with the bay breeze, forcing the bow to cut through the glassy ocean rolls that flowed into the inlet. She glided toward the bridge, anticipating the open sea. The ocean spray felt good on Tom's face and hands. He waved to the children and fishermen that lined the walls of the inlet. Casting their fishing lines, they hoped for a small bounty of the sea, done more for pleasure than for food. Tom had been raised as a sailor and enjoyed the water and the coast town of Avon-by-the-Sea. As he made his way up the inlet, he remembered his time on the wall. He too had spent many days fishing from the inlet with his father. He had been five years old then; now, twenty-five years later, he was sailing passed the wall. Avon-by-the-Sea is a quintessential seaport town of friendly people and large Victorian homes surrounded by colorful gardens and tree-lined streets. The spring and summer air, filled with the scents of flower and salt, lavender and rose, brought intimations of the Victorian era. As the seasons changed, so did the appearance of the town. Summer brought the visitors to the New Jersey shore; cars and people filled every guesthouse. Fall brought serenity and colors of orange, purple and red to the fall sky, and winter brought the solitude. Snow lined the beaches and yards as the wind brought the ocean to life. Fierce and strong, the wind blew and the ocean reacted. The North Atlantic Ocean was no place for fishing or sailing in the winter months. But it was summer now and he knew it would be a great day as soon as he arrived at the docks and noticed that most of the other sailboats were out for the day already.

"How you doing, Tom?" came from atop the bridge as the boat maneuvered through the opening.

"Hey there, Mr. Carlton," he yelled back to the bridge master. "Great day."

"Watch the point at low tide, Tom," Mr. Carlton yelled back, the *Blue Heron* clearing the bridge as the bells rang and the bridge began to lower.

"I will." He yelled back, cupping his hands. "I heard about the new wreck already."

Mr. Carlton turned and waved in acknowledgment, and began waving the cars to proceed across the bridge.

Tom turned the winch, tightening the lines, and turned the rudder. Jibbing, he made a sharp turn north, heading along the town's shoreline. The wind was at his back and filled the sails. He sat watching the pristine beach, the houses that lined Ocean Avenue and the pavilion where he ate lunch on many occasions.

"Today's going to be a great day!" he yelled to the blue sky and dark, bluish-green water of the North Atlantic.

As the boat danced on the rushing water and began heading out to sea, he noticed a lone girl standing on the beach near the jetty. She watched the *Blue Heron* glide over the water like a seabird in flight. He stood up and watched her standing there on the shoreline. *She seems so peaceful,* he thought, as she slowly waved. Tom waved back and smiled as she turned and began walking down the beach. Tom watched her as the sunshine played on the water, making it sparkle like stars in a clear night sky. Her white sundress moved with the soft breeze as she continued her walk. The hint of flowers and sea mixed with the air, bringing to mind a perfect sunny day in a new land.

He sailed all day, up from the Shark River Inlet, around Sandy Hook's point, into the bay and up the Navasink River, then back down the coast to the Inlet. It was a fantastic day for a sail and Thomas relished the solitude of being on the water alone. The setting sun made an ending to a perfect day as he tied up the *Blue Heron* to the dock and prepared the sloop for another day. Fishing boats began bringing in their catches as the sun lowered in the sky. The seagulls arrived, anticipating a free meal from the fishing boats. The sky began its change from light blue to purple, as the sun became a bright orange. Throughout the day Tom's thoughts had turned to the lone girl on the beach. He'd not seen her in the town before and could not get her image out of his head. He even wondered if he was imagining the whole thing.

"Howzit?" she called nervously. "So how was the day? As good as you hoped?" Then there she was walking down the dock toward him.

"Hi. Yeah…it was really nice." Tom smiled. He understood her English but wondered about her accent. He was surprised to see her at the Belmar Marina and walking toward him. She had changed from her sundress to a pair of faded jeans and a white cotton shirt.

"That was you on the beach earlier?"

"Yes. I was out for a morning walk."

"Nice day for a walk as well as a sail," he stammered. *She has the face of an angel,* he thought as he jumped from the boat to the dock. The setting sun played on her dirty-blond hair and blue eyes and he watched her slender body as she walked closer.

"My aunt asked me to purchase some fresh fish for dinner," she blurted out without thinking. "I...I don't really know what to buy." She fumbled her words. Her smile beamed with life and her eyes mesmerized him as he looked at her.

"I heard they had a good tuna run today. Probably get a nice price from the fishermen over there." He pointed to the end of the pier.

"I'm Jessica Sinclair." She extended her hand. *He's tall and big like my brothers,* she was thinking. As they shook hands, she looked into his brown eyes.

"Jessica." He said without thinking. "Well, hello, Jess. I'm Thomas. My friends call me Tom." She smiled when he said her name. It had certain warmth to it, reminding her of John Hanson and her father. She felt butterflies in her stomach.

"I like Thomas better." She smiled again. "What is your surname?"

"Jennings. I live in Avon-by-the-Sea, where I saw you on the beach."

"Well, Thomas Jennings, it was nice meeting you. Thanks for telling me earlier it was going to be a great day. You're the first person to yell at me since I arrived here." She giggled, knowing he was just yelling out to the sky as he sailed.

"Did I yell loud?" he said, laughing. "I was happy to be out sailing. I tend to be a little loud from time to time, people say."

"Oh, do they? Well, I think whoever was still sleeping woke up at that point. I thought it was God talking to me until I saw your sloop gliding across the water."

"How'd you know it's a sloop?"

"I live in a fishing town called Gansbaai in South Africa. I've been around boats most of my life."

"Me too!" he exclaimed. "I mean, I...where...you're from where? South Africa? I was wondering about your accent."

"*My* accent? *I* don't have an accent; *you* do." She grinned.

"No...I mean, I didn't..."Tom stammered, realizing she was toying with him. Then she raised one eyebrow and made a questioning face. She crossed her arms and tapped her foot in anticipation of his response. He stood for a moment, thinking, she's a smart girl. I'd better watch what I say from now on.

"Jessica! Jessica!" rang out from the street above where they stood.

"Oh...it's my Aunt Sarah. I forgot about the fish," she said, turning, she started up the dock. "Hey, Thomas Jennings," she yelled as he watched her walking away.

"Yeah!"

"Better tie that starboard line a little better to that cleat before she goes adrift on you." She said laughing.

"Where you living?" he yelled as she and her aunt went toward the fishing boats.

"Here!" She turned and smiled at him. "I'm living here for the summer."

He watched the two women as he gathered his gear and walked to his truck. *My lucky day,* he thought, seeing them drive off. Jessica waved once more as the car left the marina and headed for Ocean Avenue. The sun set as the tide came in and the seagulls returned to the sandy beaches. They waited for what the sea would offer in the night and watched the light fade behind the western hills and trees of Shark River Heights. Night came as the day retracted its light. The stars glittered in the night sky as the constellations appeared. Mythical gods of a thousand civilizations asked for the meeting of night and day as the stars danced to the rhythm of the cosmos.

***

Two days passed and the rain seemed to never end. Jessica watched the raindrops play on the sea as the fishing boats went out for their daily catch. She thought back to Gansbaai and its proud fishermen, strong Afrikaners who braved the Atlantic and Indian Oceans for their livelihood. Generation after generation had lived and died by the sea but now the fishing industry was changing and many of the fishing factories had closed their doors. Jessica was sitting reading a book when the doorbell rang.

"Jessica, could you please get that?" Aunt Sarah yelled from the kitchen.

Jessica went to the door, opening it to find a dozen red roses and, behind them, a delivery boy from the florist shop. The scent of roses filled the air.

"I have some flowers for a Jessica Sinclair." The delivery boy placed the flowers on the table next to the door.

"That would be me."

When the boy had gone, Jessica sat on the couch, placing the flowers on the coffee table in front of her. She closed her eyes and smelled the blossoms, touching the soft velvet of their petals.

"Jessica, who was it?" Aunt Sarah came out of the kitchen. "Oh, roses!" she exclaimed. "Who are they from?" She pushed the ribbon around the stems to the side, revealing a small note. "I don't think they're for me." She handed Jessica the note.

"This will make the day less dreary," She went on. "Oh...this rain...will it never end? Well, open it, my dear."

Jessica quickly opened the note.

To: Jess

In all my life, I never did see

A seashell on the seashore
As pretty as thee
Sunshine above and
Starlight at night
My heart is forever
Yours at first sight

She read the poem and smiled, knowing whom it was from. Placing the poem in her pocket, she ran to the closet, retrieving her yellow raincoat and blue Yankees baseball cap. She looked in the mirror. "God, I look like an American in this baseball cap!" She giggled.

"Well, who was it from, Jessica?

"The boy. The boy at the docks." She excitedly said turning and ran to the front door. "I'm heading out," she shouted. "I'll be back later." The door slammed behind her. Sarah smiled as she stood watching Jessica run happily down the walkway in the rain, remembering roses she had got as a young girl, many years ago.

"Must be love. The girl's in love."

Thomas heard the rain pounding the deck of the *Blue Heron*, wondering if the roses had arrived yet. His heart raced at the thought of Jessica receiving his gift and he felt maybe it was too soon. Maybe it would scare her away. Maybe he was one of many guys who sent her roses and she would just laugh at him. He hadn't dated since his longtime girlfriend Megan had died two years earlier. His heart had been broken when he heard the news of her death and he had never felt the need to look for anyone else. He sat in the dimly lit cabin, nervously wondering what was next. Wondering if he was ready for someone in his life. But he knew the feeling in his heart, and the excitement he had felt when he saw Jessica on the beach, at the dock, and when she had spoken to him that day. But, again, in his heart he still felt the pain of losing Megan that cold December morning. Could another person take away the pain and sadness he felt? Was another person supposed to take away the pain? This he did not know, but he did know that his heart, once again, was beating faster. Something he never thought he'd feel again: Love. He never wanted to lose his love for Megan, and never wanted to meet someone, and go through that pain and sorrow of losing someone again.

The clouds began to clear as the seagulls circled above the marina. Rays of sun began to break through. It seemed majestic, like a painting of Van Gogh or Monet; bright, colorful, it transcended one's comprehension of beauty. The clouds seemed to move with the hand of God as beams of sunlight broke through, bringing hues of yellow, orange, purple and blue. Tom quietly sat listening to his heartbeat as he heard the sound of thunder in the distance. The storm was going out to sea and change was in the air. He could smell the newly fallen rain, fresh and clean. It washed away the hurt and brought life to his soul. It was a summer's rain. Jessica quickly walked down the ramp toward the *Blue Heron*. She too felt the storm depart as her heart lifted with each step. Thomas opened the hatch and came up from the cabin to find Jessica standing next to the boat on the dock. They looked into each other's eyes for what seemed a lifetime before either one said a word.

"Why are you crying?" he asked.

"I'm not crying." She wiped her cheeks. "It's rainwater." She looked into Tom's eyes, hoping. Hoping that he felt the same way she did. He jumped to the dock and went up to her. She looked so cute, he thought, in her little yellow raincoat and blue baseball cap. She searched his eyes for a sign. Tom placed his hand on her face and wiped away the rainwater from her cheek. As they stood there on the dock, looking into each other's eyes, the sky cleared, shining its light about them. She looked up at him, wondering what he felt. He looked at her and felt love in his heart. She placed her hands on his hips as he slowly slid his hand to the back of her head and gently kissed her on the lips. It was a long kiss. Their hearts raced with excitement and Jessica felt weakened from his touch. Then she became dizzy and her mind clouded into darkness. Thomas clutched her body before she fell to the dock. When she woke, she found him sitting at her side. She was in the cabin of the *Blue Heron* lying on the bunk.

"Are you okay? He asked, nervously. "I mean...I didn't know what to do. You fainted."

"Yes, I...I'm okay, I've been getting these dizzy spells lately," she said, remembering the kiss. "Did you kiss me?" Her eyes opened wider.

"I...I, I did. I hope that was okay. I mean, I didn't mean to if you didn't want me to. I didn't..." Thomas fumbled his words. She reached up and kissed him.

"I'm not usually forward but there's time for talking and time for kissing." She smiled. "I would think that this is a time for kissing, wouldn't you?"

Thomas leaned over and pushed her hair to the side. Their lips touched for the third time. Their hearts felt the sun shining and the clouds depart as the storm went out to sea. The smell of freshly fallen rain began to mix with ocean mist as the seagulls played. Life had come with the storm and now the storm would traverse the sea. It would bring life to others and death to some as it rolled across the savannahs, deserts and plains of distant lands.

***

The days and weeks passed, bringing renewal to their hearts. The sandpipers dashed and darted with each crashing and receding wave as seagulls waltzed in the blue sky. Mr. Carlton watched the inlet as the *Blue Heron* glided toward the bridge. As the bridge opened, he waved, looking down. Tom and Jessica waved back at him standing above.

"Enjoy the day, Tom! See you caught something already!" Mr. Carlton yelled as they sailed through the opening and headed out to sea. It was a new day and a time for healing for both Jessica and Thomas. It was their time for love and their time for each other, a moment the world would soon never forget. As the sloop tacked from side to side, Tom played the wind like a song. The sound of the rushing water, the banging of the hull, and the whooshing of the wind composed a rhythm of life. The love of nature was about them and in them. One a child of Africa and the other a child of the sea, they both felt the call of nature, the destiny of their hearts and the longing and love for life.

The day passed with grace as the sun sank in the western sky.

Tom held Jessica in his arms. "What a fantastic day. I can't remember a better one."

"Me neither, Thomas," she whispered softly. "It's like a dream, like some ancient dream. I had a dream where I was running down a beach and then I began flying into the sky. It was weird. There were people there, just standing on the sand dunes watching me in the air. They were holding candles."

"Sounds like a nice dream to me. Maybe the beach was where I first saw you and the flying is now, gliding over the water."

"No. I was home in Gansbaai. I remember. It seemed so long ago; so distant. The people were singing, singing an African song. I could hear them singing as I..." She stopped talking abruptly. Her eyes seemed distant, remembering the dream. *What did it mean? Did it mean anything at all?* She looked out over the water and watched the sun, starting to head toward the horizon. It seemed so strong and majestic, yet it moved with such grace. It had a quiet fortitude she admired. A tear ran down her cheek.

"What's the matter, Jess?" Thomas looked into her eyes. She seemed to drift away; drift to a place he did not know. "What, Jess?" Thomas rubbed her arm. "Are you okay?"

"Yes," she said quietly. Distant but not forgotten were her pains and sorrows. "I was just thinking about someone I once knew and some people I once knew in Africa."

"You seem sad." He brushed the hair from her face. *What made her so sad?* He thought, looking into her eyes and brushing away the tear.

"I'll be fine. It's getting late. We better get moving."

They held each other tight as they slowly made their way west, under the bridge and up the inlet, heading back toward the dock.

"You have to tell me about Africa someday, about your home. I want to know everything about you," Thomas said. Jessica pulled away from him as the *Blue Heron* neared the dock. He watched her as she helped guide the boat into the slip and secured the tie lines. Had he said something wrong? Was he moving too fast?

Jessica turned to him and grinned. "All tied up, Captain! Sorry for getting moody on you. It was a nice day and I had a great time. I'm just a little tired." She reached for Tom's hand and held it tight. She didn't want the day to end, and knew that good things sometimes came to an end, whether she liked it or not. "I'll tell you all about my home tomorrow." She kissed him softly on the lips, closing her eyes as they kissed, feeling the tears building up as she stepped away, grabbed her day bag, and headed up the dock. "Let's go, big guy! It's going to get dark soon!"

Thomas watched her. He sensed something was wrong but didn't know what it could be. *It has been a great day,* he thought, grabbing his bags and walking behind her, wondering about the peaceful girl, the quiet girl he had first seen on the beach. The night began washing over the day as they walked toward the car.

***

Jessica lay in her bed, listening to the birds chirp and sing as the morning rays broke through the green trees, filling her room with a warm loving light. The sounds of the waves breaking on the shoreline could be heard in the distance as she watched and listened to the day begin and she thought about the previous day. Sailing with Thomas filled her heart with warmth. And she remembered the loss she had felt as she recalled Africa and the people she had loved and lost.

Dear God, she prayed, *please take this pain from me and help me understand why, why there is evil in the world.* She turned on her side and closed her eyes, listening to the waves and feeling the morning light on her face.

"Jessica! Are you awake?" Sarah cried out. "Come on down and get some breakfast, young lady!"

Jessica sat up, lifting her arms high, stretching them to the ceiling. She remembered sitting in her tent in Angola one morning doing the same thing. Her mind turned to that morning, as breakfast was cooked at the fire. She could hear the eggs and bacon simmering and smell the coffee as if it were that day. The tent was already hot from the morning sun, the heat beginning to climb. As she walked from her tent, she saw a little tribal boy sitting below a nearby tree. She looked at him as he sat, quietly playing in the sand. He was so at peace as he played but seemed too quiet to her as she walked to him. "What are you doing?" she asked.

"I hurt," he replied in his native language, words she had heard many times before and in many African dialects.

"What do you mean, you hurt?" She came closer.

"My foot hurt," he replied as he looked between his legs.

Jessica walked up to him, and found that his leg had been severed from a land mine explosion. He was in shock, disorientated. *He must have been making his way to my tent for help,* she thought. The mine, left over from countless years of civil wars and unrest, was a cruel reminder of the devastation and brutality of war.

"John!" she had screamed out as she grabbed the boy, his leg, and ran for the medical tent. She remembered never eating the breakfast as it burned on the fire that morning, and she remembered seeing the same little boy crying that horrible day in the schoolhouse as General Mobutu fired shots over their heads and murdered the elderly tribesman, the boy's grandfather. Tears filled her eyes as the memories of the past haunted her soul. It hadn't been till later that day, while talking with John, that she had realized she had been awakened by the muffled blast of the mine. John, too, had heard the blast, and was running toward her tent when he saw her holding the small, bloodied boy.

***

"Jessica! Are you coming to breakfast?" Sarah yelled.

"No, Aunt Sarah. Not today," she answered in a sad and distant voice, which faded to a distant past as she looked out the window at a nearby tree. The room was already building from the morning sun as the day's heat began to climb. Feeling dizzy again, she rushed to the bathroom and vomited. Afterwards, she lay down on the bathroom floor for a long while. The cool floor was comforting as she lay there, remembering the healing rains and life-giving waters of Africa.

***

Thomas was sanding the deck of the *Blue Heron* as Jessica arrived at the dock. It was a hot July morning and the sun was high.

"Hey! Where've you been all morning?" he said sarcastically as he put down his sander.

"Doing things around the house. Had to help my aunt take care of some chores."

"I was thinking of taking a ride into the country." Thomas watched her standing next to the boat. "What do you think?"

"Why? Don't you like the beach?"

"I do. I just thought we'd head out and explore. Maybe see some horses. Take a walk in a field. You know, get away for the day." Jessica looked to the open sky. Not a cloud could be seen.

"There's a place not far from here where there are horses." Tom went on, "why don't we get a lunch from the sub shop and head out there. I'm going to jump in the shower and clean up. I'll just be a minute." He winked at her as he opened the hatch, and went below-deck. Within minutes they were in Tom's truck and heading west on Route 33 to the rolling hills and farmlands of New Jersey. To the south, were the Great Pine Barrens, a vast area of pine trees, rivers and lakes that encompassed much of southern New Jersey's land. They drove west for an hour and turned north onto Route 206 to Gladstone. The lush rolling hills, the farms and streams filled Jessica's mind with wonder. Everywhere she looked, she saw miles and miles of green trees, farms and blue skies.

"This is still New Jersey?" She looked with wonder at the open rolling hills. "There are trees everywhere."

"All this is New Jersey. It's not called the Garden State for nothing." He grinned as he drove. "We're almost there."

"Where are you taking me?" She looked at him as he turned off the main road onto a dirt tree-lined road.

"It's just beautiful," she said. "It's really wonderful here."

"Where I'm taking you is a surprise. I hope you like it when we get there?" Thomas made a sharp turn up and then around the side of a low mountain, turned one last time and drove down a tight winding path. He stopped next to an old barn and jumped out of the truck.

"What do you think? Nice place for a picnic!" he said as he began unloading the truck. A large tree stood in the middle of a great field. Oak, pine, maple and birch trees filled the forest as far as she could see. She watched water running over the stones of a nearby stream, making them appear soft from years of wear. Another large field, once plowed for crops was now a sunny meadow, and everywhere were, trees and flowers and life. The crowns of the trees captured the sunlight as the birds played, swerving and diving from side to side. It was a beautiful valley tucked away and hidden from view.

"It's lovely, Thomas! Just lovely." She went to him as he finished unloading the truck. "This place is magical. I could spend a lifetime here." She swung around with her arms in the air as a bird dancing upon a warm summer's wind.

"I'm glad you like it." He chuckled, watching the expression on her face. She seemed happy and that made him happy. "Let's head over to that chestnut tree there in the distance. Looks like it has nice shade."

"Thomas." Jessica said looking into his eyes. "Thanks for bringing me here." She put her arms around his neck and looked into his brown eyes as they softly kissed.

"Come on, let's get some food into our stomachs before we pass out from starvation." He grabbed her hand as they walked to the distant tree that stood in the field.

As they sat and ate their lunch, they enjoyed the view of the rolling hills, the sound of silence and of nature and of love. Off in the meadow, deer came from the woods and passed before them as they watched in silence. Chipmunks and squirrels played in the trees as black crows squawked in the distant sky. A lone hawk glided high above, feeling the unseen air currents that provided hours of flight as it searched for a meal. It was a special day for their love to grow and it was a special spot, Thomas had taken her to see. "So, do you like it out here?" he asked, looking around the field.

"This is an amazing place. I can feel nature here. It's so alive and knowing. I haven't felt that since I was in Africa. It feels like it knows we are here. And it is letting us be here. We have permission. But in Africa, there's more feeling of danger."

"What's it like there?" he said, not knowing if he should ask so soon. He felt something was bothering her inside that had made her cry. "I mean, I've seen the Discovery Channel and 'Wild America' and all, but I really don't know that much about Africa other than it has a lot of blacks."

"Thomas!" Jessica was stunned. "That's not nice to say. I don't like when people talk like that!"

"Well, isn't it true?" Thomas sat upright. "Aren't there a lot of blacks?"

"People, Thomas." She was now upset and confused at Thomas's statement. "There are many different people in Africa, Thomas. Not just the black people. It's very diversified, like here in the United States."

"I know, but what about all the troubles" Thomas exclaimed. "You have all that apartheid stuff happening in South Africa?"

"Yes, but it's not everyone. Not everybody who's white and lives in South Africa is a racist. Just like here in the States, you're not all racist." She had become defensive as she thought back to her homeland, movies she'd seen and talk she'd overheard in America. "You know, Thomas, it's easy for people and countries to point the finger at South Africa. But you and other people don't live there. You haven't seen with your own eyes. Look at your own country, the United States. What they did to the American Indians. Look at Australia and what they did to the Aborigines. Other countries and peoples of the world have done things to survive, to grow and to control lands, but now everyone points their finger at the South African whites. I'm not saying that what was done was right, but Africa is a place of survival of the fittest. The animals and its people know that this is true, both black and white people there know this is true. My father and brothers fought to keep the borders free from terrorists for all the people of South Africa and help eliminate the crime, drugs and killing in our country. They put their lives on the line for our country's safety. My brother Ian hasn't been the same after coming back from the Northern Transvaal. He used to be happy and cheerful but now he's withdrawn and quiet." Her voice rose. "I just don't know why everyone keeps coming down on South Africa."

"I'm sorry, Jess. I didn't mean to say anything bad," Thomas said as he held her hand. "I didn't mean to upset you," he added softly.

"It's just that I've heard people talk about this here and I don't understand why they are saying bad things about us. We're just like everyone else in the world. We want to survive, live a happy life, free of terrorists and killings and wars. I've seen war and…"

Jessica began to sob uncontrollably. She cried for what seemed an hour. Thomas felt her pain and sorrow. He brushed her hair back and wiped away some of her tears, but more followed like water in a stream. They washed over her cheeks, making them soft, but underneath the tears, was a rock that would hold true to herself, a rock that would not be changed by life's hardships and life's sorrows. He remembered the hatred he had in his heart for the two black men who raped and killed his girl that cold night in December two years earlier. He felt the hate in his heart, the hate he had for the race. He would never feel any love for their kind, but he did not mention to Jessica the hatred and pain he held in his heart, and the cause of his girlfriend's death. He looked at the great chestnut tree they sat under. What would it take to heal the anger and pain he felt for a whole race because of two evil men? What would it take to again have innocence in his heart and mind?

Jessica told Thomas about the work she had done with the Red Cross in Angola, the atrocities and horrors she had observed that day at the schoolhouse and the beatings she had undergone in the jail cell, holding back that she had been raped. Thomas held her as she told the story of the tribal boy, his father and the solders. It had been a dark time for her and this was the first time she had talked to anybody about the pain she had experienced and the horror of war. His anger for the black race broadened, knowing what had happened to her, and he felt it build in his heart.

"So what happened to this Mobutu guy?" he questioned.

"I don't know. I stayed in South Africa for some time after that to heal. I checked the papers and the Internet about Angola, but nothing was said about him. I do know that the civil war was over, and there was peace again, just as my father said there would be. Thanks for listening to me, Thomas. I haven't told anybody what happened." She hugged him.

"You're lucky to be alive, Jess. If I ever see this Mobutu guy, I'll kill him."

She became alarmed at what he'd said. "You shouldn't say such things.

That man is an evil man and God will deal with him, not you. Now stop talking like that."

"It's just not right that people like you should be hurt by people like that."

"Just remember what I'm saying, all people should be treated equally. There are bad people and good people in all races in the world. It's not right to view things that way. In my country, Apartheid and hatred are coming to an end. Now maybe, just maybe we can bring unity to all the people of South Africa: Black and white."

"Well, there are just some things I don't understand," he said, leaning back against the tree trunk.

"There are things that are meant to happen in this world, she said with passion. "Someday we'll understand why things happen the way they do. My father always said that everything happens for a higher purpose. I believe he's right."

"Okay, Jess...maybe you're right, but with all the pain in the world... there are a lot of people suffering and hurting...I just hope God knows what he's doing."

"He does, Thomas. He does."

After some time, as the two sat under the tree, Thomas's anger began to settle. She could feel that he was upset by what she had told him and was glad she'd not told him everything. He looked up at the great tree. Sunlight broke through the upper branches and leaves.

"This tree we're sitting under...it's a chestnut tree," he said softly. He stared up at the bright green leaves and white sunlight. "At one time these trees lined the eastern seaboard of the United States. People would say that a squirrel could walk from Maine to Florida on top of the chestnut trees. Now they are few in number, and this one was saved only by cutting this huge field around it."

"Why?" she asked.

"Because someone made a mistake. A disease was introduced from the East that killed only the chestnut trees. So today there are only a few of them left. There are researchers at work trying to grow a chestnut tree that can withstand the disease before it's too late and we don't have any more left in the world. That's one of the reasons I bought this piece of land."

"Thomas!" Jessica's eyes opened wide.

"Yep! I purchased it a few years ago. I plan on building a house here someday. I think it would make a nice place to live. Just like this field and tree, I can put my arms around you and keep you safe too. I mean...I'd like to if you want me to," She felt the love growing in her heart and wanted to hold him forever, too, but she also knew she wanted to go back to the land she loved.

"We'll see." She knew that she still needed healing. She looked at the darkening sky, thinking about her tears and pain, the children and people of the tribe, John Hanson and Mobutu. Anger filled her heart with the thought of Mobutu and the uncertainty of whether he was still alive. They watched the constellations move across the sky as the night passed.

***

As the days went by and summer came to its end, the sun shifted north as it rose in the east and setting a little farther south with each fading day. The sky and ocean began to change with the coming fall and the ocean, as if enraged at the changing of the season, came to life. The sky, too, celebrated the changing with bright oranges, reds, purples and blues as the sun lowered in the western sky. The gods and mythical powers were at play once again. A lone Hottentot stood on a distant shore. He looked to the changing light, the moving constellations and the change in the air and gave thanks. He lifted his head high and lifted his arms high to the gods above. He was ready. He knew the cycle of life was at play. It was written in the heavens. He was ready to continue with life or die. Only the gods knew his destiny. Just as the Cape Lion stood long ago, he too would stand proud. Time was ending for the Mamzibi, the mosquito people and their way of life. The Great Karoo would last forever but the nomadic way of life would fade in time. The world seemed to be closing in on them from all sides. Would they too diminish into history, only to be remembered in folklore and books?

CHAPTER 5

Conrad Sinclair walked outside and looked toward the western horizon. He held a letter from Jessica. She had stayed two years in the States and was arriving home to South Africa. It was a time of political change. Apartheid had been ending when she left for the States and political tension was still in the air. Nelson Mandela became the new president of South Africa, and the new government was now in power. But the same problems persisted in the country: Crime, drugs and the ever-increasing rise of HIV; and now the instability of the new government, and the newly changed regime, added to the chaos. Conrad watched the changing times with caution. He saw the change as inevitable, for in Africa, like the universe, change was a constant and it reminded him that humankind was just along for the ride. Civil war had erupted in Rwanda and other bordering countries. Angola's civil war came to an end after months of death and destruction and the loss of many innocent lives.

Conrad waited for his daughter; happy she had seemed to find peace of mind and healing of heart in the United States. It had been over two years since her unfortunate troubles in Angola and he was still worried about the impact that such brutality would carry in her mind and body.

"Ready to go to town." Mary Sinclair came out of the house, anticipating the arrival of Jessica at Cape Town International Airport. She longed to see Jessica and could not wait to show her the changes they had made to the house. The only room that hadn't been touched was Jessica's. "It will stay the way it was till she returns from the States," Conrad had declared one night at the dinner table.

"You seem a little nervous today, Conrad?" Mary remarked cautiously. She knew her man, knew the way he thought. With thirty-five years of marriage behind them, they knew each other well.

"I'm fine, Mary. I was just thinking of Jessica the night we found her in that prison cell. Jessica had been hurt badly and I still don't understand a few things about it. As the medics tended her, Jessica was fading on us. She kept saying she saw a Mamzibi. She kept saying, 'I saw him on the rock,' over and over again. That night as we approached the town, Duncan and some scouts were sent out ahead to secure the area. As he walked near the back side of the town, he heard a clicking noise to his right. He turned to find a small, light-skinned Hottentot crouched down near a bush. Duncan immediately turned and pointed his rifle at the man, but something told him not to shoot. Duncan said the man pointed to an area yards ahead, just to the left of where he was walking. When Duncan looked at the spot he saw someone light a cigarette. It was dark and it was obvious he would have walked into the trap. When he turned back, the Hottentot was gone. Duncan said he seemed to vanish into the night. And he thought the Hottentot was one of the Mamzibi tribe. After the shooting and fighting commenced, Duncan entered the jail cell where he found Jessica lying on the floor. He picked her up and began carrying her out of the room. He turned one last time as he exited the room. He said there on the floor was a dead guard. The guard's gun was next to Jessica when he picked her up. And there was an arrow in the guard's chest."

"What do you make of it?" Mary questioned.

"I don't know," Conrad opened the car door for her, "I really don't know," he softly said, looking toward the Drakensberge Mountains, thinking of the Hottentots and the Mamzibi. The Great Karoo lay on the other side of the mountain range. There were still places unexplored in the Great Karoo, he thought, and he knew that the Hottentots or Khoikhoi, as they are called, still roamed the vast plains of the Karoo and other nearby countries. There weren't many of these nomads left in Africa and the Mamzibi were no exception. Their way of life was fading with time.

The ride was quiet, both Conrad and Mary deep in thought as the car headed toward Cape Town International Airport.

"Let's stop for lunch," Mary said as she placed her hand softly on Conrad's arm. "We have time and it will give you a chance to relax."

"Sounds good," he said as they arrived in Hermanus.

The day was overcast and rain clouds came in from the ocean. They stopped for lunch at the Marine Hotel and Inn, and enjoyed the afternoon together reminiscing about their lives together, the children and the state of the country. They'd seen many changes in the 35 years of their marriage and watched the country's political situation change as crime and drugs increased over the years. But Conrad remembered the better times and smiled; he recalled their lives together, raising the children and the vast beauty of South Africa.

The airport bustled with people coming and going as the two walked to the arrival terminal. Conrad hoped Jessica was as well as she sounded on the phone and from what he read in her letters.

Suddenly, loud voices erupted from the departure area. Conrad turned to see two white Afrikaner men arguing with three black uniformed police officers. From what he could hear, the white men were being detained for questioning. Tempers flared as the men resisted the police officers' interrogation. One of the officers radioed for backup as the argument continued. Two more uniformed officers arrived and handcuffed the two men. Then two well-dressed black security agents arrived, one clearly a high-ranking officer, who commanded authority. He poked at the white men and slapped one across the face as they escorted them into an interrogation room. The head security man stood outside the door smoking a cigarette.

"What do you think is the matter?" Mary asked, Conrad.

"I don't know but I don't like the look of that head security agent. He seems a little rough, smacking that fellow and dragging them off to that room."

"What do you think they did?"

"Probably nothing. I heard there's a new person in charge of security now, a Director Something; I can't remember his name, a man from up north somewhere. I think that's him. I saw a picture of him in the paper last week." Conrad watched the security agent hit the man again. "I'm not liking this situation, Mary. We better move over to the other side of the arrival area."

"I read in the newspaper that the old security director lost the position."

"Yes. New people are replacing most of our government officials. With the new government in power, there are a lot of new faces. Mostly blacks. I just hope they uphold the peace and abide by the laws of the country. However, I don't think that's going to happen." Conrad stood up and watched the uniformed police yelling at the two white men in the room. The head security agent turned and looked directly at him. Conrad could feel his arrogance and the coldness of the stare through his dark sunglasses. Conrad held his stare. He was a proud Afrikaner, a man of means who backed down from no man.

"Why don't you sit down?" Mary asked as she grabbed and pulled at Conrad's hand. "Come on, honey, sit down. There's nothing you can do," she said nervously as she watched the security officer continued to stare at Conrad. Conrad sat down and turned to see if the security officer was still looking.

"I don't like the looks of that man, Mary. He's trouble. What if that was our son being questioned? I don't like this at all," he said looking one last time. The head security officer laughed, still looking directly at Conrad. Then he turned and walked into the office where the two white men were being detained for questioning.

"Look! There she is!" Mary shouted as Jessica walked through the customs gate. Conrad grinned proudly, seeing his little girl safe and smiling as Jessica walked toward them.

"Howzit!" Jessica yelled running to them. "Hi, Daddy! Hey, Mom!" She hugged them both. "I've missed you guys."

"We've missed you too, Jess. How was the trip?"

"Fifteen hours on a plane is long enough for me. And if the pilot said, 'We may experience some turbulence' one more time, I think I would have jumped off the plane in the middle of the Atlantic Ocean." She looked around the airport. "This place crowded or what, man?"

"Yes. There have been a few changes since you left—" Conrad looked toward the security room.

"Now, now, let's not get into that right now," Mary interrupted. "Let's get your luggage and get you home for some supper."

"Thomas is finishing up with customs and will be bringing the luggage," Jessica said, winking at her mother.

"Thomas!" Conrad became alert. "The same Thomas your Aunt Sarah told us about?"

"Yes, Daddy. I have a boyfriend now and his name's Thomas. I told you I had a few surprises."

"You sure have!" Conrad looked at Mary. "Did you know about this? And what do you mean, a few surprises?"

"You'll see!"

Mary grabbed Jessica's hand and began to walk toward the luggage area. "Yes. I knew all about it."

"How come I'm always the last to know?" Conrad sulked as he followed.

"It was my wish for you not to know, Conrad." Mary said. "You know how you get sometimes." She and Jessica giggled as Conrad followed, searching for Jessica's American boyfriend, Thomas. He wasn't completely surprised; he knew his daughter and had known she'd surprise him someday with this kind of news. She was a strong-willed girl with a free spirit. He walked behind them, turning from time to time, watching the security office door in the distance.

"Thomas! Over here, honey!" Jessica yelled across the conveyor belt as the luggage moved in front of them. People scrambled for their belongings, pushing and shoving as they grabbed their bags and saw loved ones.

"Honey!" Conrad muttered from behind them as Jessica went to Thomas.

"Conrad!" Mary shook her head. "Be nice. The girl's in love."

"Oh, now it's love, is it?" Conrad smirked.

"Hello, Mr. and Mrs. Sinclair. I'm Thomas Jennings," Thomas said with a wide smile, shaking hands with them. Firm handshake, Conrad thought.

"Please call me Conrad," he said. "Being called 'sir' sounds old. I used to call my father 'sir'." Now Conrad was smiling.

"Conrad it is, then."

"And you can call me Mary," she said.

"What's going on over there?" Jessica was looking toward the security office and the men standing outside its doors. In the room behind them were the two Afrikaans men, sitting in chairs against the back wall. Both had blood on their faces, one, his head hanging, had blood running down his forehead.

Jessica stared into the room at the two men. "Daddy. What's happening?" she again asked.

"I don't know, Jess." Conrad watched the head security officer watching them as they passed the security office. "Let's just keep moving; a lot of things have changed here since you've been away, I'll explain later." Jessica and Thomas looked at the men in the room as the security officer closed the doors. Jessica felt the coldness of the head security officer's stare, his dark sunglasses and stern expression piercing her soul. She studied his face for a moment as she walked toward the terminal exit.

She could feel the cold stare from the head security officer behind them as they neared the exit door. She went back in time to that horrible day in Angola, remembering the rain, blood and horror she had endured.

Turning, she looked at the security officers one last time before she, Thomas and her parents walked out of the terminal. The security officers stopped at the doorway.

"Oh my God…it's Mobutu. It's Mobutu," she said as tears began running down her cheek. Her hands began to tremble and she thought she heard the dark, evil voice of Mobutu say, "White whore, I know you. I know you."

"Are you okay, Jess?" Thomas said with concern, seeing the tears. I knew you'd cry when you saw your parents." He rubbed his hand on her lower back.

Puzzled, Conrad looked at his little girl, then back through the exit doors at the two security officers. "Have you seen those men before, Jess?" he asked.

"No. Let's just get going, I'm just tired, Dad." She wiped away her tears, the past horrors seeming to haunt her again. She could feel her legs shaking and her soul yearning to scream out, "It's him—he's the killer—get him before he kills again—before he hurts the children."

Something is wrong, Conrad thought, as they loaded the luggage into the car. He glared back at the entrance doors as they began to drive off, then surreptitiously removed the .45-caliber pistol from the door and placed it next to his seat. Mary watched with concern.

Mobutu, watched the car drive off, remembering the South African fighters who had killed his men. He remembered the white whore he had ordered killed. He had questioned her disappearance from the cell and the death of his guard. Now the pieces were coming together. He ordered his man to follow the car. Secure in his new position as Director of Security, he would not let anyone tamper with his new life in South Africa.

Jessica watched the countryside pass as the car headed for home. She seemed distant, remembering back to all the horrors she had seen and experienced in Angola. The trip to the United States had been long and she felt she had been away from her country a lifetime, but her memories and pains of the past seemed like yesterday. She still heard the screams of the people, the firing of the gunshots and the horror of seeing John Hanson lying in the mud, dead from a gunshot wound to his head. She remembered his blood dripping and mixing with the mud as the rain fell that day. She rested her head on Thomas's shoulder as they drove toward home. While in Gansbaai, she resolved that there, she would search her soul and heart for answers once more. There she would find the innocence she once had known in her youth.

Conrad looked at her in the rearview mirror. The happiness he had seen when she had first arrived at the airport was gone. Something was wrong and he knew now his little girl was still wounded; her mind was somewhere else. He remembered the day he saw her standing near the edge of the cliffs. She had the same look on her face: distant, sorrowful and troubled. He knew she'd seen the evils of war and the pain of losing people she loved and cared for. But there was something else that he did not know, something that had triggered her emotions at the airport. Was it seeing the men in the room? Was it being back home in South Africa? Was it seeing the security officers? He watched curiously in the mirror at the truck that followed in the distance.

The afternoon waned as the sun began to settle on the western horizon. The clouds moved inland, over the Drakensberge and into the Great Karoo. Though there was little chance of the rain falling, God had made the land dry and harsh for a reason. The Khoikhoi believed it was the place where the deities created mankind by mixing the dry orange-colored soil with the blue waters of life. They believed this was why their skin was orange in color and their eyes blue at birth. After a few weeks of life, their eyes changed to brown, signifying the water draining from their bodies and returning to the earth. There was little water in the Great Karoo and when it did arrive, it was a blessing from the gods. They cherished and lived by the waters of life.

By the time they arrived at the estate in Gansbaai, both Jessica and Thomas were fast asleep. Mary looked at them sleeping and was happy for Jessica.

"Hey, guys, we're home."

"We're home already?" Jessica smiled tiredly. "Thomas, wake up, honey, we're here."

Thomas turned from side to side, opening his eyes and looking around, wondering where he was. He'd never been so far from his home in the United States and jetlag played upon his awareness. "Where are we?" He looked around.

"We're in Gansbaai, my home. Welcome to my home, honey, and welcome to Gansbaai," Jessica said softly, hugging him.

Thomas looked through the car windows as they came to a stop before the large Dutch Colonial house in Gansbaai. The whitewashed walls and copper-colored clay roof radiated from the sun setting over the ocean. He then realized how far he was from home. "I can smell the ocean," he said. "It smells clean here."

"We're very near the ocean, Thomas." Conrad grabbed the bags and began unloading the car. "Where are my boys when you need them?" he chuckled, looking around the estate. "They haven't seen their sister in two years and they aren't here to meet you." Near the back of the compound the guard dogs barked. Conrad and Thomas picked up the luggage and headed for the house. "I'll have a word with my brothers when I see them, Daddy," Jessica sarcastically said as she and Mary followed. They placed the bags on the front porch, off to the side near the rocking chairs.

"Wait till you see what we did with the place, Jessica." Mary said. "You're going to love the new furniture."

"We redecorated most of the house except your room," Conrad said. "I wanted you to pick the furniture out yourself."

Jessica hugged him.

"Someone's home," Jessica said. "I smell something cooking."

"Jara. I told her you would be hungry. She's probably put something on the stove for us."

"Well, Jess," Conrad said, "head in and see what we've done with the place." Jessica opened the door and everyone followed her into the dimly lit house. Suddenly, lights flicked on and she found herself in a room filled with people.

"Surprise!" erupted from the crowded room.

"Howzit, little sister." Ian was smiling from ear to ear. "Welcome home!" he signed with his hands.

"Welcome home, Jessica." Duncan smiled broadly as he went up to her, picking her up from her feet in a strong hug. "Jesus! You eating in the States or what?" he said, swinging her from side to side.

"Put her down before you break her in half, Duncan." Mary smacked him on the back. "They've had a long trip."

"What do you mean, 'they'?" Duncan put her back on her feet and looked at Thomas standing silently near the door with Conrad. "Hey! Who's this here?"

"So!"—-he went to Thomas—"you the one not feeding my little sister, hey!" He grinned. Jessica stood and watched her older brother act tough as Thomas held his ground, looking around and seeing that everyone was still smiling. He knew that Duncan was just acting.

"Well, I tried feeding her but she said that your barbecuing killed her taste buds." Thomas grinned in delight of his quick comeback. Everyone began to chuckle as Duncan looked around the room.

"Well, for one thing, it's called a briaa here, Yank; and for two, I cook the best briaa in the whole Cape." A roar of coughs and laughs came from the family and friends. With a broad smiling face, Duncan said, "Hey! You know it's true!" He turned toward Jessica and winked in approval of Jessica's new boyfriend. She mouthed a silent "thank-you" in return.

"I'm Duncan, Jessica's oldest brother. Welcome to South Africa, Thomas." They shook hands vigorously and Duncan placed a large hand on Thomas's shoulder. "Come. I'll introduce you to Ian and the rest."

Thomas looked at Jessica and smiled with relief, then was introduced to everyone. Duncan proudly introduced him as Jessica's boyfriend from the States. "We have a Yank here." He laughed.

Thomas admired the large house's decor. Dark wood beams extended across the ceiling, four large Bombay fans revolved slowly above. It had a warm and welcoming feeling and he immediately felt at home. On the whitewashed walls hung the heads of various species of animals: Springbok, Thomson gazelle, and hyena heads lined the walls. Above the massive fireplace was a larger-than-life lion; its head and extended black mane told of its life as king. Conrad came to Thomas side.

"Mighty are we that live, for it will come a day that we too will perish from this land," Conrad said, staring at the great beast.

"It's amazing." Thomas looked up into the lion's face. "Even now its face tells its story. I can feel its wisdom and pride. It's really amazing. I've never seen a lion head that big."

"And you will never again, Thomas: not alive, that is." Conrad looked up at the great beast with pride. "That is known to be the last Cape Lion that roamed Southern Africa. They were the biggest of all the carnivores of Africa in its time. The last of these mighty lions perished in the early nineteen hundreds. This one was hunted and shot by my father when I was a boy.

"I don't see any other lions here, or elephants or rhinos. Why?"

"Because I don't hunt the big five," Conrad said, looking up at the great lion, he squinted. "The big five are almost extinct and it's time to preserve these great animals: The elephant, lion, leopard, rhino and buffalo are the big five here in South Africa. Just in case you didn't know." He winked.

"No, I didn't know. Thanks."

"Before my father's death, he said the only regret he had in life was killing this Cape lion because it's believed to have been the last one alive. He knew that this lion wasn't just a kill, but extermination. Zoologists in Cape Town are now searching the world over for any that may have been kept alive, transported out to other countries…but no luck yet in finding any.

"Your poor father…he must have felt really bad."

"It was one of his last thoughts before he closed his eyes and died."

"Hey! What are you guys up to?" Jessica came up to them with two glasses of wine. "Here, have a glass of South African wine. It's becoming some of the best in the world."

"Thanks, Jess. We're talking about the big five."

"Cool!"

Mary joined them, "Did he tell you he hunted and killed that thing? Because he tells everyone he hunted and killed it a long time ago with his father. Don't believe him, Thomas." She winked at him, grinning.

"I didn't say that to him!" Conrad said defensively.

"Sure, Conrad. Come on, let's leave these two alone for a while," she said, dragging him off to mingle with the other guests. Jessica placed her arm through Thomas's and held it tightly.

"I love my mom and dad," she said.

"They're good people, I think your brothers like me, as well. Ian is a little quiet though. I don't know if he likes me yet."

"They do." She looked into his eyes. "I know my brothers and they like you already. Ian is a little quiet so don't take it as a sign that he doesn't, okay? He lost most of his hearing while fighting years ago, and now he reads lips really well. He's learned to use sign language too." She kissed Thomas, and he brushed her hair to one side and kissed her back softly on the lips. "I love you, Jess."

"I love you too, Thomas." She kissed him again, this time passionately. The firelight danced in her eyes as her heart lifted. She did love him and wanted to spend the rest of her life with him. She wanted to grow old with him and someday bear his children.

Thomas looked deep into his heart and soul and knew that he was ready to spend the rest of his life with her. He would never forget the pain of losing his first love, but knew he wanted to try again. Life would give him a second chance, life would give *them* a chance together, a chance to live, love and grow old together. They knew that what they felt in their hearts was love, true love that only God can give to them, and only God can take from them.

Thomas woke early to a warm sunny day. He could smell breakfast cooking in the kitchen, the bacon sizzling and coffee perking on the stove. He stood on the outside porch watching the sunrise over the mountains. The ocean twinkled as the light danced on the incoming tide. He smelled the clean ocean air and watched the seabirds glide across the unseen air currents; gliding high in the sky, they seemed to be celebrating the sun's return. He watched the rolling waves break on the shore, the ocean seemed part of a fortress of sorts: The ocean in front, and mountains in the rear, made a nice, secure place to live.

"Hey! You're up?" Conrad came around the corner of the house. "I thought, after that flight, you two would sleep until next week."

"This is such a great place you have here."

"Yes. We are lucky to have it. My father built the main house and we've expanded the compound a great deal since."

"I noticed that you are protected both by the ocean and the mountains," Thomas said.

Conrad watched Thomas surveying the area. "That's one of the reasons he built it here. Back then there were tribal threats and other dangers. But today, with the weapons people have, it serves just as a home. However, I still feel very secure here. It's been my home since I was a young boy and it's been Jessica's home since her birth."

"She always talks about it. Now I can see why she missed it so much. I had a completely different picture of Africa in my head before today."

"Well, make yourself at home. I have a feeling you will be around for a while."

Duncan and Ian came from the back of the main house. They seemed disturbed about something, Thomas thought, as he watched them.

"Howzit, guys?" Duncan said.

"Hey Duncan. Hey Ian. Good morning." Thomas said.

"Howzit, Thomas?" said Ian, "you're up early."

"Dad, we checked the back perimeter wall." Duncan said. "You were right; there was someone there last night. The guard dogs must have scared whoever it was off."

"Okay, boys. Thanks," Conrad said. "Have some of the men check the area and keep watch over the next couple of days. I saw a car following us from the airport yesterday. Maybe it was someone looking for a free meal."

"Okay, Dad," Duncan nodded, "I'll get right on it."

"Not a word about this to Jessica." Conrad said quickly.

"Hey, guys!" Jessica came up to them. "What a great day." She was grinning as she looked at the four of them. She noticed Thomas seemed to be relaxed.

"Man, you've become Americanized," Duncan said. "You didn't say, *Howzit.*

"Oh, you're funny, Duncan." She punched him in the arm playfully. "I'm as much of an Afrikaner as you, loser." She hugged Ian. "Duncan, you don't get a hug." She sarcastically smiled scrunching her nose.

"Hey, Jessica, you have to tell us about America," Ian said. "What's it like?"

"It's big, Ian, and very green. I'll tell you about it later. Thomas and I are going to hang out a little today so maybe we'll talk a little. I haven't been feeling well lately."

"What's the matter?" Conrad asked.

"I don't know, Dad. I've been feeling rundown. Sick at times." She grabbed Thomas's hand and kissed him. "Morning, honey."

"Morning honey!" Both Duncan and Ian said, laughing.

"Shut up you two. See what I have to put up with, Thomas?"

"Probably the American food you're eating." Duncan laughed. Ian and Thomas began laughing as well. Conrad looked at her, worried. She looked skinnier than she had three years ago.

"What else are you feeling, Jess?" he asked. Sickness was no joking matter to him. He was raised in tougher times and knew that the hospital system wasn't as good in South Africa as other parts of the world.

"It's nothing, Dad. Really!"

"Maybe you should see Doctor Vieter."

"I know, Dad. I'll be fine. Okay, what's up here?" She asked him. "You guys are way too quiet, man."

"Nothing's the matter, Jess. Why do you ask?" Conrad said.

"I saw Ian and Duncan near the back wall with the guard dogs, that's why." She smirked.

"They were just checking the wall, that's all." Conrad said calmly. "We've had a lot of new people in the area and we make checks from time to time,"

"That's all?" she persisted. "They're not lying to me, are they, Thomas?" She turned to him.

"No, Jess. They're not lying to you," he said, placing his arm around her shoulders, hugging her.

"Breakfast!" Jara yelled from the open window.

"Come on, guys, let's get something to eat," Conrad said. "And Thomas, I'd like to talk to you later, if you don't mind."

"Sounds good, Conrad."

Later, Thomas contemplated his conversation with Conrad, Duncan and Ian. What was it that troubled them about the back wall and who could have followed them from the airport? The estate was built like a fortress. A six-foot-high wall surrounded the compound. Barbed wire lined the top of the wall and guard dogs didn't hesitate to inform the family about intruders. Thomas knew South Africa had its troubles but Apartheid had ended. It seemed there was more that he needed to learn about the land. It was a wonderfully sunny day, hot, with not a cloud in the sky. But storms can sometimes roll in from the ocean with little warning, though not all storms are from the sea but come from the land.

CHAPTER 6

Jessica sat in the quiet waiting room of Doctor Vieter's office in Hermanus. Her visit would be a secret. The smell of medicine was in the air, a familiar smell that reminded her of vitamins, penicillin and sick people. One lone African woman sat near the entrance door. She seemed worried as she stared out the window, silent and lost in her thoughts, fumbling her thumbs as she waited to hear her name called. Jessica watched the rain trickle down the windowpane and wondered about the woman.

"Are you okay?" she asked softly. The woman said nothing, watching the door. "How are you feeling?" Still no response, Jessica leaned back in her chair and cleared her throat, watching the woman's thumbs circle around and around each other. The minutes passed as the thunderstorms rolled overhead and into the distance. *They're heading over the Drakensberge now,* she said to herself as the door opened.

"Mrs. Maziba, you're next," the doctor said, looking at the charts. The woman quickly stood and crossed to the door. "Jessica!" The doctor grinned. "Well, hello, you're back? I didn't know. Come on in here and let's have a look at you." He turned to the African woman. "Sorry, Mrs. Maziba, you'll have to wait just a little longer. Come on in, Jessica."

"She was before me, Doctor Vieter," Jessica said nervously, looking at Mrs. Maziba, who stood in the middle of the room, her head now lowered.

"No, you come on in, Jessica," he said again.

"Really. I insist, Doctor Vieter." Jessica grabbed Mrs. Maziba's hand and led her to the doctor. Then, turning, she looked into her eyes. As the rain trickled down the windowpane, Jessica could see the tears building up in the Mrs. Maziba's eyes. She was hurt and needed attention. "Treat her. I can wait a little longer," she said, walking back to her seat.

"Okay, Jessica. As you wish." The doctor led Mrs. Maziba into the examination room and closed the door behind them. Jessica sat watching the remaining drops of water work their way down the glass as the minutes passed. She searched through the magazines and read an article about the ending of Apartheid: "The New South Africa." Ironic, she thought, glancing toward the door. It would take some time for the country to heal its wounds; however, it was now on the right path, and with the proper care, would eventually heal its past troubles.

The exam-room door opened. "Have a good day, Mrs. Maziba," Doctor Vieter said with a warm smile. "Watch your step going out." He turned to Jessica. "Well, now, Ms. Sinclair, what brings you here?"

"I've been feeling a little sick. Just thought I'd get checked out while I was still in South Africa. I've healed pretty well, I think. I mean, my scars have healed and I don't hurt anywhere," she said softly. "But...I've been feeling sick at times...I mean nauseous...to the point where I'm vomiting and things."

"What do you mean...and things?"

"Well, I'm losing weight and, and...it seems I can't breathe as well as I used to."

Doctor Vieter watched her face and studied her eyes as she spoke. He remembered Jessica as a young girl. Being the family doctor, he knew the Afrikaner families well. "Let's step into the examination room and we'll have a look at you."

Nervously, Jessica followed the doctor into his office. She knew there was more to her illness and the doctor would find out. He gave her a clean robe to wear and asked her to sit on the table. "I'll be right back," he said, leaving the room. A few moments later, a nurse came in, a pleasant-looking Afrikaner in her forties systematically circled around the table gathering needles, gauze pads, test tubes and band aids. After a jolly, "Hello, Ms. Sinclair," said in strong Afrikaans voice, the nurse moved a small table to the side of the examination table and placed the supplies on it.

"Jesus, what's he going to do to me? Operate?" Jessica said jokingly in Afrikaans.

The nurse just smiled at her. "No, just taking some blood; readings of your blood pressure; weight; and a urine sample—usual procedure, Ms. Sinclair. The doctor will be in, in just a moment, so relax. I'll be doing most of the work. So, let's get your weight."

Jessica shook her head. "What did I get myself into?" she said, standing on the scale.

After a few moments, Doctor Vieter came in. He inspected the chart the nurse had prepared, gave a couple of grunts, rubbed his fingers across his chin, and stepped to the end of the table where Jessica sat. "Did you get a blood sample?" he asked the nurse. She nodded. "Okay. Thank you, Helen." He gestured for her to leave the room. Doctor Vieter stood in silence for what seemed a couple minutes, glancing over the charts of Jessica's medical history: Broken arm when she was eight, stitches in her right foot when she was eleven, fever when she was fifteen and so on.

"Well," he muttered once and came to her side.

"Well what?" she questioned nervously.

"You have lost a lot of weight?"

"Yes. And…"

"Let's take a listen to your heart and chest." He placed his stethoscope on her back. It felt cold to her skin. "Give us a cough now. Again, again." He was moving the stethoscope around on her back. "And again," he said one last time. Placing the stethoscope on the little table, he began marking her chart. "Well, it seems you have some fluid build-up in your chest."

"I have been having trouble breathing, but just this last month or so."

"Yes…yes…I think that the blood and urine tests Nurse Helen took will tell us more. How long have you been feeling sick, Jessica?"

"A while now…maybe nine months or so…"

"Jessica!" he exclaimed. "That's not good!"

"I know!" She fidgeted. "I was in America and I didn't have any medical insurance. Plus, I was just a little sick. Like an upset stomach; vomiting from time to time; feeling a little dizzy at times…I…I thought it would just go away."

"What other symptoms are you having?"

"I've been bleeding."

"Where?"

"When I go to the bathroom. It began about a month ago," she said uncomfortably. Her mind raced with uncertainty; time seemed to telescope before he asked the next question. There was a moment of silence that filled the air. She could smell the medication and vitamins. That smell, she thought. He placed his hand on her shoulder. She could hear Nurse Helen in the hallway just outside the door, opening and closing cabinets. She felt uneasiness in her heart. Her mind raced, contemplating what the doctor would ask next. What she didn't want the doctor to ask.

"Jessica." He carefully studied her eyes. "Has this been happening since your troubles?"

She sat quietly for what seemed a long while. She looked out the window and saw streaks of water droplets on the window, a reminder of the storm that had passed. Her eyes clouded. Her mind seemed to drift to a rainy day in Angola when the storm had come to the land, to the people. She cried openly as he rubbed her shoulder. She could not stop the flow of tears. He knew her pain was deep. He knew that this young girl was hurting inside; still, he needed to probe her for answers, to find out to what extent she was hurting.

"I thought it was over," she sobbed, her body shaking.

"I know you did." He placed his hand on her cheek and brushed the hair from her face. "Does anyone else know about this?"

"No."

"Maybe we should let your parents know?" he said. "There's more happening here than just a fever or cold."

"No!" She looked up at him. "I don't want anyone to know yet. We don't even know what's wrong yet. Do we?" She looked back into his eyes for an answer.

He watched her stare and knew she was scared. He had an idea what was wrong, but she was right, they needed to submit the tests and wait for the results.

He frowned, then, saw her face light up as she watched his frown turn into a soft smile. "You're right, we don't know anything yet. Let's see what the test results bring us and we'll take it from there, okay?"

"Okay. Thanks, Doctor Vieter. Just please don't tell my parents anything yet, okay?"

"Okay. Now you wipe those tears away or my other patients will think I'm a mean doctor," he joked, rubbing her arm.

"Okay." She wiped the tears from her eyes. Doctor Vieter left the room, concerned for her. He knew that her symptoms were not a good sign and he needed to have the test results sent in immediately. He instructed Nurse Helen to take the tests to Cape Town immediately and wait for the results. Without hesitation, she left with the blood and urine samples and the chart indicating what tests needed to be run on the samples: Tuberculosis, HIV and others were checked off. She looked at the scribble on the bottom of the chart: Possible HIV infection and initial internal organ breakdown.

The ride home from Hermanus was longer than usual. Jessica drove silently, watching the lines that divided the road and oncoming cars. The lines seemed to melt into one another as her thoughts receded to another place in time. She daydreamed she was walking along on an open plain watching springbok, Thomson's gazelle and wildebeests running and playing. The sun was high and the heat played on the land, bringing haunting images of drifting trees and rocks that moved like water; mystical illusions that played upon her mind as she looked out across the grasslands. The visions swayed in her head as she watched the collage play.

Off in the distance she saw a man running across the plain, closely pursued by a large lion. The man did not seem to tire as he approached where she stood watching him. He ran at a steady speed with the lion close behind him. She knew he would never make it to safety. Her mind questioned their presence as they came closer to her. She watched him, wondering how such a man could run that long a distance without tiring. The lion gained on the man. Just as the man was within twenty yards of her, she saw that he was a Hottentot and that the lion was no ordinary lion, but the larger Cape Lion. She looked about her and knew there was nowhere to go, nowhere to run or hide. Her heart raced. She could feel the heartbeat of the man, the lion and her own heartbeat become one. She could feel their souls. As she watched, the lion overtook the man, but instead of the lion bringing the man to the ground, the man became the lion, which charged toward her at a great speed. She watched his black mane bounce and his huge muscular body move as the wind moves the clouds above. There was power and dignity in his face. He moved with such grace. With great grace his body lifted from the ground like a tornado erupting from a storm and leaped at her. Her hands lifted before her, not in self-protection but in acceptance, in knowing her fate. As she did, the lion's image seemed to become one with hers. As two light waves blend to make one color, so it was that the man, the lion and Jessica became one.

Her heart was racing as she broke from her daydream, only to find that the truck was now running close to the edge of the road. Below to her right was the ocean and to her left were the Drakensberge Mountains looming high in the blue sky. She turned the wheel, steering the truck to a safer course as she noticed the sweat on her hands. She watched the cliffs alongside the truck as she headed for home.

***

The sea ran at high tide as Conrad and Thomas watched the swells finally meet their end as they crashed on the rocks bellow. Their long journey across the Atlantic Ocean was not in vain, Conrad thought. Everything has its purpose in life, even the waves of the ocean. The two men sat conversing for most of the day, enjoying a glass or two of wine from the green, hilly vineyards of Stellenbosch. Their conversation was interspersed with moments of contemplation. They enjoyed each other's company and Conrad liked Thomas. He was a sincere and kind man and would make a fine husband for Jessica someday. He wanted the best for Jessica, and Thomas seemed to have more in mind than just dating her.

"God, Jessica's been gone all morning," Conrad said.

"Didn't she say she was going to town for a while?" Thomas asked.

"Yes, but it isn't good to be out driving alone. It will be dark in a few hours," Conrad, watched the sky, thinking that it wasn't good for a girl to be alone at all.

"She has a two-way radio in the truck, doesn't she?"

"Yes. If she needs to she'll call, but there are times that a girl shouldn't be out alone in this country. It's not safe," Conrad said. "You see, Thomas, South Africa has a way to go before we are on a good road. This is all new to us here. There are a lot of people coming into this country who have little regard for other people and little regard for life. Years ago, it was secure. We protected our people and had it comfortable here. Now, with the changes and the new government in power, it's going to take a while to get things in order. There are people jockeying for position and making a mess out of things now."

"Tell me, Conrad, with Apartheid ending, do you see a future for South Africa? You've seen a lot of change."

"We've come a long way here in South Africa. I see a future for us here, for all South Africans, white, black, colored and other peoples who have made it their home. But first we need to work out our grievances and build a proper judicial system, a society that works together. With this change taking place, we'll know in the coming years if we are going to make it or not, but I see the new government trying, and that's a good sign. Nelson Mandela is a good man and the end of Apartheid is a good thing. But there's one thing that has always ruled Africa, and that is that the strong survive and the weak and sick, die. It's been that way since the beginning of time. There's no changing that, it's Africa."

"Yeah. I've watched 'Wild Kingdom,'" Thomas grinned.

Conrad looked at Thomas, and then began laughing. He knew he sometimes became engulfed by his thoughts of South Africa and its people. He shook his head, "What have you seen or heard about us here? What do some of the Americans think? I know it's a broad question, but tell me, what's the word out there about South Africa?"

Thomas thought carefully about his response. "It varies, Conrad. Some people saw Apartheid as a police state where the government ruled the people with an iron fist. Some people saw it as a remnant of the sixties and seventies strife that plagued, not just South Africa, but most of the world. I had a conversation a few months ago with a friend's girlfriend. She was opposed to white people being in South Africa, so I asked her why she felt the way she did. She said, because they don't belong there. I asked her, do you think that we, *white people*, belong here in the United States? She said, why, yes! This is our land. I wondered at her response, so, after a few moments, asked her, how long do you think white people have been in Africa? It doesn't matter, they don't belong there, she said. I said, what do you think about the extermination of the American Indians? I mean, we, *white people* basically wiped them out in the late 1800s, put them on reservations, took over their lands by means of superior firepower, and starved them to death. And, what do you think about the Aborigines of Australia? Same thing happened to them, basically. She looked at me crossly, sipped her coffee and said without remorse; I don't know about the Aborigines, but this is *our* land."

"It's interesting," he went on, "that a lot of people have the same views. They haven't been to South Africa, or Tibet, or Cuba, or *any* Third World country, but they'll stand in the street with a sign that says: 'Stop the atrocities.' You know, Conrad, if more people traveled in this world, I think it would be a better planet."

"I think so too," Conrad said, sitting back in his chair, slowly shaking his head. He knew bad things happened during the Apartheid years and was glad that the change had taken place. But he also knew that danger comes with change, and chaos sometimes caused all the peoples of a country to suffer. Deep in his heart he wanted it to all end in peace. There was a new beginning happening and the old ways were ending in Africa. He knew Thomas understood more about the world than most people, and knew he understood that there was both good and bad in the world as well. If people are going to have an opinion on something, someone or some country, then they should find out the facts first, he thought. They sat sipping their wine and watched the sun and ocean before them.

Jessica had stopped on the way home to sit near the rocks and watch the ocean. It had been a difficult day for her and her thoughts raced nervously about her examination. She was sick and didn't know what to do or who to tell, thought she would tell Thomas when the timing was right. It would have to wait till another day. He was so happy being here in South Africa, at the estate, and he was enjoying the time with her family. Everyone seemed to like him.

Just before dinner, Conrad announced to Mary and the boys that he had something to say before they ate. "Listen up." He said, when they were all sitting at the table. "I have a word to say." He grabbed his wine glass.

"Here we go again. Now the meat's going to get cold," Duncan joked to Ian.

Conrad threw a cross look at Duncan. "It will not be a long speech, Duncan, don't worry. And don't interrupt me either." He drew a breath. "Okay, as we know, Jessica is now back home for a while and, she has brought Thomas. Welcome to our home Thomas." Everyone reached for their glass. "A toast, to Jessica, your safe return to South Africa, and to Thomas, a newfound friend of our family."

"Hear! Hear!" Duncan yelled.

Mary raised her glass. "And to those who are in our hearts but cannot be with us today."

"Yes," Conrad said softly, smiling at Mary. "To all our family." Mary looked across the room toward the window as he raised his glass again.

"Okay, okay," Conrad said, "the surprise I had in mind is: I think that it's a good time for the Sinclair family to go on safari."

"That sounds great!" Duncan yelled, reaching again for his glass.

"When?" Ian asked.

"Soon, I think." Conrad smiled broadly as he looked at Jessica, anticipating her reaction. Like her mother, Jessica was looking out the window toward the hill and her sister's grave, her mind elsewhere. Thomas knew something was wrong.

"Jess, is everything okay?" he whispered, while everyone talked about the safari and didn't notice the sadness that had overcome her. "Jess, are you okay?" he asked again.

She broke her stare from the hill and turned him, "Yes, everything's... okay. Safari sounds great." She smiled, and squeezed his hand tightly. He knew something was bothering her. He had seen that look on her face before. Conrad watched them from the other side of the table. He too knew something was wrong, but did not understand fully the hurt in her soul.

"Hey, Dad, where we going?" Ian said.

"I think we'll go to the Great Karoo." Jessica's head turned toward her father. It had been a long time since she had been in the Karoo and had dreamed about crossing the Drakensberge and seeing the Karoo again.

"When do you think we'll go, Daddy?" she asked.

Conrad wondered what she was thinking. "Maybe a week or two, Jess," he said as he watched her expression change. Thomas leaned over and kissed her on the side of her face. She smiled at him and her father, but it was a half-hearted smile.

"Let's eat." Conrad said, watching Jessica and Thomas. They seemed so right for each other and it was apparent that Thomas treated her well. He was happy for his little girl, and wanted the best for her. But, he knew that she had undergone a serious trauma in Angola, and there was that nagging, gut feeling that something had happened at the airport at Cape Town International. What had she seen that made her cry? What pain did she still have in her heart? Would her secret hurt reveal itself before their departure to the Great Karoo?

***

General Mobutu sat in his chair, wondering about the girl. He stared out the window of his office in downtown Cape Town. He'd thought she was dead. Sure, they hadn't found her body when he and his men returned after the battle in Angola, but he assumed that whoever attacked that night took her body away. Now he knew that his men were right when they said the trucks flew the flag of South Africa. Seeing her at the airport threatened his very existence in the new South Africa. He had received the job as Director of Security because of his outstanding record as military leader.

He flicked his cigarette into his ivory ashtray. It was filled with cigarette butts, ashes and hours of thoughts on what to do about this situation. After some investigation, it was apparent that he would have to take care of this thing quickly. Conrad Sinclair was no man to anger; a military commander in the South African army for years, now retired, he still had the means to reach across borders with military personnel and defeat his men. No, Conrad Sinclair was a man of skill.

Mobutu remembered back to how his men were systematically killed that night. Conrad Sinclair could destroy him here in South Africa too, he thought, watching the traffic outside his window. He flicked his cigarette again, missing the ashtray. He knew the Afrikaans people and their controlling ways, their political views, and their Apartheid suppression of the African people. He would not give up his position of power by any means.

With the Truth and Reconciliation Committee in place, it could be possible that Conrad would either be thrown in jail or, maybe, gain power again as a commander. Mobutu could not take the chance to find out; he had to move and move fast before something happened. But what could he do to such a man as Conrad Sinclair; a man who was guarded and protected by the new laws of South Africa, guarded and protected by the Afrikaner people who held him in high esteem as their own military leader.

Mobutu reached over to his intercom and summoned in his two most trusted men, men who had seen their bloodied comrades lying dead after that night in Angola. They would be angry knowing who was responsible for the death of their friends.

"Something has happened." Mobutu swung his chair around, facing his men. They looked at each other and then at him. "We have come up against an adversary here in South Africa that we did not know existed."

"Who, General?"

"There is a man here who killed our friends and comrades when we were overtaken that night a few years ago, just outside Cacolo. Do you remember?" He looked through his dark glasses at his men. Anger began to build on their faces. He knew they would do anything for him and that these added visions of their dead friends would help stroke their anger and hatred for Conrad and his family.

"Yes, General. We remember," one of the men, remarked. "They were all killed. My brother, Semeal, was killed that night. I found him with a knife hole in his chest. He still had his eyes open as if to say, revenge me."

"Yes, well, I know the family who did this to your brother and comrades. Their name is Sinclair and they live in Gansbaai, along the coast near Hermanus. Do you know where that is?"

"Yes, General. But there is a large Afrikaner presence there."

"Yes, I know, but we have to find a way of killing them, without making it look like we did it—-understand?"

"Yes, General."

"And we have to do it soon."

"Yes, General."

"So I need the two of you to take this situation in hand and kill these people."

"Yes, General. Would you like us to head out there now?"

"Yes! Now...Did I not make myself clear!" Mobutu yelled, knocking the ashtray from his desk. "Damn it! Take some men and do what you have to." His men gathered their things and began heading for the door. "Just one more thing." Mobutu stood up, towering over the two men, his look commanding and strong. His dark glasses hid his eyes but his cold-hearted stare cut through them like a sharp knife cuts through butter. He stood there in silence, contemplating, and knowing what he had to do first. He raised another cigarette to his lips and drew on it. The smoke made him look like a dragon before fire erupts from its mouth. "The girl. I need you to kill the girl first. Her name is Jessica Sinclair." Smoke streamed from his nostrils. "Kill her first, and I'll see to it that you get promoted. Go kill the girl now."

When they had gone, General Mobutu went to the window. Across the street was a park. In it children played, both white and black children, laughing and yelling, jumping and running as they played with one another. He watched them like a falcon flying high above. His cold, hard stare brought a cloud of darkness over their future. He watched one black child and one white child holding hands as they walked together. Their mothers quickly walked to them and separated them, bringing them to the opposite sides of the playground. Mobutu puffed his cigarette, and then dropped it on the floor. He grunted as he placed his foot over it and crushed it. Uncertainty was still in the air as the smoke lingered.

***

Thomas and Jessica were walking near the back wall of the compound, Jessica was deep in thought as she picked wildflowers and watched the setting sun. The light brought a beautiful array of yellow and orange to the western sky as she watched the seabirds playing in its glow. Thomas watched her strolling, remembering back to the farm he owned in New Jersey, and the wonderful day they'd spent together there.

"Are you happy?" he asked. She looked at him and softly smiled and walked toward him.

"Why do I sense something's on your mind?" He had grown to know her well over the months they had spent together. He cherished the time. She would make a wonderful mother, he thought, and he longed to grow old with her.

"I love you, Thomas, you know that?" She hugged him gently. His body towered over her little frame. Like a male lion with a female lion, he knew he would always protect her and care for her. It would be his job to always take care of his girl.

They headed out of the compound toward the rolling hills that were filled with wildflowers and followed the path up one hill to a group of trees near the edge of the property.

"I want to show you something," she said, looking toward a small-gated area at the top of the hill. Grabbing his hand, she led him to a small, well-maintained grave. Beside the small headstone were older graves, the Sinclair family's, with the names of Jessica's grandfather and grandmother.

"Your grandparents?"

"Yes," she smiled, "they were good people."

"This one, Sarah Sinclair, who is she, an aunt?"

"No, it's my twin sister."

He looked into her eyes and could see the tears building up in them. He hugged her as she began to cry softly. "It's okay, let it out, Jess. I know the pain and hurt death can bring to a person's heart."

She rubbed his back with her hands, feeling protected and loved, and she knew he loved her. But she knew that what she had to tell him could break their love apart.

She tasted the saltiness of her tears as they reached the corners of her mouth. She smelled the clean ocean in the distance and the flowers that surrounded them, as they stood there alone on the hill.

The little grave read: *Sarah Sinclair, She has our love with her in heaven. We will wait another day for her to see our smiles and feel our love. Taken from us at birth, she will always be in our hearts.* Thomas read the inscription and could not help feeling the sadness that Jessica and the family must have felt.

Jessica wiped the tears from her eyes and was sad. She felt so much love for him and only wanted the best for them, but there was something she had to tell him that would test their love for each other.

"Jessica, I know you love it here in Africa and you feel it in your soul. I just want to tell you that I never want to lose you."

"I know you love me, Thomas, and I love you, too, but...but...there's something I have to tell you," She saw the uncertainty in his eyes. He did not know what she was about to say, but she had to tell him, especially now.

"What is it? Are you going to stay here in South Africa?" She walked to her sister's grave and knelt, placing the wildflowers in front of the stone. She placed her hand on the stone and began to cry. Thomas put his hand on her shoulder, rubbing it softly.

"We have to talk about this, honey," he said, looking around at the field of wildflowers. He wondered how many times she'd walked these fields since she had been a child. Who was he to take her from her homeland? Who was he to think he was good enough for her? He turned and walked a few feet away.

"I'm dying." She stood up. Thomas stopped and turned toward her, suddenly confused...

"I don't understand...how?" Pain filled his heart and soul. "How do you know you're dying?"

She cried in his arms, knowing he loved her and that her dying would end their love. That she would never have the one man she loved with all her heart.

"I'm dying of AIDS."

"AIDS!" Shocked, he broke away from her. "How did you...? When did you...? When did you find this out? I don't understand? There's no cure for AIDS." She could see the look of confusion and fear in his eyes. "I don't understand—-tell me—-tell me this isn't happening!" he said once again.

She didn't know what to say or do. She just cried, standing there with her arms limp at her sides.

"I've been feeling sick. I went to Dr. Vieter's office and got tested." She sobbed. "He called...the tests came back...I'm HIV positive."

He looked at her and knew she was hurt. He knew his girl was in trouble and needed him. He embraced her with all his love.

"I'm so sorry, Jess," he said. "I wasn't thinking."

She felt the warmth of his body and the love he had for her as she stood there in his arms. She had wanted to go through life with him, have his children, and make him happy. It wasn't till his next question, a question anyone would ask, that they realized the full spectrum of the crisis.

"Did you somehow get it from me?" If she was infected with the HIV virus, then they both were.

Jessica's hands went to her mouth. She suddenly felt so ashamed. "Oh my God...Thomas...Oh my God!" she cried.

Thomas held her in his arms as they both cried. This sacred place, this hallowed ground, was now a place they would never forget. The field wasn't as green and flowery, as it had been just minutes before, the sky seemed darker and the air heavier as they stood there alone, hurting and in love.

"How did you find out, Jess?"

"From Doctor Vieter."

"How did it happen?"

"I was getting sicker so I went to Hermanus to see him."

"But *how*, Jess?" Thomas placed his hands on her face. "*When* did this happen?"

"In Angola. I was raped in Angola." Her body shook uncontrollably as she cried before him. "I'm so sorry, Thomas, I didn't know I was sick, and now I got you sick too. I'm so sorry."

"Okay…okay, come on…we'll work this thing out, Jess. There's medicine in the States that can help deter this. We'll head back and get it checked out."

"You think they could help?"

"Yes, I think that it's a good possibility that we can catch this before it gets any worse," he said.

Inside he knew there was little hope of surviving the disease if it was not caught in time. He'd heard enough stories and read enough articles about it. But he silently prayed that it was not too late for them, for her. He remembered back to the time they spent together in the States and the love that had grown between them. Twilight had come at a time when they had least expected it. The shadow crossed the land and filled their minds with despair. Thomas took a deep breath as he looked out at the ocean.

CHAPTER 7

The Khoikhoi knew the Great Karoo as the land of thirst, an arid area that made life hard for its inhabitants. With little to no water during the course of the year, its species evolved differently. But life was in the Great Karoo and life would remain in it for a long time. Like the animals, plants and insects of Madagascar and the Galapagos Islands, life evolved in the Karoo, learning to make do with little or no food and water. It was this evolution that made it a place of mystery. The Khoikhoi walked the land, it seemed, since the beginning of time, and their way of life was one of little means. It was the home of the Mamzibi, one of the last ancient tribes of the Khoikhoi. Their numbers were few and they were seen little by the outside world. From time to time, park rangers from the Natel-Zulu National Park, the Kalahari and other bordering parks of the Great Karoo saw a Mamzibi, usually from a distance and mostly at dusk. They were a pleasant race of people and raised little threat to anyone who saw them. It was said that anyone who saw a Mamzibi would capture some of their spirit, for they walked the way of nature and had a oneness with the land. Countless stories, over the years, were told of the Mamzibi, and there was always a certain mystery about the encounters.

"I swear it was a Mamzibi who saved me," or "The spear came from nowhere. It was a spear of the Mamzibi warrior that killed the lion who was going to eat me alive."

The trucks rolled north on highway N2, heading for the Great Karoo. After some time, they turned off and onto a dirt road. It took a whole day before they arrived at their final destination, a campsite the Sinclair family had used in the past. Everyone seemed to enjoy the ride, singing songs, telling jokes and watching the landscape roll passed the windows like a picture—thought Thomas—from "Wild Kingdom." African music played on the radio. Ladysmith Black Mambazo's African rhythm brought it all to life with their music; a soft rolling beat and African dialect mixed with an array of tribal instruments, it made for the perfect music for a safari. They neared the Great Karoo as darkness began to climb over the eastern horizon.

"Daddy, will it be too late to set up camp?" Jessica said from the back seat. "Maybe we'll have to sleep in the trucks tonight."

"Maybe," Conrad said, winking at Mary. "If it's too dark when we get there, we'll set up in the dark, or wait for morning."

"Yeah, but I think everyone's a little tired after the long ride," she said.

"I know, dear," Conrad grinned. "It's customary to make the newcomer set up camp for everyone—-so Thomas, I hope you're feeling up to it?"

"Stop that!" Mary said, nudging Conrad's arm. "He's only kidding you, Thomas. Pay no mind to him, dear."

"I'm not worried, Mrs. Sinclair, I was in the Boy Scouts of America...I know how to set up camp, make fires, and even barbeque...I mean braai, as you call it here in South Africa," Thomas said.

Both Thomas and Jessica had decided to try to enjoy the trip to the Great Karoo. They both knew what had to be done when they returned to Gansbaai. They would break the news to the family that they had an emergency and needed to return to the United States sooner than they had planned, that Thomas had to return to work because of some special project that would call on his skills as an engineer. Still, from time to time, Jessica felt sick and needed to rest, but Thomas would watch her and take care of his girl. Doctor Vieter had confirmed that Thomas, too, had the disease, and had most likely contracted it from her. Doctor Vieter had been saddened as he told them the news, but agreed with them that there were better medications available in the United States. He had also agreed to hold their secret with him.

As the truck rolled and bounced down the dirt road, Thomas could not help but remember the two days he and Jessica had spent in Hermanus. After seeing the doctor, they had stayed at the Amanzi Inn. It was a quaint little place that overlooked the turquoise-blue Atlantic Ocean. Each morning they had walked along the cliffs and paths, passed the museum, and down to the boat landing to watch the fishermen. They'd listen to stories the fishermen told about the sea, while eating the bolton and dreboerewors they purchased from the open market in town. He admired the Afrikaner fishermen. They had a certain strength and innocence about them. He could tell they were good, hard-working people who lived and died by the sea.

On one night they had purchased tickets to the fishermen's annual dinner, during which, they listened to Seventies music, danced, drank wine and laughed. Once a fisherman found out he was an American, everyone called him Yank. He got a kick out of this and enjoyed some of the jokes they told about Americans. It was one of the best times he'd had in South Africa, and the people of the De Kelders would always hold a special place in his heart. He felt sad for the people who labored on the sea to bring food to the tables of South Africa and to the world.

"Daddy, there seems to be some light up ahead?" Jessica said, as the truck rolled up the road toward a small hill. It was now, around ten, and they were all tired from the long ride. Thomas hoped Conrad was kidding him about setting up the camp. He too was starting to feel weakened from the sickness, but didn't have the heart to tell Jessica that he had been feeling sick.

"Yeah, I see it!" Conrad replied.

"What do you think it is?" Mary asked.

"I don't know."

"Maybe we should tell Duncan and Ian, so they can get prepared."

"Prepared for what?" Thomas said.

"You never know," Jessica said, wondering why her father was so calm.

"I'm sure it's okay, Jess." Conrad turned the wheel and headed for the site. "It's just over this small hill."

"But, Dad, it could be dangerous. Someone is definitely at the site, I see firelight." Jessica squirmed in her seat, edging toward the front between Conrad and Mary. "What do you see?"

"I don't know, Jess." Conrad's voice thickened and he became tense as the truck rolled over the small hill and into the camp.

"There are men here, Daddy."

"I know, Jess," Conrad said firmly.

"Your father will find out who they are. Sit tight," Mary said as Conrad got out of the truck. Duncan and Ian's Hummer rolled up. In the light, Jessica could see that Conrad had a handgun in his hand. She watched, knowing that being away from civilization could mean danger. The firelight blinded them from seeing much of what was taking place. Conrad and the boys walked up to the men. They were talking, but Jessica could not hear what was being said because the truck's motor was running.

"Damn! I can't hear a thing," she said. "What's happening, Mom?"

"I don't know, dear," Mary said. "Wait and see." She looked into the rearview mirror at Thomas, who caught a mischievous look in her eyes, and a faint hint of a smile. Should he be outside with the men? He felt like a child sitting in the backseat of his parents' car. It was darker than most nights he'd seen in Africa and the firelight played upon their weary eyes. The voices outside the truck erupted into what sounded like an argument. Everyone moved about in the orange glow of the firelight, but now they could not tell the men apart.

"Maybe I should get out!" Thomas motioned to exit the vehicle.

"No, Thomas, we need you here with us," Mary said.

"Maybe he should see what's going on, Mom?" Jessica said excitedly.

"I'll go."

"Jessica...stay put."

"But..."

"Look. Here he comes," Mary said quickly as one of the men walked toward the truck.

The truck door swung open and the man got in. "Howzit!"

"Uncle Pete! Ah...you jerk! You scared the hell out of us, man!" Jessica yelled.

"Scared? It's just me!" he replied. "Hello, Mary. How's my sister doing?" He smiled, kissing her on the cheek.

"Hi, Pete. How was the ride in?" Mary asked.

"You knew about this!" Jessica smiled, "Mom!"

"Yes, dear. We planned this a week ago. Thomas, camp's already set up."

"So this is Tom?" Pete extended his hand. "I hear you two are going to marry soon."

"Uncle Pete!" Jessica said, embarrassed.

"If there were more light in this truck, we'd see her blushing right now, huh Thomas."

"I think so."

"Hey, Jess!" Conrad said. "How's it feel to be out in the bush again?" Jessica gave her father a cross look.

"You wait," she mumbled, "you wait."

It was a fine camp and the African bush amazed Thomas. He had noticed that the landscape changed as they entered the Great Karoo; it seemed drier, but there were hills and bushes and trees, even a mountain range off in the distance. The land had an orangey look to it and reminded him of the Grand Canyon. Different shades of orange, brown, gold and yellow played on the landscape as the truck had rolled toward the camp. He could see and feel the natural beauty of the Great Karoo and feel the life force about him. It gave a sense that the land knew they were there and it was okay. He watched everyone talking and laughing at the table. Conrad and Pete sat by the fire smoking their pipes and Jessica was smiling and laughing more than she ever did as they talked about past safaris, outings and old times with her family.

The night was warm and inviting and the stars crossed overhead, making an ocean of sparkling lights in the sea of darkness. After dinner they settled in for a well-deserved sleep and anticipated the first morning of the safari in the Great Karoo.

***

The car crept along as it neared the estate. Lights could be seen in the distance, indicating that someone was home. Mobutu's men, four of them, dressed in black, softly closed the car doors and walked toward the back wall of the estate. It was silent and dark, as clouds had rolled in from the ocean earlier that day, making it a perfect opportunity for murder. They would avenge their comrades and brother for what Conrad Sinclair had done. But they remembered Mobutu's words: the girl must die first. They climbed the wall silently and jumped into the compound. At once the guard dogs barked in excitement as they ran toward the four men.

Jara sat quietly as the water filled her bath. She had the house to herself for the first time in ages. She sipped the wine she had secretly saved from the party and enjoyed the sounds of the African beat that played on the radio. It was a warm day, she thought, as the clouds advanced from the ocean. She had prepared a nice dinner for herself and anticipated a relaxing bath. She'd been a maid most of her life and the Sinclair family treated her as one of their own. Coming from Crossroads Township, she enjoyed the peaceful feeling of the Sinclair house, but longed to return home to her people on the weekends. But this weekend was special for she had the house to herself, and she would relax, pretending it was her home, a home she knew she could never afford. But she didn't dabble in politics and the gatherings against her white countrymen, for she was a friend of the Sinclair family, and she was loyal to them out of love.

The two dogs charged straight at the intruders. The men stood their ground as the dogs neared. Then, with a few well-placed shots, the two dogs lay dead. The gun's silencers had muffled the sounds and there was silence once again in the African night.

Jara turned off her bath water and dipped her fingers into the warm water. It would feel so good to have a candle lit, she thought.

She placed the lavender scented candle near the edge of the tub and gently stepped into her waiting bath. Refreshing, she thought, closing her eyes, and submerged her body into the warm oiled water. *We don't have tubs like these in the Township,* she thought, *not like these.* She rolled her shoulders, submerging her head again.

The minutes passed as she enjoyed the water's warmth before she noticed the candle vigorously flicker. Jara noticed the air current moving the flame. Being from a land that knew danger, she immediately knew something was wrong and reached over to the radio, turning it off. She slowly leaned back in the tub and listened to the sounds of the house. It was quiet, too quiet, she thought. There were no sounds from the dogs and the field crickets were silent. Off in the distance she heard a passing truck roar down a road.

"There's evil in the air," she nervously said to herself. "The Tokoloshe is here." She lowered her shoulders. "I did something I wasn't supposed to," she said, as guilt and fear filled her head.

The back door of the house slowly closed. Three men entered the Sinclair house and made their way through the dimly lighted rooms. They crossed the great room and walked down the hallway toward the bathrooms.

"It's too quiet," one man whispered, raising his gun to fire at anything that moved.

"Shut up, there's someone here," another, the leader, whispered. "Follow me and be ready to shoot."

They knew nobody was in the kitchen, or the living room, because they had looked in the windows before entering the house. Whoever was there was in the bathroom.

They were like a pack of hyenas on the hunt, stalking their prey with cunning and daring. They were there to murder. Nothing else.

The bathroom light was on and the door was ajar as the men approached. They'd kill the first thing that moved. One of them kicked open the door and they entered the bathroom, their guns in hand, ready to fire. It was payback time. Conrad Sinclair and his family would die tonight. Midnight struck and the grandfather clock behind them began to chime. Startled, they immediately turned and fired down the hallway.

Jara hidden behind the open bathroom door, waited to surprise her attackers, jumped from her hiding with force. Whether it was the Tokoloshe or intruders, she would fight for her life. She swung the door into the men. As the door smashed into the men, one of them accidentally fired on his friend.

She pushed the door again and the two men fell to the floor. The other intruder lay bleeding with a gunshot wound to his stomach as she ran down the hallway, passed the grandfather clock, and into the great room. She'd run for help, she thought, as she ran out of the front door. She began to run down the front stairs, as an arm smashed into her throat.

She fell backwards to the ground, choking and gasping for air.

The man stood above her, placing his foot on her neck, making it even harder for her to breath.

"Got her!" he yelled to his fellow assassins. "I got the girl!"

Jara lay on the ground looking up at the tall dark figure. "It's the devil," she cried to herself. "I've done something wrong."

The other two men ran from the house to where she lay on the ground. They circled about her like a pack of hyenas. Murder was on their minds. Revenge was in their hearts. Jara looked up at them, gasping for air. Her heart raced as they stood above her.

"Who are you?" a man asked. He lifted his foot from her neck.

"Answer him, lady! Are you Jessica Sinclair?" Jara's mind raced with fear, but she then realized that these men were not the devil, but sent to kill Jessica. These were evil men. She coughed and cleared her throat. She would not let them know who she was. She would gather her courage and fight them off. She began to kick and scream and punch as hard as she could.

The men began kicking her with their boots. Her throat was again closed by the man's boot.

"Answer us, bitch!" one man yelled at her as they looked around furtively to see if anyone else was near.

"You'll tell us before your family returns." The man said kicking her side. She coughed again and blood dripped from her mouth.

"Bring her in here," said one of the other men in a quieter voice. "Let's have some fun with her before we kill her." The men dragged her body to the house.

She began kicking and screaming again in her African dialect, but they paid her no mind as they threw her to the floor. Her strength was not enough to overcome the beatings and she became weak and bruised.

She fought the best she could before her battered body could not fight anymore. Her clothing was torn from her and scattered, and her blood now stained the floor and furniture of the great room. Above her was the head of the large Cape lion. These hyenas would not live if he were alive, she thought, as she closed her eyes.

"Once again! Who are you?" The man said placing the gun to her head. She gasped for air and prayed. Her mind became clouded and dark. "I've lived a good life," she cried to herself before uttering her last words.

"I'm Jessica Sinclair."

The gun fired. Her blood spattered onto the wall of the fireplace and began trickling from the back of her head. Darkness closed in around her as she breathed her last breath and the warm Cape wind carried her spirit away.

***

At the Karoo camp the next day, Jessica and Thomas woke to sunshine. Clouds had come over the Great Karoo during the night and with them an uncanny darkness that made the morning colder than the day before. But as usual, rain had not fallen in the night and the clouds had rolled overhead like great spirits on the move. The Karoo was dry and hot and at times unbearable, but this day was as beautiful as they come. The morning clouds began to move across the sky and into the distance as they began their day. At times the sunlight broke through the clouds, bringing a heavenly golden glow to the landscape. Uncle Pete had breakfast cooking on the open fire. The smell brought images of past hunts and older times.

"Nothing like bacon cooking on an open fire," Thomas said as he and Jessica walked from their tent.

"Howzit, kids?"

"Morning," Thomas said.

"Morning, Uncle Pete," Jessica looked around brushing the hair from her face. "You're up early."

"You two are up early, too." He said, flipping the bacon and checking the scrambled eggs. "Want a cup of coffee?"

"Sounds good."

"Where you two off to so early?" he asked, handing them cups of hot coffee.

"We're going for a walk to that hill over there." Jessica pointed to the hill not far from camp. "It's a great day, isn't it?"

"Doesn't seem like much rain falls here," Thomas said.

"First time in South Africa, Thomas?"

"First-timer here, Uncle Pete. We have to watch this one," Jessica joked, leaning over and kissing Thomas.

"The others will be up shortly, so if you two want some privacy, you'd better head out soon."

"Good idea."

"Hey, Thomas, do you have a firearm on you?" Pete said.

"No. Do I need one?" Thomas looked at Jessica.

"Yeah. Take mine." Pete laughing shook his head. "You're right, Jessica, we have to watch this guy." He handed Thomas his Colt .45 pistol and holster. "Know how to use that thing?"

"Yeah, I think I watched enough TV to know what to do," Thomas said. "Like a cowboy." He put on the holster and grabbed the handle of the gun. "Just call me Slim."

"Okay, Slim." Jessica laughed. This was one of the things she loved about him, a natural comedian. "Let's hit the trail, cowboy."

"I'll see you in a little while," Pete said. "Oh, and Slim, don't go blowing your foot off with that thing."

Thomas brushed his hand over the holstered Colt that hung at his side. He liked the feel of the pistol. He'd never used a handgun before, though he had used a rifle in the past, and was a pretty good shot at that. How could he ever kill a man, or for that matter, an animal? Sure, he could kill if he had to, in a war or something, but to kill another being was barbaric.

Somehow, the sky had seemed larger and bluer when he was younger. The orange and brown soil of the Karoo was dry and dust like. He saw the small bushes, rock formations and cacti of the land. The dirt seemed to get into everything: shoes, socks, pockets and pants; it even irritated his eyes a little. He thought of the Middle Eastern people who covered their heads as they shielded their faces and eyes from the sandstorms.

As they walked, the old trail split, one branch heading toward the hill's top and the other running along its base. Jessica took the trail to the top but Thomas stopped at the fork. Jessica turned to see what he stopped for. "Why are you stopping, honey?"

Doing his best John Wayne impression, he leaned his hip to the left, placing his right hand on the gun, and raised one eyebrow.

"You take the high road and I'll take the low road." He gave a wry look, lifting his left hand and pointing toward her. She shook her head, laughing at his impression. She always found him funny, even in tough times.

"Come on, silly, before some Indians come charging over the hill and shoot you with an arrow." She turned, laughing.

"Then I can be a one-way sign," he cracked.

They reached the top of the hill and studied the terrain. The plains and hills seemed to go on forever. It was rocky and jagged in some places, but soft and rolling in others, with steep mountains to the west. The mountains towered over the land, majestic and ominous, grand and threatening, far off but near.

"What mountain range is that?" Thomas asked.

"That's the Drakensberge. We came over that far end during the night."

"Too bad we didn't do it in the daytime. I would have liked to see the view from the top."

"Yeah. It's a beautiful land." She shielded her eyes from the now-rising sun. The Karoo glowed a golden orange. The landscape began to come alive as the light played on the bush and rock formations. Birds flew to and fro and rock lizards darted back and forth like people gathering their things before leaving for a long trip. As they looked across the plain, Thomas noticed a small rock formation in the distance. Its shadow appeared to grow as the sun slowly lifted off the eastern sky.

"Hey, Jess, look at that rock over there."

"Where?"

"Over there." He pointed. "It looks like a lion, doesn't it?"

"Yeah, it does…kind of. Let's go check it out."

"Wow. This thing is huge," Thomas said, after they'd reached the rock. He ran his hand across its base. Jessica circled around to the other side, looking at the cuts and grooves of the rock.

"I think it was carved. A long time ago, I'd say," she called to Thomas.

"Yeah. I think you're right." He looked in amazement at the large rock. "There's some sort of painting here, I think…it's old and faded."

She walked around to where he stood under the lion's weathered head. There, cut from the rock, was a small ledge. They looked up at the old rock painting and studied it for a moment.

"Looks like a hunt scene or something," he said

"I think it is a hunt. Looks like a man with a spear and a lion." She pointed. "But what's that above them?"

"Looks like a fly or a mosquito or something."

"It's the work of the Mamzibi, I would think."

"The who?"

"The Mamzibi. They're one of the nomadic tribes here in South Africa. They're part of the Khoikhoi peoples. There aren't very many of them around anymore but from time to time, people see one or two of them near the mountains. This rock painting could be one of theirs...or maybe the San or maybe one of the Bushmen's. It's old and it's hard to tell."

Thomas studied the painting. "I didn't think there were any Cape Lions in this part of Africa anymore."

"You're right. They've been extinct for a long time. But my father says that the Khoikhoi believe that when the lion returns, the people of Africa will be saved, and Mother Earth again will smile on Africa." she thought of her father, of the mystical tales he told, and the Cape Lion above the fireplace back home.

She turned to him. "Lets keep this our secret."

"Why?"

"I don't know, I think it'll be cool knowing that we found something like this, together."

"Sure," he said, kissing her, "if you like."

"Let's call this place Hope of the Lion," she said. "I'm so glad you're with me, Thomas."

***

After three days of being in the outdoors and five days away from home, they all began to relax and enjoy each other's company. Conrad decided to take Thomas and Pete a little farther east of the camp to an area called the Valley of Desolation. It was known to be the primary area of the Mamzibi peoples, and prior to this safari Conrad had made contact with them while out hunting a few years earlier. They were a gentle race of nomadic hunters and gatherers who were dedicated to a life of solitude and peace, a mysterious tribe who lived the way of the land. Conrad admired the Mamzibi warriors for their values. They were strong warriors and mighty hunters who were also the spiritual keepers of the land. In his eyes the Khoikhoi *were* Africa, and he believed that they were the true owners of the land. The three men began to set out for the hunt and readied the truck for the journey. It would be a long ride to the hunting camp.

"It's a bonding thing." Thomas said to Jessica as he loaded his bags onto the truck.

"Yeah, I know, but?" Jessica said.

"We'll be back in a day or two, I'm sure. Take care of our lion, kiddo. See you in a few days." He put his arms around her waist, pulling her close. "I'll be fine."

"Go and have fun...just watch yourself out there. This isn't the United States you know."

"Let's go, lover boy," Conrad said. He winked at Mary. "I'll see you in a day or two. If you need anything, use the radio."

"Okay. Be careful." She kissed him and brushed his wavy blond hair with her fingers. Mary knew Thomas would be fine, for Conrad had been on many hunts before. He loved being in the outdoors and, after years of being in the bush, the effects were on his face. He was a rugged man with a hundred-seventy-pound, well-defined build and he carried himself in such a way that men looked up to him. He'd done it all, military commander, hunter and traveler. Conrad was a man of Africa and Africa was in his blood. He truly was one of the last great hunters, a man who respected the land, its people and its animals. He looked out over the plain before climbing into the truck. It was all changing before his eyes and he knew his way of life would end if the world didn't react to the changing environment. Reflecting back to his younger years, he longed for a time of renewal, a time when there would be no wars, a time when humankind would take note of what it was doing to the lands and seas. He took a deep breath and swung into the truck.

"Let's get going!" he yelled.

Mary watched Conrad, Pete and Thomas drive down the embankment and off into the distance. *There goes my guy,* she thought, *off again, off into the unknown to be closer to his soul.* She looked over at Jessica, Ian and Duncan as they calmly talked near the fire. Her heart lifted as she remembered the years.

***

Mobutu's men arrived back in Cape Town and headed for their boss's office with the good news. They had killed the girl, the Sinclair girl was dead, and Mobutu would be happy.

Mobutu sat behind his desk, looking out the window. His large frame, dark glasses and decorated uniform made him appear bigger and more powerful than he really was. The smoke from his cigarette, the pile of ashes, and the cigarette butts revealed his anxiety. He'd been waiting for news about the girl and wondered why his men hadn't called. He tapped his fingers on the desk and flicked his ashes into the ashtray.

"General." Mazi, who was his lead inspector, saluted. He stood erect, proud of his men for accomplishing their mission. The girl had been alone and easily overcome. He was proud because he was the one who shot her in the head. He knew she was dead and this meant he'd get a promotion. Mobutu stood up, towering over his men. His presence was numbing, and they feared him. The light danced on the smoke as it hovered above their heads, like a cloud of evil on a sunny day. Their hearts blocked whatever light they had in their souls. They had served with Mobutu in Angola and knew that he was hard and heartless. He was their general and they'd seen what happened to soldiers who disobeyed or screwed up his plans. But today they had returned with good news.

"Well?" Mobutu barked. "You are here. What happened?"

"We killed the girl," Mazi said, saluting again. "I shot her myself."

"Where?"

"At the estate where you said she'd be. She was alone in the house. We surprised her."

"Is this true?" Mobutu said, looking at the other men. He leaned over the desk, grinning.

"Yes, General," they answered.

"We snuck in over the back wall, killed the guard dogs, and entered the house. She put up a fight but we got her, and killed her."

"Good, good," Mobutu said, smiling wickedly. "Good!" He began laughing.

"You will be commended for your work, Mazi. You have always been a good soldier." He walked around the desk and stood in front of them. "Now that we have that cleared up, we can be assured of our new place in this country."

"Thank you, General," Mazi said, smiling broadly.

"Did the white bitch die crying?" With that, Mobutu's men stopped smiling. They became quiet and fear filled their eyes.

Mobutu's voice changed. "What-what is it? Tell me." He looked into Mazi's eyes. His cold, dark stare brought fear to Mazi's soul and he knew that they'd killed the wrong girl and the General would be furious. What could he do? What could he say? He seemed to sink in height and began to fidget; sweat began to seep from every pore of his body and he felt the heat building around his neck. He swallowed his saliva to clear his throat.

"Well, Mazi, what is it?" Mobutu questioned again.

"The girl, General," he muttered. He lifted his shoulders to protect his head. "The girl we killed was black."

With a powerful fist, Mobutu struck Mazi across the face. Mazi fell to his knees as the General stood over him. "You idiot!"

"Sorry, General." Mazi quivered.

"She's a *white* girl, you idiots, God help me!" Mobutu said, standing in front of them with clenched fists. "You get back there and kill the right girl!" He walked back behind his desk. Mazi didn't dare get up until Mobutu said to. Mobutu's face was hard and his anger could be felt throughout the room. His men cowered as he continued screaming and banging his desk, yelling how incompetent they were, and how he'd have their heads if they didn't do it right this time.

"Stand up, Mazi!" he yelled. "Get out of here and get the job done. It's one girl, a white girl, and a settler at that. Go kill her *and* her family, if you can!" He turned and stood at the window of his office and looked into the distant ocean. Roberts Island lurked in the mist of the ocean. Below his window was the playground where children, both black and white, played, laughed and giggled. It was foreign to his soul and he despised their laughter.

***

The four-hour ride to the hunting camp was bumpy, hot and long and the sun's heat was unbearable. As the truck made its way toward the hunting camp, the old road curved from side to side as it made its way through the small brush. Thomas looked from his window and admired the large mountain range off in the distance. High and majestic, it reached out of the dry earth like a hand extending to God. Along one part of the mountain's top, a jagged edge ran for what seemed like miles, like a fierce dragon's teeth, he thought.

"Four o'clock!" Pete yelled back to Thomas. The truck's motor revved and roared as it bounced from side to side, climbing the now steeper hills of the Karoo at the mountain's base.

"We're almost there!" Conrad yelled, turning on the radio, listening for any incoming calls.

Thomas wiped the sweat from his forehead with his sleeve. Dark stains of perspiration marked his shirt and he felt uncomfortable from the sweat. The backseat seemed hotter than the front, and the one stop they had made during the day was not enough to revitalize his now saturated body. Conrad looked in the mirror, grinning to himself as he watched Thomas's face.

The truck turned up a small hill and then down the other side and came to a stop.

"Well, we made it," Conrad said, as he too wiped the sweat from his forehead. "You okay, Thomas?"

"I'm good," he lied.

"Pete?"

"I'm good. I could use a cold beer"

"Me too." Thomas grinned.

Pete jumped from the truck. These two sixty-year-old men moved as if they were in their thirties, Thomas saw. He remembered the first time Conrad shook his hand; the strength and wear from years of hard use could be felt in the shake. His hands were hard and felt like stone.

Night came quickly and camp was set up just before the sun lowered over the mountains, making a magnificent array of colors as it lowered over the dragon's body. The night brought coolness to the camp and the campfire was comforting. The three men sat around the fire talking of past hunts, the Afrikaans people and the Khoikhoi.

"I've met some of the Mamzibi," Conrad said, watching the fire roar. "They're being seen more and more these days. Civilization is closing in on them from all sides."

"When did you see them?" Pete said, turning. "I hear they stay up in the mountains mostly."

"Yeah, they do, but they come down to hunt, I guess. I saw two of them about three years ago. I was hunting not far from here with Duncan and Ian, walking along a dried-up riverbed, and one of them was sitting on a rock watching me as I walked."

"Were you scared?" Thomas said.

"No, no, they're not a dangerous people. The Mamzibi are a peaceful tribe," Conrad, squinted his eyes as he looked at the fire, remembering back. "They were friendly to me. After a few hand and face gestures, I figured out that they were trying to tell me that I could find game over the next ridge. They drank some of my water and offered me some of their food and water. I remember it like it was yesterday. The water they offered me was in an ostrich eggshell. The nomadic tribes here place water in Ostrich eggshells and place them in designated spots along their hunt route. They bury them in the sand until they need them. I walked up to them just as they dug one up."

"And the water, what did it taste like?"

"Water. Just water."

"So, did you find any game over the ridge?" Pete asked.

"Yes. I killed two animals that day, a mountain zebra and a springbok. The amazing thing is, I left the mountain zebra on the rock where I'd seen them, and the next day when I returned, it was gone. They left stones, I guess a thank you note in their language."

"Do you think we'll see them here?"

"Maybe. But first you're going to have to remove those keys dangling from your belt." Pete laughed. "With those keys jangling, they'll think the Tokoloshe is coming for them."

"You see, Thomas," Conrad said, "the joke here in South Africa is that we can see and hear a tourist from a mile away by the things he wears, and by the keys dangling from his belt."

"Oh man, I'm going to kill Jessica," Thomas said, shaking his head. "She looked at the keys the other day and laughed. I asked her what was so funny and she said, 'you'll find out.'"

"It's okay." Conrad patted him on the back. "Thank God you're with us, and not Ian and Duncan."

Thomas slowly pulled the keys from his belt and put them in his pocket.

"By the way, Thomas," Pete said, "if you do see a Mamzibi, please don't shoot him, okay?"

"Okay, Pete." Thomas laughed.

The waning moon brought a quiet night to the camp. Conrad radioed Mary, Jessica and the boys, letting them know that they had made camp, and were settling in for the night. It was clear and cool, and the men found comfort in the night air as they lay on their cots. Thomas thought of the lion rock, and the paintings he and Jessica had seen, and wondered about the Mamzibi.

CHAPTER 8

The next morning brought unusual clouds to the Great Karoo. Rain could be felt in the air and Conrad didn't understand why he didn't smell it coming. *But this was the Great Karoo,* he thought, *and anything could happen here.* Must be the mountains. He looked up at the darkening sky. Pete, up early as usual, had breakfast on the burners, but he was nowhere to be found. Conrad yelled his name and Pete yelled 'hello' as he came over the ridge of a nearby hill with an armful of wood.

"Looks like we'll need this tonight," he said looking to the sky. "It's going to rain tonight, I think." He placed the wood under a large plastic sheet.

"Yeah, it looks like rain." Conrad poured himself a cup of coffee and sat on a large rock. He looked up at the sky once again just to make sure he wasn't seeing things. "The forecast didn't say anything about rain, did it Pete?"

"Na, nothing from what I saw." Pete was now tending the cooking food. "You hungry yet?"

"A little."

"Where's lover boy?" Pete chuckled. "Looks like the ride got the better part of him."

"Yeah. I think he's been doing too much since they got here. Jessica's had him running around from Gansbaai to the De Kelders to Hermanus. I don't know what's up with those two," Conrad sipped his coffee. "You'd think they'd spend more time with the family. God, she hasn't been here for over a year, and we don't even see her."

"Ah, they're just in love. You can see it on their faces. Probably just finding a little time to sneak off. You remember sneaking off with Mary, don't you, old timer?" Pete laughed.

"Don't remind me." Conrad looked toward Thomas' tent." I just can't help but think there's something else going on with them. I don't know, they've been going to Hermanus a lot these last two weeks and...well, I can't help remembering the trouble she had in Angola."

"She'll be fine." Pete slapped Conrad's shoulder. "He looks like a good kid. He'll make a fine son-in-law someday." He sat down on the rock next to Conrad and the two men watched the burning fire. Conrad squinted his eyes as he looked deep into the violently leaping flames. The smell of the burning wood and the bacon on the grill reminded him of past safaris.

"She'll be fine. Relax a little," Pete said, as he poured Conrad a fresh cup of coffee.

"Yeah. I know," Conrad mumbled.

"It's about time!" Pete yelled." We're hungry." The flaps on Thomas' tent opened.

"Hey, guys," Thomas, walked over from the tent, rubbing his eyes. "What time is it?"

"Around eight or so."

"God, you guys get up early." Thomas grinned.

"Cup of coffee, Thomas?"

"Sounds good." Thomas looked around the camp and out across the rolling hills. It amazed him how colorful everything looked. He never imagined the Karoo looking so colorful, with its small, gray scrub bushes highlighted by flowering plants of red and yellow and blue. The green cacti reminded him of the deserts of Arizona, back in the States. The orange and reddish soil seemed endless to his wandering eyes as the cloudy, blue-gray sky stretched into the distance. "This place is amazing," he said, as Pete handed him coffee.

"It's a mysterious place, for sure." Conrad smiled. "Pete, is that grub ready?"

"Sure is."

"Good. Then lets eat and head out for a hunt." He grabbed a plate for Thomas and handed it to him, noticing Thomas' safari clothing. "You just go shopping, Thomas?" he questioned. "You're looking a little like Hemingway in that outfit." He winked at Pete.

"Did I overdo it?" Thomas looked at his tan, short-sleeved shirt, brown shorts and boots. "I went shopping before we came to Africa," he said, as Pete served him scrambled eggs, bacon and boerewors.

"Ah, we're just having some fun with ya."

"Have some chutney with that boerewors." Conrad smiled as he spooned some peach chutney onto Thomas' plate. "You look good Thomas. It just looks new."

"Yeah, it is." Thomas laughed. "Jessica *told* me not to dress like a mighty hunter. She said you guys would notice. I didn't care."

"Hey, Thomas, when your done with the hunt, can I have those boots?" Pete teased.

"Hey, hey, I want them there boots when he's done with 'em, pardner."

"Oh...I see you guys have been watching a few cowboy movies," Thomas intervened. "I'll tell you what, you give me that old, worn-out ostrich skin hat you have on your head before I leave, and I'll give you these boots."

Both Conrad and Pete erupted in laughter, enjoying that Thomas was not afraid of or uncomfortable with a little teasing, appreciating his quick-witted rebuttal.

The day drew on as the three men made their way into the bush. During a brief instruction on rifle technique, Conrad realized that Thomas had used a rifle before, and that weapons were not foreign to him. Over the weeks since Thomas and Jessica's arrival, he'd watched the two of them during their stay at the estate. He admired Thomas for being an upright man, and enjoyed his company. The two of them had formed a certain bond in the short time, and, being very much alike-innately confident and gentle, with similar views and philosophies, they felt a certain comfort with one another. But one thing Conrad did not understand was Thomas' dislike of the black race. He had noticed it a week before as the two men talked about Apartheid. Thomas become agitated as they discussed the black and colored people and made many generalizations. Conrad watched Thomas' eyes as he spoke and knew there was some hidden anger in Thomas' heart. From where, he did not know, but it was certain that something had happened in Thomas' past that triggered such hatred. His face began to redden in anger, as if he was recalling some past memory, some past hurt he had experienced. Or was it that Jessica had told him about her troubles in Angola. He did not know.

Clouds lined the sky as far as the eye could see and the landscape seemed to know that a change was in the air. The three men walked a distance from camp, searching for animal tracks. Thomas watched Conrad and Pete discuss the dryness of the land, saying that it was dryer than most seasons. Here and there, the men could see old animal tracks as they searched at the orangey-red soil for signs of life. Conrad, an experienced hunter, would show Thomas the tracks, explaining the difference between them: "These are springbok tracks here," he whispered once, as they walked around a small hillside, "and these are eland tracks here. It's said that the Bushmen and Hottentots believe that if you kill an eland, the hunter captures its soul. They revere the animal. You would be lucky to have such a kill on your first trip to Africa." He winked at Thomas. "These tracks are fresh, maybe a day old."

The morning turned into afternoon as the clouds moved off into the distance. The day's heat began to build as they decided to rest and have a quick lunch. Pete, a park ranger for most of his life, had a rugged-looking face, tough as leather from years of being out on the land. Thomas had seen the same weathered look on the fishermen back in the States, but Pete, like Conrad, was an Afrikaner, born and raised in Africa, from Dutch descendents who migrated to the land for trade. They were tall, well built men who worked and hunted the land, standing proud and strong in their heritage and Thomas knew he was in good company. Both men knew the land and understood its ways, spiritual and giving. They'd learned to respect Africa.

"Hey, Thomas, what's hunting like in America?" Pete said, eating a sandwich.

"Well, to tell you the truth, Pete, I don't hunt much in the States." Thomas drank from his canteen. "I hunted when I was younger with my father, but haven't hunted for a long time since."

"Does it take all day to track animals...I mean, do you remember stuff like that?" Pete asked.

"Yeah, I remember some. We'd sit in a tree stand all day, waiting for the deer to walk by, and when they did, we'd shoot them."

"That's it?" Pete laughed.

"Well, it's different in the States. From what I know, if you were in Alaska or the Rocky Mountains, then you'd track the animals as we are doing now, but in the eastern part of the country, there isn't as much land, so there are laws that we have to follow in order to hunt. There's some good hunting there as well but times are changing."

"It's happening here too." Conrad said, placing his sandwich on his knee. "The land is closing in on us here as well. Remember when we were young, Pete? We'd hunt for weeks, and the hunt was good. Today, the land's divided like a puzzle, separated with fences and wires and stones, only the Great Karoo is still vast and even that is shrinking. Things have changed here for sure."

"Yes." Pete nodded. "But we aren't seeing much game because there's a drought on the land. It's drier than most seasons here in Africa and the Great Karoo is even drier than most years. The animals go to the water now."

"True," Conrad said, gazing around, "but there are fresh tracks and these animals probably know rain is on the way. It's a good sign for us if it rains, because the animals will walk freely afterward. Still, times have changed, I guess here as well as in America. Everything is changing and moving too fast these days. What bothers me most is the polluting of the lands and oceans. The fishermen are seeing very little reward from the seas these days, the catches are smaller and the fish are smaller. I think there's something wrong. And now, these past couple of years, the drought on the land...it's not good...not good at all."

Just as the other two were finishing their lunches, Thomas walked some yards off to look over a nearby hill, watching the land for signs of life as Pete and Conrad talked about the past hunts of yesteryear. As they talked, a shot rang out from Thomas' rifle. Both men jumped in alarm, not expecting Thomas to shoot anything without first consulting them.

"Jesus!" Pete yelled. "I hope the hell you didn't shoot a Mamzibi?"

"What is it, Tom?" Conrad said, as they ran toward him.

"Looked like a large deer." He shouted. "I got him."

"You sure you dropped him?" Pete asked excitedly.

"Yeah...He fell over there, near that rock." Thomas pointed.

"Damn, boy!" Pete yelled.

"Lets go have a look." Conrad proudly slapped Thomas on the back and led the way to the large rock a hundred yards away. Conrad looked at Pete in amazement at the distance of the shot. "If you shot him at this distance, Thomas, then we underestimated you." He guffawed. Pete winked at Thomas as they walked to one side of the rock.

"There's blood!" Pete said.

Conrad looked at Thomas, raised one eyebrow and smirked. "Son of a bitch...you got him...then he got up and ran for a bit."

"Don't mind him, Thomas," Pete said. "He's jealous you got the first shot off."

"I'm not jealous. I'm happy for the kid." Conrad winked. "Okay, Thomas...now's time to track...follow the blood trail and other markings on the ground."

Thomas walked around the rock searching the ground. The blood trail was splattered, not just on the ground, but on the rocks and bushes as well. They walked about thirty feet before Conrad saw the dead animal lying near a small clump of bushes.

"I can't believe it!" Conrad said, in shock.

"What!" Pete mirrored Conrad's uncertainty. "God, will you look at that, he got a eland."

"That animal you said had mystical powers?" Thomas asked, as the men walked up to the dead animal. Its body was still. Conrad checked the antelope for the shot hole and found the bullet had pierced the animal's chest and heart. He knew the eland's chest was hit because of the blood on the brush as well as the ground. As they tracked the animal, he had noticed that the blood was redder in color, indicating that the lungs had been hit. As they stood there checking the eland, the sky began to darken.

"Congratulations Thomas!" Conrad smiled broadly, extending his hand. "You got the first kill of the hunt—and a eland at that—I can't believe it."

"Great job, Thomas." Pete took out his knife and handed it to Thomas. "Now, start gutting this thing so we can eat fresh meat tonight."

Conrad looked at Pete and the two men watched Thomas as he began gutting the eland.

"I may need help with this," he said, turning to them.

"Here," Pete said, leaning over and removing the knife from Thomas' hand. "You relax and I'll take care of this for you."

"Thanks, Pete." Thomas stood, walking a short distance away. Conrad watched him pour canteen water over his hands as he rubbed them together to clean off the bloodstains. He sat on the rocks and looked out over the land as the rain proceeded to fall from the sky for the first time all year. The Great Karoo would see life again as the rain replenished the dry soils. Thomas sat thinking about the eland and what the great animal must have been thinking when smelling the coming rains. *Was he thinking that life was in the air, or did he know that this would be his last day?* Thomas had seen the eland look at him and he'd lowered his rifle as if to say, run. The eland had watched him, standing on the hill, and turned his proud head as if to say, I am finished, before the shot rang out.

On a hill, not far from the three men, a lone man stood. He'd seen the great eland fall and the mighty hunter who captured his soul. He saw the rains fall from the sky as the animal's blood mixed with the soil. Life was taken and life has come to the Great Karoo. The Hottentot, a Mamzibi, ran off into the distance with the news. There was change in the air and the rains have come to renew life. Tonight, the Mosquito people would celebrate the rains, and with the rains would come the Mosquito of the Great Karoo.

Evening came as the rains receded and the clouds could be seen moving into the northern sky. The brief storm had replenished the dry land and the night brought coolness to the air. The three men sat at the fire as the night unfolded around them eating the fresh cooked meat of the eland. A multitude of stars began to appear in the dark sky. The moon hung low on the horizon just above the rolling hills and jagged rock formations. Full and large, its presence could be felt, like the watchful eye of the great lightning bird, *Impundulu.* They sat discussing the day's hunt and Thomas' luck in finding and bringing down the mystical eland. It was a great ending to the two-day hunt, something they would never forget.

"One shot!" Conrad yelled. "I can't believe you got the eland with one shot."

"Thing is"—Pete smiled—"he shot it straight through the heart as well."

"And at four hundred yards too," Thomas replied.

"Alright, now you're pushing it kid." Pete laughed, spitting whiskey into the fire. The flames leaped into a fiery yellow glow.

They'd had a great day and would return to the main camp with the good news of Thomas killing the eland. The news would excite the rest of the family and they would braai the rest of the meat when they arrived home the following week. But tonight, they would talk and bond, as men do, watching the orangey red glow of the firelight, feeling its life-sustaining heat, and sitting under a star-filled night like their ancestors did so-many years ago. It was primordial and raw, rough and peaceful, calm and exciting, and the men could feel the power of nature around them as the night waned.

Until that night at the camp, Thomas had never fully understood why people longed to return to Africa once they'd visited it. He watched the fire glow and the stars shine, and the moon hang over the distant hill as they talked; there was an old feel to it all, a primitive, ancient and innocent feeling. Now he knew why men like Conrad and Pete lived here in Africa. He thought about Jessica and how she longed to return to her homeland, and now he too would long to return someday to Africa. Some night in the future as he is stoking his fireplace, and watching the red glow, his mind will drift to this night, to this hunt, and to this safari in Africa. Thomas now felt the soul of the black continent and would never forget the feeling he now had in his heart.

"There's something moving over there," Pete said, quickly reaching for his rifle. Conrad instinctively grabbed his own gun and moved away from the firelight securing the perimeter. Pete walked toward the movement as a lion defending his lair. The men moved quickly as if they've rehearsed this a million times. Thomas left the firelight as well but did not bring his rifle. Conrad whispered to him from the shadows and he followed the sound of Conrad's voice. The two men watched Pete walk to the edge of the fire's light, his rifle pointing into the night. The night became still and their bodies became cold as they stood in the shadows, away from the heat of the fire.

First, Pete spoke to the darkness in Afrikaans. Thomas didn't understand what was said, but knew from the tone of Pete's voice that it was threatening and hard. There was no reply from the darkness as Thomas watched Conrad's squinting eyes. It was as if Conrad could feel the darkness. His head moved to every sound of the night. The moon created light but their eyes were still adjusting from the bright firelight. As Thomas looked into the dark, the landscape played upon his mind, things appeared to move and sounds evoked his fears. Even the littlest sounds from the dark became ominous and foreboding.

"Stay low," Conrad whispered. "I'm heading over to Pete."

"Okay, but I don't have my rifle."

"I know. Just stay low."

"What do I do if we're attacked?"

"Stay here next to this rock." Conrad crouched down like a stalking lion. He moved quickly and silently into the night. Thomas watched him disappear into the black shadow. The moon began to fall behind the hills as the landscape became even darker. Again Pete said something in Afrikaans, this time even louder. His frame looked large and threatening as he stood his ground. He knew not to show any fear, and he knew he'd placed himself in harm's way to protect his friends. This is what the Afrikaner people were like, proud and fearless in times of danger; the blood of the Boer people ran strong in them.

Suddenly Thomas saw Conrad walking from the darkness toward Pete, speaking another language that sounded more like clicks to Thomas' ears. Conrad lowered his rifle, and asked Pete to do the same. The two men walked back to the fire and waited, whispering to each other as they watched the dark landscape around them. Thomas watched as his heart raced. He could feel coldness in his body as his eyes adjusted to the darkness. He could make out more shapes in the blackness and hear more sounds of the night as the minutes drew on. Conrad made the noises again, mixing this time with what sounded like some African dialect.

Out of the African night came distant sounds from many directions. Then Thomas could make out two men walking from the bush. Small in height, they walked as silently as a mountain leopard stalking its prey. The men walked from the darkness into the light, straight toward Conrad and Pete. Conrad and Pete looked large and ominous with the firelight flickering behind their larger and taller bodies. Thomas could hardly hear the dialogue between the men, but Conrad lowered his rifle even further. Pete walked to the fire, picked something up and returned to the group. After a few moments, Conrad turned toward the rock and called Thomas to the fire. The two smaller men gestured to the darkness and more men appeared from all directions. Turning, Thomas found a five-foot, light-skinned black man standing two steps behind him. The man smiled a large smile as their eyes met. Thomas smiling back uncomfortably, knowing that the man had been standing behind him the whole time.

"It's okay, Thomas," Conrad said, "come on out."

"Who are they?" Thomas said, coming from his hiding place.

"Mamzibi warriors." Conrad greeted the man, who followed Thomas as they approached. "They saw you kill the eland earlier."

"Ah...is that good...or bad?"

"We're going to find out," Conrad said, winking at him. "They want to meet the warrior who killed the mystical beast."

"Oh great," Thomas said, concerned. "I see myself frying on an open fire by morning."

"You watch too many movies." Conrad laughed. "Come on."

Conrad, Pete, Thomas and the Mamzibi warriors congregated around the fire. Conrad fed the fire with fresh wood and the flames became brighter, lighting up the surrounding area as the men sat. Some of the warriors sat on the ground and others stood near the fire, warming their hands and feet. Thomas could not help but think that the warriors looked like children as they smiled at him. They seemed to be friendly people, smiling and laughing, as they talked and ate the cooked meat. Pete, the official cook, put on more meat for their newly arrived company. Conrad sat near one warrior, talking in what seemed a mix of African dialects. He seemed to understand most of what the man had to say.

After some informality, Conrad turned to Thomas. "This is Ghanzi. He saw you kill the eland. He said you and the eland became one and that he saw you give the eland a chance to live." Conrad looked at the warrior and repeated what he had said in the Mamzibi's tongue.

The man nodded and smiled at Thomas. As Thomas looked into his eyes he could see the innocence of the man. There was a kind and spiritual way in the warrior's eyes, and softness in his look. As Thomas extended his hand in a gesture of friendship, the warrior's eyes fell on the tattoo on Thomas' arm. Grabbing the arm, he pushed the rest of Thomas' sleeve up, revealing the lion. The warrior stood up and backed away from Thomas, calling to the rest of his men.

"What's happened?" Pete said, alarmed, as he watched the warriors surround Thomas and Conrad. The Mamzibi became excited and the clicking sounds increased. The warrior pointed to Thomas' arm and his eyes became excited, his voice louder before they all fell into a sudden silence.

"Well, Thomas, it seems you're not only a great hunter, but a part of their legend." Conrad chuckled.

"What do you mean, legend?"

"It seems that you are now the lion that has returned to their land." Pete turned and walked back to the fire, laughing. "Your tattoo" he said.

"What about it?" Thomas rolled his sleeve up again. The warriors moved in to look at his arm. A soft roar erupted from the Mamzibi warriors as they saw the tattoo of the lion.

"I'm going to burn at the stake tonight right," Thomas said.

"No." Conrad shook his head. "You're not going to burn at the stake." He laughed. "They have a legend about the lion returning to them. Your lion tattoo is a sign of the lion's return."

"Jessica told me about that when we found the rock the other day." Thomas remembered.

"What rock?"

"We found a large rock near the other camp. It was carved like a lion but it was old and worn...underneath it was a painting of a lion, and some other things...a mosquito, I think."

"Really?" Why didn't you two say something?" Conrad said.

"We just thought we'd keep it a secret, that's all." Thomas looked at the warriors while Conrad pondered what Thomas had said, knowing that some things in life were not coincidence but destiny. But how Thomas' lion tattoo played a part, or would it play a part, and to what degree, he did not know.

The Mamzibi warriors huddled near the fire, eating the eland meat and quietly talking amongst themselves. Conrad made out some of their discussion but not enough to understand everything they were saying. He had learned the clicking language from some of the now domesticated Bushmen and Hottentots who worked on the estate back in Gansbaai, but he did not fully understand it. Not all the native Africans lived in the bush and many of them had become educated and were now a part of the African working class. Only a small number of them still lived the old ways.

Ghanzi and another, higher ranking Mamzibi warrior named, Gobab broke away from the warriors and sat in front of Thomas. Conrad and Pete sat beside him. Ghanzi introduced Gobab as the Inkosi's first son and next in line of chiefs of the Mamzibi. They talked to Thomas as if he knew the language and watched his face for a reply to their question.

"Thomas," Conrad said, turning to the warriors, squinting his eyes, "I think they want you to go with them to meet their chief."

"You're kidding me, right?" Thomas said with a wry look at Conrad. "I don't think that would be a good idea...I mean, I don't even understand what they're saying."

"Well, they want you to attend some kind of ceremony tonight at their village." Conrad giggled. "Now don't let them see you getting nervous. They're just asking that you be their guest." He smiled again at the warriors.

"Well...I...tell them, I want you to go as well. Can you do that?"

Conrad spoke to Gobab in what sounded like a mixture of distinct clicking noises and hand jesters. Gobab sat motionless, in thought, as the group watched. The village was a secret, and a well-hidden place that outsiders did not know, but this was the lion's return and the chief, his father, would be happy that they'd found this man, and that he had the spirit of the eland in him. Gabab looked up at Thomas and Conrad and smiled. He agreed to Thomas and Conrad going to the village, but Pete would have to stay back. Pete didn't care and just shrugged his shoulders. He knew that someone had to watch the camp anyway.

Conrad agreed. He turned to Pete and spoke Afrikaans. Pete nodded and returned to the fire once again to tend the cooking meat. "We'll be back by late morning," Conrad told Thomas as he gathered his gear. "I hope you slept well last night, because you're going to be up all night tonight."

Thomas knew he was in good hands with Conrad, and even though he neither trusted nor liked the black people, these Mamzibi seemed nice enough. He gathered some gear and they headed off into the darkness with the Mamzibi warriors. Some of the warriors ran ahead with the news of the hunters and that they'd be bringing meat of the eland. More important, they'd be bringing the returned lion. It would be a special ceremony tonight at the Mamzibi village with the ceremony of the mosquito; dormant during the dry months, the mosquito of the Great Karoo was now awake from the newly fallen rains. With that had come the return of the lion, as the ancient legend foretold.

***

Jessica sat by the warming fire as Ian placed more wood on the now high flames. As she sipped her coffee she watched him, wondering what he'd seen during his fighting in the Northern Transvaal ten years earlier when South Africa had to protect its borders from its less civilized neighbors. Since his return he'd changed from a happy, smiling boy of twenty to a quiet, introverted man. But, though his face seemed older, his movements were still sharp and keen. For a thirty-year-old man he was in good shape and a strong Afrikaner like his father.

He looked out into the darkness from time to time, carefully scanning the surrounding darkness for movement. He never said anything about the fighting, the guerrilla warfare that came to be known as the Bush Wars of the Transvaal. She'd heard stories about the South African troops fighting hand-to-hand combat, night after night in the rough terrain. Many of her countrymen never returned from the borders. The night fighting was the worst, she'd heard, because the men just seemed to disappear into the night without a trace. Yes, he was different, but he was still her brother and she loved him as such.

Ian sat down next to her and warmed his hands in the fire's warmth. He glanced toward the table where Mary and Duncan played cards. They had all been out hiking that day and after a hardy supper, were resting their legs and feet.

Ian placed his arm around Jessica and hugged her close. They smiled at each other.

"How you doing, Ian?"

"Ah...good," he said in their native Afrikaans language, looking at the fire. "It was a good walk today, huh?"

"Yeah, it was nice hanging out with everyone," she smiled. "I'm glad to be sitting now."

"I know...Duncan really likes to walk, doesn't he?"

"Yeah." She frowned. "He thinks he's the king around here sometimes. And since Daddy is out on the hunt with Uncle Pete and Thomas, he gets a little bossy."

"Yes, I know, but that's just the way he is. So, how are you doing...I mean after that stuff happened to you in Angola, how are you?" Jessica looked into the fire and sipped her coffee. She didn't know what to say and became unsettled. Ian could see he'd unnerved her and placed his hand on her shoulder.

"Sorry."

"It's okay, Ian. I...I was thinking about what happened, and I...." A tear ran down her cheek.

"I know. I have felt the same way at times. I cannot get some things out of my head, and I don't know what to do about it. I'm sorry." He rubbed her shoulder. Jessica put her head on his and wiped her eyes. She knew he didn't mean anything bad and only cared for her. Ian was always her favorite brother, and they had a special bond. And now, with the things she'd seen and experienced, she too, knew some of the feeling created by killings and war.

"Was it bad up there?" she whispered.

"Yes, it was bad," he replied, looking deeply into the fire, remembering back to those dark nights in the Transvaal. She rubbed his back and looked into the fire as well. The pain of war was in their hearts and the sorrow of the things they'd seen. She knew Ian had killed protecting their country's borders from terrorists and she understood why he did not want to kill again. She now understood why he was quieter and more introverted and avoided confrontations. She remembered her confrontation with General Mobutu that rainy day in Angola, and remembered his face at the airport the day she and Thomas arrived from the United States. He was an evil man who hurt and killed for power. Would she have to confront him again now that he was here in South Africa?

***

Conrad and Thomas walked behind the Mamzibi warriors. The night swallowed them as they went down an embankment and Conrad heard water trickling from the limestone rocks. Bearing their spears and bows, the warriors walked in silence, like cats along a forest path, quiet and alert. Thomas felt safe knowing Conrad was with him. As they walked, he felt the ravine close in on them as they descended a path. Conrad, too, felt the gorge about them and whispered his thoughts to Thomas. "I didn't know there was such a gorge here," he said. "It runs deep." The group walked for about two hours until they reached the cave. Every fall of a rock or trickle of water could be heard as they entered the cavern. The Mamzibi lit two torches and proceeded deeper into the cave. Limestone formations could be seen from the torchlight, and the glints from the metal spearheads danced as the group moved down into the cavern.

"It's getting warmer," Thomas said.

Conrad nodded. "I know the Mamzibi are secretive but this I did not imagine," he said. "We are going to a place I don't think any white man has been before."

"How many of these Mamzibi are there...a lot?"

"I didn't think there were many left," Conrad said, avoiding a small boulder. "The Hottentot people usually travel in groups of ten to fifteen, but they sometimes meet in larger groups."

As they talked, they walked from the cavern and into a large, open area. In the night sky, the stars shone and the Milky Way's path spread overhead. Conrad and Thomas looked around the canyon in amazement as Gabab and Ghanzi lead them through the village. There were forty to fifty reed huts scattered over the canyon floor with one large lodge near the far end. The steep cliffs towered ominously overhead, making a perfect fortress, hidden from the plains above, secluded from the outside world. The rest of the warriors disbanded as Gabab barked orders. Some of the village people came to greet the warriors as they walked to the main lodge.

"This is amazing," Conrad declared. "I never knew the Mamzibi had such a village."

"It seems there are more of them than you thought," Thomas said, smiling at Ghanzi. Ghanzi smiled in reply, not understanding a word Thomas had said. "They're friendly."

"Yeah, they're friendly but they're also warriors," Conrad said. "I also know of many battles in history that the Mamzibi fought. Of all the Hottentot people, the Bushmen, who are an enemy of these Hottentots, feared these warriors most because of their fierceness and cunning fighting skills."

"See, I told you we're going to burn at the stake tonight."

"Maybe you chunky, not me." Conrad laughed. "I'm old and wrinkly, they don't want me for meat."

"Chunky!" Thomas frowned. "I'm not chunky!"

"To them you're chunky."

The men walked behind the two Mamzibis, who led them into the main lodge. Conrad noticed a large black pool of water just off to the right side of the lodge doorway. Inside the center of the lodge, they found a ten-foot round, well-lit fire, and were surprised to see that there were as many as forty Mamzibi people inside. The noise came to a sudden halt as the four men entered the lodge. Gabab walked directly to the chief, who sat at the far wall, and knelt before him, talking freely to his father as the other men waited in silence. The chief was a small, older Hottentot who sat on a small chair, simply decorated, not evaluated like most chairs of men of rank. Still, the chief's bare feet dangled as if he were a small boy at a kitchen table.

Gabab spoke to the chief, pointing at times to Thomas. The chief nodded and looked passed Gabab curiously to the man with the mark of the lion. Gabab went to Thomas and summoned him to the chief, who sat motionless and proud. He was the spiritual leader of his people, and would make the final decision about the lion's return to his lands.

Thomas walked up to Gabab's father. "Smiling seems to be the thing around here," he said to Conrad as he watched the chief.

"I don't think you can go wrong with a smile. Just don't over do it, or it's going to look like you're growling at him, and trying to scare him." Conrad joked.

With that, Ghanzi laughed, and walked to the chair were the chief was sitting. The chief got up, walked passed Conrad and Thomas and sat with the rest of the Mamzibi warriors behind them. Ghanzi sat in the chief's seat and spoke to Conrad and Thomas.

"I am Ghanzi, chief of the Mamzibi, as you have called us," he said slowly in English. "I had to make sure you were good people before I could reveal myself to you. I now know the lion has come to us again and I know this from looking into your soul. You have been sent to us from afar and I know your heart is of the lion of the sky."

Conrad stood up and came next to Thomas. He wondered how it was that a Mamzibi warrior knew such English. "I'm Conrad Sinclair," he said to Ghanzi, "I'm a little confused. How do you know such good English?"

The chief laughed and with that the Mamzibi people followed suit. Ghanzi stood up before the two men. Thomas and Conrad towered over him and looked even larger with the roaring fire behind them. The fire's light flickered off the walls of the lodge, making a hunting dance of the reeds and beams that lined the walls and roof.

"I learned it in school. I was educated by one of your Afrikaner people when I was a boy." He looked around at his people and smiled. "I was lost once and one of your people found me wandering. They fed and helped me to learn your ways. I was in your world once, but when I grew, I decided to return to my people here. We have lived here for many years and this is my true home."

"Thank you for your hospitality Ghanzi," Conrad said, "was it you I once saw while hunting here years back?"

"Yes, Conrad, it was I who pointed you to the game for your hunt. And now you return with the eland and the lion on the night of the mosquito's return."

"The mosquito?"

"Yes. Our legend has it that when the lion is in the sky and the mosquito comes with the first rains of the season, our people will be saved. We will once again become as strong as in days of old. You have brought the lion on the night of the mosquito. Tonight is the ceremony of the mosquito and the lion stands here in our land, and in the sky above, the stars show us the sign of the lion. It is a special night, and we have seen the changing of the sky, the changing of the weather, and the changing of the land for many years now."

"What do you mean 'your people will be saved'?" Thomas asked. He looked around the lodge and then into Ghanzi's eyes. "Your people don't look like they need saving."

Ghanzi looked at Thomas, and then at Conrad, his face becoming humbled. "We are living because we chose to be separate from the outside world, your world. Most of the African people are dying of the great disease. We have seen it. We do not have the disease here in our village yet. "

"What disease?" Conrad questioned.

"The great blood disease, the great evil that is killing many of the people."

Thomas turned and walked away a few steps, lowering his head. Conrad and Ghanzi watched him standing near the fire. He seemed to be mulling over what Ghanzi had said of him being the savior of the African people. Conrad knew Thomas did not like the African people and thought this was upsetting him.

"You okay, Thomas?"

"Tell them I'm not their savior, or lion, or anything...I mean...Ghanzi, I'm not a savior," he mumbled nervously, looking deep into the fire. Conrad walked to him and touched his shoulder.

"Hey, don't let this stuff get to you, it's only some Hottentot legend," Conrad said calmly. "We're going to see a ceremony and be out of here by morning."

"I think we should go now!" Thomas said agitatedly, raising his head and looking at Conrad.

"Hey, what's with you, Thomas?" Conrad squinted his eyes studying Thomas' face. "Relax. Relax a little—we'll be out of here in an hour or two."

Thomas quickly reached up and smacked his neck, killing a mosquito. "Jesus, I'm being bitten alive in this fuckin' place." He walked closer to the fire.

Conrad turned to Ghanzi and shook his head. Ghanzi looked at Thomas and wondered what he was so worried about, and what made him angry. Thomas watched the fire and thought of Jessica. He knew they'd have to leave for the States as soon as they got back to Gansbaai. She would need the best treatment that money could buy, and he'd see to it that she had it. He would not lose another love to something these people did. But there was no cure for HIV and he knew he would also put these people in danger if one of these mosquitoes bit him and then bit one of them. "Damn these mosquitoes, they're fuckin everywhere."

"It's time for the ceremony!" Ghanzi shouted. Turning to his people, he spoke to them in their tongue. "The mosquito is awakening from its sleep and the water will come alive with them soon."

With that, some of the younger boys of the tribe, painted white, began to wash the paint from their bodies.

"We go outside," Ghanzi said aloud. "The lion is in the sky!" A sound of clicks and movement rolled throughout the village. The lodge began to empty.

Conrad said to Thomas. "You alright?"

"I just don't know if it's a good idea for me to be here, Conrad," Thomas said, warming his hands at the fire.

"Why, what's up? I thought you'd like this stuff...it's something most people dream about seeing."

"I know, but I'm not feeling well." He hesitated, thinking if he should tell Conrad about Jessica and him being infected with HIV. He looked at the fire in silent thought.

"You sure you're okay...I mean...do you need to talk or something?" "What's bothering him," Conrad wondered as he looked at Thomas staring into the fire.

"No. I'll be fine." Thomas turned to him smiling falsely. "Lets get this ceremony over with so we could get back to camp."

"Hey, that's the spirit." Conrad grinned. "These people seem to like you. You're not going to burn at the stake tonight."

"Just get me away from these mosquitoes. They're biting the shit out of me. I'd rather burn at the stake than have these insects suck my blood dry."

"Just stay close to the fire. I don't have any insect repellant with me, sorry."

"Aren't they biting you?"

"No. Seems they like you better." Conrad laughed. "Come on, let's head outside to the ceremony."

The two men left the lodge and found that many more Mamzibi were outside near the pool of water. Thomas stood near a large fire, hoping that the mosquitoes would stay away from the heat and wondered why Conrad and the others did not seem to be troubled by the insects. "Little fuckin' bloodsuckers should all die," he moaned to himself as he warmed his hands and swatted and killed mosquitoes. The ceremony commenced.

The night sky could be seen clearly from the canyon floor and Conrad noticed that the constellation Leo was directly overhead. He puzzled over what Ghanzi had said concerning the lion in the sky and the lion tattoo on Thomas' arm. Was it coincidence or destiny, he thought, as they walked to the large fire roaring by the pool. The fires throughout the village played upon the canyon walls bringing a haunting glow to the village. It was like nothing Conrad had ever seen before and he wondered how long the Mamzibi had this place as their village. Knowing that they were a nomadic people, he wondered if this place was used only for the ceremonies and meetings of the Hottentot people.

Thomas surveyed the village, he too wondering about the people. They seemed so happy and innocent to his eyes, smiling and playful, of little harm to anyone, but he did not like the black race and his deep imbedded hurt would not easily leave his heart.

The tribal boys painted in white were now standing near the water's edge and the white paint was being removed from their bodies. There were four of them and they appeared as children to Thomas because of their height. The color of their skin was orangey brown, and their hair a lighter color like most of the black people Thomas had seen in the United States. Ghanzi said a kind of blessing before them as a few tribal women brushed their bodies with some sticky substance.

"Exactly what is going on here?" Thomas whispered to Conrad.

"I think they're coming into manhood and this is some sort of initiation ceremony." Conrad was watching and listening to what Ghanzi was saying. As the fire roared, the Mamzibi people began to chant and dance near the water's edge. They moved around the boys who were jumping up and down and waving their arms as if flying. Each time they landed, they exhaled forcefully bringing their arms to their sides. The canyon reverberated with the pounding of drums and the sounds of the Mamzibi people.

"Look at the water!" Thomas said, his eyes widening. "Is that fog... or...?"

"Mosquitoes," Conrad said softly in disbelief.

"Mosquitoes!"

"That's the largest swarm of mosquitoes I've ever seen."

"I was being bit often before, but now...oh shit! I've got to get the hell out of here."

"Just stay put next to the fire and you'll be okay," Conrad said as he walked toward Ghanzi, who was watching the water and the dancing and the fire where Thomas stood. Ghanzi knew this night was special and it was the time for his people to again be healed.

Conrad thought about the possibility of getting malaria or some other sickness as the insects swarmed and whined around the camp. Maybe Thomas was right in that they should leave and return to their camp. They'd hunted and got the meat of the eland. The hunt was over. The trip was a success. But, more of a mystery, he wasn't being bitten and didn't understand why.

"Ghanzi, we have to go," he said reluctantly. "We are not accustomed to this and it's late for us, after being up all day on the hunt."

Ghanzi smiled softly watching Thomas frantically swatting at, and brushing away the mosquitoes flying around him.

Conrad, seeing Thomas' distress, knew they'd better be going right away.

"He will be asleep soon." Ghanzi said.

"What do you mean 'asleep soon'?"

"After the first bites of the Mamzibi mosquitoes, he will sleep."

"I don't understand, Ghanzi?"

"We, you and I, are not being bitten by the mosquito." Ghanzi said, grabbing Conrad's exposed arms. "See. You are not being bitten. My people are not being bitten by the mosquito either."

Conrad turned to the boys near the water and watched them. "They're being bitten."

"Yes, because they are new to the village. They have never been here and the Mamzibi mosquitos have never bitten them before. They will be part of the Mamzibi tribe now, and will bear the markings of the Mamzibi till death."

"I don't understand. Why am I not being bitten, then?"

"Because you have been bitten before by the Mamzibi mosquito."

"When."

"When you were here last. Years back, you hunted not far from here. It was the time of the mosquito then too. Once a year the mosquito comes. Once you are bitten, no other insect, no other mosquito will bite you again, ever."

Conrad thought back to the time he had hunted the Mamzibi land and the time he had seen Ghanzi. The mosquitoes were biting him, and no mosquito had bitten him for years after that day. He had never paid it any mind.

The noise settled and the chanting stopped. Conrad turned to find that the tribal boys were now lying on the ground, asleep. He saw a few tribal women tending Thomas, too, slept on the ground next to the fire. Conrad remembered he had hunted the Mamzibi land years back, getting tired and falling asleep, too. After waking he found Ghanzi and the other Mamzibi warrior minutes later. Could it be that this mosquito's bite was different from the rest of the mosquitoes of the world, the ones that brought disease and death from malaria, yellow fever and other sicknesses? What is it about these mosquitoes that are different? Conrad questioned.

"There is little food here in the Great Karoo. What little we have we need to preserve. The mosquito is doing as we do and the ancient ones did. We keep and mark our food supply and protect it from others."

"You mean it's injecting us with something that repels other insects, so that we are their only food supply?"

"Yes."

"That's amazing." Conrad looked around the village. The people were walking to their huts as the fire began to die. The mosquitoes swarmed off into the canyon. He knew that there were places in the world where species of animals and insects evolved differently, places like Madagascar, the Galapagos Islands and places in South America, but he never knew such things to happen here in the Great Karoo. Why not, he thought. Why not here, where man ventured little. This was a place that time had forgotten, open and vast, this was why he loved it so.

"Look!" Ghanzi pointed to the star-filled sky. "Look to the lion. It now sleeps as well."

Conrad looked to the canyon wall. The constellation Leo had moved to the other edge of the canyon wall, and was now setting, as if sleeping, on its rim.

The night had held the legend of the return of the lion to the Mamzibi lands and the hatching of the Mamzibi mosquito. He wondered about all that had happened, and if Thomas' part was over. He knew he had a lot of explaining to do to Thomas in the morning, and he knew Jessica would be upset with him for taking Thomas to such a place. When they returned, Thomas would have to see Dr. Vieter to see if he had Malaria or any other type of disease, see that he was okay and able to return to the States.

CHAPTER 9

The next morning the two men walked silently to their camp where Pete waited. Both were deep in thought and the walk back seemed longer than the night before. The sun was shining low and the day's heat was building. Not a cloud could be seen and the blue sky seemed to go on forever as they looked out over the landscape. Groggy as he was, Thomas tried to make sense of what had happened during the night. The last thing he remembered was Conrad talking to Ghanzi as the never-ending barrage of barbaric mosquitoes swarmed over his body in search of their next meal. "Damn little bloodsuckers," he muttered as he walked, scratching every bite on his body. "Sure, I didn't get burned at the stake. I was a human barbeque; I knew I should not have stayed at their village."

Trudging into camp, exhausted, they knew they'd be resting out the day. Without even a smile, or acknowledgement of Pete's offer of breakfast, Thomas walked straight to his tent, and collapsed.

Conrad sat next to the fire and poured himself a cup of coffee.

"You two look like shit." Pete said, handing Conrad a plate of warm food. Conrad took the plate, nodded in confirmation and began eating. Pete knew Conrad well and knew he would talk when the time was right. Conrad was, occasionally, a quiet man who took time to contemplate things and understand events, before voicing his thoughts. Pete knew this and continued to make idle talk, receiving grunts and nods of acknowledgement in return. Minutes passed before Conrad looked up. He seemed distant and tired to Pete.

"Are you okay?"

"I'll tell you, Pete, I don't think I've ever experienced anything so strange in my whole life."

"What happened? Did you guys go to the Mamzibi camp?"

"Yeah, we went to the camp, alright. It was bigger than we thought."

"What do you mean, bigger?"

"It was a village in a canyon to the south of here. We walked for about two hours until we came to a cave."

"A cave!"

"Yeah, to get to the canyon, we had to go through a cave. And when we came out the other side, I could not believe my eyes. There were Mamzibi everywhere, huts, and a center lodge, and a small lake."

"A lake! Here in the Karoo?"

"Yeah. I couldn't believe it either." Conrad said, looking into the fire. He thought about the night, the ceremony, and the mosquitoes and about the legend of the lion's return to the Karoo. Pete didn't need to know everything that had happened and Conrad didn't feel like telling him. He was tired. He needed to sleep before their return to the main camp and the long drive home to Gansbaai.

"I'm going to grab some shut-eye, Pete," he said, yawning. "I'll tell you about it some other time, okay?"

"Alright, Conrad, get some sleep and I'll see you later." Conrad got up and headed for the tent.

"Hey!" Pete yelled. "What about the kid. Is he alright?" He asked.

"Yeah. He'll be fine."

The ride back to the camp was long, hot and tiresome. The three men spoke little, as they made their way across the hot, dry plain. Thomas looked out the window in a daze, watching the landscape pass before his eyes. He thought about Jessica and the disease that they were infected with. From what he knew about the HIV virus, what the Mamzibi called, the great blood disease, it had no cure and it seemed a cruel, and horrible death. What would they do and how could this happen to them? He thought about her smiling on the docks that rainy day in Belmar and all the fun times they had sailing on the *Blue Heron*. He wanted to spend the rest of his life with her...and now, now that these people had infected—her and him—with the disease, his anger for them grew. He despised them for what they had done to her. The hatred manifested itself deep inside him. The next morning they drove into the main camp. Thomas could feel the colors of his mind turn from bright to black as his heart felt the anger deep within.

"Here we are guys." Pete said as they drove into camp. Jessica and Mary stood near the smoldering fire, smiling as the truck came to a stop. Jessica ran to the truck as Thomas opened the door.

"Hi!" she yelled, throwing her arms around his neck. "I'm so glad you're back, honey!"

"Hi." Thomas kissed her. "How're ya doing, Jess?" He held her tight.

"I'm good. You feeling okay?"

"I'm fine...how were things while we were gone?"

"We had a great time, hiking, playing cards, hanging out." She looked into his eyes. "You don't look too good, honey."

"I'm just tired from the ride."

"You sure?"

"Yeah. I was worried about you," he said hugging her. "I missed you, Jess."

Conrad and Mary stood a few feet away, listening. Conrad looked into Mary's eyes and softly smiled.

"You guys must be hungry for supper, " Mary said. "Ian and Duncan have some food cooking on the braai for you."

"Good!" Conrad said.

"You sure you're okay, Thomas?" Jessica said, softly rubbing her hands on his face. "Why don't you clean up, have a shave, and we'll get something to eat for you, okay?"

"Sounds good. I'll be fine in a while and I'll tell you about the Mamzibi."

"The Mamzibi? You guys saw a Mamzibi?" she said excitedly, turning and looking at Conrad. "You saw a Mamzibi?"

"More than one." Conrad said. "We'll tell you about it as we eat."

"Wow! You guys had an exciting trip, I should have gone too."

"No, you shouldn't have," Thomas said, walking away, his head down.

"Dad." Jessica turned to her father. "What happened?" She crossed her arms, tapping her foot nervously.

"I'll tell you at dinner."

"Duncan...Ian, we have more meat in the truck: Eland meat." Conrad said, evading her questioning.

"Eland!" Duncan said. "Who shot an eland?"

"Thomas."

"Thomas?"

"Yes. Thomas," Pete said. "One shot through the heart at two hundred yards."

"Holy shit!" Duncan yelled. "We have a hunter in our midst."

Jessica looked at Conrad and Mary, and then over to Thomas as he washed up near the rear of the camp.

The sun would be setting soon and the heat was unbearable. Thomas slowly washed the day's sweat from his pores and the mosquito bites on his arms, legs and neck. Looking into the mirror, he couldn't believe how many bites he had on his body. He itched and it was hard not to scratch the itch away. He closed his eyes, still feeling heaviness in his eyes and limbs. His body felt fatigued and heavy, but he was glad to be back at the main camp and in Jessica's arms. Her spirit always seemed to lift his.

"What the hell, man!" Jessica said, standing behind him. "What the hell happened to you? Look at all these bites." Thomas opened his eyes and frowned in the mirror. He gave her a wry look and closed his eyes again as he washed his face. She reached into a nearby bag and began applying antiseptic cream to his back and neck.

"Can't wait for tonight," he joked sarcastically.

"Dad!" Jessica yelled, turning to her father, where he sat at the dinner table with Mary. She went to him and grabbed his arm to inspect it for bites. She inspected his neck as well. No mosquito bites could be found on Conrad's body.

"Didn't you think to give Thomas some repellant too?" she angrily said. "He was bitten alive, man. Jesus Dad, he's going to be itching for a week."

"I'm sorry, Jess. I'll tell you all about it when you sit down, okay," he said, reaching for her hand. "I'm tired. We're all tired." He held her hand and gave her a fatherly look. "Trust me, you'll know everything tonight."

"Mom." Jessica implored, turning to her mother. "Do you have any more antiseptic cream? This one is almost empty."

"Yes, dear." Mary replied, looking into Conrad's eyes as she got up from her chair. "I'll get it for you."

The night came quickly as the sun lowered behind the western mountains. They all sat down to eat and talked about the hunt: Thomas killing the eland, the meeting of the Mamzibi, and the ceremony of the mosquito. Mary, Jessica, Ian and Duncan listened to the story Conrad told them, what Ghanzi had said about the legend of the lion's return to the Great Karoo, and what it meant to the people of Africa. He also told them of the great blood disease that sickened the people of Africa, and the world. Jessica glanced at Thomas and lowered her head as she listened. He glanced her way sadly and winked, assuring her that neither Conrad nor Pete knew HIV had infected them. Her heart was in sorrow and it showed on her face.

After dinner they all sat near the fire and enjoyed each other's company. The fire's heat felt good as the night air began to chill as they talked more of the week's events. With a little nudging, Duncan edged Thomas to talk about the killing of the eland, and joked about him being the returned Cape Lion of the Karoo.

"So, you have become famous here in the Karoo, Thomas," Duncan joked. Conrad smiled as he watched Thomas and Duncan's exchange.

"Yeah, that, and a buck fifty, and I'll be able to get on a subway in New York," Thomas joked. "I'm amazed that these people have kept so well hidden over the years here in the Karoo."

"It's not like *no*body knew they were here, Thomas," Conrad interrupted. "We just didn't know that they had a village as they do."

"So it was that big, Dad?" Ian asked.

"Yes. It was quite big, and hidden in a canyon, as well." Conrad sipped his wine. "I must have been hunting right near it a few years back, like Ghanzi said. I remember feeling tired and sleeping just after the hunt. It was some story about the mosquito and how it selects you as its own food supply."

"So once you're bitten you won't get bitten by any other mosquitoes again, ever?"

"Seems that way, Duncan. No other mosquito has bitten me since that day. I wasn't bit once last night at the Mamzibi village, either. Its like, they feed on you once and move on, like a swarm of locust"

"Why, though?" Ian asked. "Why would that happen?"

"I don't know, Ian," Conrad replied. "I guess like the cheetah hides its food in a tree, or like some animals bury their food in the ground, the Mamzibi mosquito somehow protects its food supply."

"So when it bites you, you become its only food supply, and no other mosquitoes can use your blood as food?" Duncan said.

"Seems that way, Duncan."

"So what are we waiting for? Let's get over there and get bitten. Shit, if you haven't been bit since your last hunt, then I want this natural repellant as well." Duncan laughed.

"Yeah, we could save on bug repellant," Ian added.

"Sure, but I don't know what other diseases these mosquitoes carry. I haven't been checked and Thomas hasn't been checked either. Mosquitoes carry all kinds of diseases, like yellow fever, malaria and others that can kill us."

"You two will have to get checked, when you get home," Mary said softly. Jessica looked at Thomas, her eyes seeming to fill with tears. Sadness filled her heart.

"When we get back..." Thomas hesitated. "We will be heading back to the States. I'll get checked there."

"What do you mean, you're heading back to the States?" Conrad stood. "I thought you two were staying another few weeks?"

"No, Daddy!" Jessica said, looking at Thomas, then Conrad as she reached over and held Thomas' hand. "We're going to head home to America. We need to take care of some things that have come up and we need to go there to do it."

"But this is your home, Jessica." Conrad said sternly.

"Conrad!" Mary interrupted.

"Look, Daddy, I'm a grown girl now. I know that South Africa will always be my home, but my home is also America...with Thomas."

With that, Conrad sat down and watched the burning fire. The light played upon his face and the darkness could be seen building around them as the minutes passed. He wondered what it was that they had to leave for and why so soon. Thomas sat quietly watching the fire and held Jessica's hand tightly. Mary rubbed Conrad's back and watched the fire as well. The minutes passed slowly and the fire flickered and crackled in the cool night air as they all sat quietly watching its glow. The smell of burning wood filled the air around them.

"I didn't mean to startle everyone," Thomas said finally. "It's just that things have come up back home with work and I have to return. I found out just before we left for the Karoo and we didn't want to ruin the trip by telling you before."

"We understand." Conrad said, as he walked away from the fire.

"I'm sorry, Thomas…Jessica," Mary said. "He'll be alright. Just let him walk it off. He loves you two and just wanted to spend more time with you."

"Sorry, Mom, but this is something we have to do." Jessica smiled sadly. "We'll be back in a few months…I promise you."

"I know, dear." Mary reached over and placed her hand over both Thomas' and Jessica's hands. "You do what you have to and we'll see you when you get back."

In the darkness, Conrad watched the night. It seemed so cold and lonely. He wondered what was so important that they'd have to leave South Africa so soon.

Moments later, he emerged from the darkness and went to the fire. Everyone looked at him. His head was lowered as if in thought, pondering for a few silent moments. Then he spoke.

"You see…" Conrad said hesitating as he lifted his head, looking over the fire at the group. "I have learned a lot in my years. I don't attest to knowing everything and I really don't understand much about the outside world, being here in Africa my whole life, but I do feel one thing's certain." He looked at each person at the fire and held his stare at Jessica and Thomas as they held hands. "I do understand that there comes a time that a daughter will leave her family. And…and I want you two to know that even though I wanted to spend more time with you, Jess…Tom, I realize that my daughter is in good hands."

"Thanks, Conrad," Thomas said.

"Wait. I'm not done," Conrad smiled broadly then chuckled. "I just want everyone to see that I'm happy for you two. Now, I realize you're not engaged yet." Conrad said, laughing.

"Daddy!" Jessica interrupted.

"But I hope the best for the two of you as you go through life together."

"Oh, Daddy." Jessica stood and went to her father. "I love you." She began crying. "I'm going to miss you."

Conrad looked over Jessica's shoulder at Thomas, who also seemed sad at what Conrad had said. Mary sat quietly near the fire smiling. She knew Conrad was saying something he'd practiced many times, anticipating this night. Jessica was in love and Thomas was a good man. He'd take care of her and watch over her, here, and in America. Conrad rubbed Jessica's back as they hugged. He was proud of his little girl and he wanted the best for her and for her future.

"Hey! Wait a minute!" Thomas said. "I have something to say too."

"It better be good, Lion King," Duncan said, laughing. "You killing the eland and being called the lion by the Mamzibi is making us all look bad."

Everyone began laughing. Thomas smiled and winked at Duncan. Ian got up and placed more wood on the fire as Mary poured more wine and coffee. The fire jumped to life and blazed, bringing brightness to the camp.

Thomas grinned. "Conrad, I have to ask you to unleash my girl." Conrad smiled and patted Jessica on the butt.

"Get over there," he said.

Jessica went over to Thomas. As she walked toward him they looked into each other's eyes. She had an inquisitive look about her face. He stood grinning from ear to ear as she approached. He winked at her and dropped to his knees.

"What are you doing? Thomas?" she said, embarrassed as everyone watched.

"Jessica. I never knew that life could be so complete with one person," he said, tears building in his eyes. "We've spent a lot of time together over the last year and I have grown to love you more than anything in the world. I was going to wait till we were alone to do this, but..."

"Thomas," she interrupted as tears began running down her cheeks. He held her hand tightly as she looked down at him kneeling in the sand. The fire's light blazed and the wood crackled and the stars shone in the night sky above. Conrad smiled as Mary looked across the fire at him. Pete and the boys sat quietly watching Thomas propose to Jessica, and dared not interrupt with any heckling, or jokes.

"Jessica, with all my heart, would you be my wife? Will you marry me?" Thomas said. Jessica could not help but smile as the tears ran down her face. She felt so much love in her heart. No sickness could separate them and no distance could keep them from finding each other in the world, for they were meant to be, and it was their time, and their moment for love. Everyone waited for her response and the air became silent in the night. The seconds seemed to extend into minutes as they looked into each other's souls. In their minds, they were alone, alone in the desert of the Great Karoo. The place where she captured the spirit of Africa from the Mamzibi boy so many years ago and the place where the Mamzibi held Thomas as their lion. Above them, the constellation Leo crossed the night sky, and nearby two Mamzibi warriors stood on a hill watching the fire of the camp of the Sinclair family. They were sent to protect the lion at any cost. The stars twinkled above and the firelight blazed in the night. Jessica felt his hand holding hers and she wiped the tears from her face.

"Of course I'll marry you, Thomas," she said. Everyone began yelling and clapping. Jessica looked at her family and smiled broadly. When she looked back at Thomas, he was holding a small black box, and in it was a diamond ring. She marveled as it sparkled in the fire's light. He removed it from the box and slowly placed it on her finger. He stood up and they kissed. Duncan, Ian and Pete smiled and clapped as the two held each other.

"Congratulations guys!" Duncan and Ian yelled.

"Thanks, guys," Jessica said, hugging her brothers. She turned to find her mother and father kissing on the other side of the fire. They too looked into each other's eyes. She could see the love they shared.

"Hey, you two!" Jessica yelled. They turned to find Thomas and Jessica walking toward them.

"Congratulations, honey." Conrad smiled as he hugged her and then shook Thomas' hand. Mary kissed Jessica and then kissed Thomas.

"You two take care of each other," Mary said knowingly. "For as long as you live."

Conrad looked up into the sky as everyone talked. A shooting star sped across the night sky, from east to west, across the Milky Way, through the constellation Leo and off to the distant horizon. The night ended with the celebration of the stars. As Conrad's gaze followed the shooting star across the sky, he noticed two Mamzibi warriors, their long, shape spears next to them, standing on a rock, atop a distant hill. The rock was shaped like a reclining lion.

To his surprise he found Pete at his side, watching the warriors. "They've been there the whole time." Pete said, staring at them.

"Yeah, I know." Conrad squinted into the night. "They followed us from the Mamzibi camp."

"What do you make of it?"

"I don't know, Pete. There are some things in this world that are a mystery. We'll know the reason when it reveals itself."

***

The next morning they broke camp and headed for home. The ride seemed longer and was hotter, but as they hit highway N2, the rain began to fall relentlessly from the unforgiving storm clouds, which had rolled in off the ocean during the night and now covered the Drakensberge Mountain Range. The rain poured down as they headed home to Gansbaai and the road, at times, became flooded and unmanageable. The engines roared. The hilly slopes of the mountain passes would not be easy in this weather. The two-day ride was hot and humid and the roads became dangerous to maneuver, but as they eased down the other side of the mountain the rain began to lessen for a time.

They passed the entrance gates to the estate. The estate was quiet, too quiet. Ian looked toward the back walls for signs of the guard dogs. Nothing could be seen or heard and he didn't like the looks of it. The storm clouds slowly rolled overhead and the sky was dark and threatening. The ocean waves crashed on the rocks below the estate as the trucks passed the gatehouse and headed for the main house. Conrad's truck radio squawked and he tuned the ham radio and pressed the button.

"Come in, Duncan?" he said.

"The gates are open." Duncan's voice blared over the speaker.

"Yeah. I figured one of you guys left them open...or Jara did."

"Nope...not us!" crackled a reply. "Ian says there's no sign of the guard dogs either."

With that, there came a haunting silence from the speaker. Conrad looked about the estate as he neared the house; Duncan, Ian and Pete were behind his truck about twenty yards. When Conrad's truck came to a stop in the middle of the road, Duncan applied the breaks, bringing his truck to a stop about ten yards behind his father's. He waited. There was an ominous feeling in the air as the rain fell and thunder cracked overhead. The road was soaked and the glare from the brake lights of Conrad's truck could be seen on the surface. The noise of the idling motor and the swish of the windshield wipers became deafening as the minutes passed. The radio squawked and then went silent. It squawked again and Conrad's voice came over the speaker.

"The front door's wide open," Conrad said warily. An uncomfortable feeling came over everyone as they looked. There were no lights on inside the house. There were no guard dogs and no sign of movement on the estate or in the house. Nearby, thunder cracked again and, a distant thunder cracked in reply, like two evil voices planning their demise. The wind blew off the ocean and the trees and plants tossed violently.

"Lock and load," blared over the radio speaker. Duncan, Ian and Pete quickly grabbed their weapons. The sound of guns being cocked and loaded broke the stillness as they readied for battle. There was no fear in them for they'd trained for this their whole lives.

"Duncan." The radio squawked again.

"Yes, Dad!"

"Let Pete drive. You head to the right of the house and...Ian"—there was a hesitation in Conrad's words—"you head around back and secure the left backside of the house. Go in through Jessica's bedroom window."

"Okay, Dad...we got it."

"Pete and I will take the trucks up to the front of the house and enter there. Thomas is going to keep watch and look after the women. He'll let us know if anyone comes from behind us. Watch out, if we start firing, don't either of you get caught in the cross fire."

"Ready here!" Pete said, manning the radio. Duncan and Ian now sat ready to jump from each side of the truck. Thomas looked back at the other truck as it sat idling. His palms began to sweat as the tension built. The wind blew and the thunder roared overhead as the rain increased.

"Tom, if anything happens, back out of here and head to the De Kelders for help. Mary, you know who to get." Conrad quickly pressed the button on the radio. "Guys, watch out for Jara. She could be in the house. Exit and head in on my word. This could be a trap, so watch your backs."

With that, Duncan and Ian pumped their twelve-gauged shotguns, loading the barrels for combat. Ian sat quietly near the left door. His eyes had a crazy, wild look about them as he remembered harder and rougher times in the Transvaal. He'd seen war and knew when the enemy was near; he could feel it under his skin and felt the hair stand on the back of his neck. He knew there was someone in the house and he knew that death was in the air. The storm clouds rolled overhead and thunder and lightning flashed. The rain fell from the sky as Conrad's voice came over the radio again.

"Go, boys!" The doors of the rear truck opened violently as Duncan and Ian ran for the sides of the house. Before long they were out of sight. The rain fell harder and the wind blew wildly across the estate.

"Pete, pull the truck up to mine and we'll head in together." Pete slowly moved up to the front truck and stopped next to Conrad.

"On your count," Pete said. Conrad could see a grin on his face. Pete was ready and unafraid. Pete knew danger and knew it well for he'd been in the military and a hunter most of his life. Conrad turned to Mary and winked. "Be back in a bit, kiddo," he cracked.

"Be careful!" She leaned over to kiss him on the cheek. He turned to Jessica and smiled. "Take care of my girls, Thomas."

"You got it, Conrad."

"Pete!" Conrad yelled into the microphone.

"Yeah!"

"Let's go in."

Conrad and Pete opened the doors of their trucks and walked toward the house, knowing instinctively not to walk too close together, and paced themselves as they moved to the house. Pete carried a twelve-gauge pump shotgun and in Conrad's right hand could be seen his Colt.45. The rain poured down their faces, making it hard to see. The wide-open front door was ominous and nothing could be seen or heard from inside. Pete wiped his eyes to clear the rainwater from them.

"This sucks," he said, walking alert and composed.

"What sucks?"

"This rain," he replied, wiping his eyes again. "I just bought this shirt."

"I was wondering when you got that."

"What d'ya think?"

"It's nice." Conrad smirked. He watched the door and windows for signs of movement; eyes squinted, keeping the rainwater out as he studied the situation.

"It's a hundred percent cotton." Pete wiped the rain from his face again. "Doesn't this rain bother you?"

"Must have paid quite a lot of rand for it," Conrad said, shaking his head. "It's not going to look good with bullet holes in it though."

Pete laughed aloud. "The only holes are going to be the ones in your pants when I empty this cylinder of buckshot in them." Conrad smiled as he looked into the darkened house. He knew Duncan and Ian must be in position and ready to act. Conrad was trained from years in the bush and knew the rain made it hard for hitting a target, even from inside a house. The thunder cracked and they could hear the echo in the mountains. Below them the ocean waves crashed violently on the rocks.

Whoever was inside the house wasn't too skilled at ambushing, Conrad thought, not unless they were somewhere else waiting for the assault. They could come from behind, or they could have killed Duncan and Ian already. As a military leader, he had to think of every scenario. He'd trained for this and was mentally equipped for such threats.

Shots rang out. Both Conrad and Pete jumped to the side of the road, out of the line of fire, Pete rolling to cover. Conrad dove head first into a clump of bushes. They hid their bodies well, making use of the small trees and bushes that lined the road.

They quickly returned fire, the thunder roared and the rain fell as the guns blasted.

But the gunshots continued coming from the house as Pete's shotgun and Conrad's Colt blasted holes through the windows and door. A front window shattered from inside and multiple shots erupted from it. Conrad aimed his Colt at the window and fired three shots. The fight was on.

Conrad's instincts were right, the enemy was in the house, and he'd helped save his family from certain death. But were Ian and Duncan alive? Did the enemy see them running to the sides of the house? Were they ambushed as they rounded the corner? Conrad didn't know, but knew he had to protect his family and his life from these intruders. The shots continued, the rain made it hard to see. Pete cleared his eyes again and reloaded the shotgun, jumped to his feet and emptied four shells into the doorway.

"Come on you, fuckers!" he yelled.

Conrad fired at the doorway and the windows with his Colt. The hail of gunshots mixed with the rain. The thunder made the firefight sound more like a war, canons firing in the distance, claymores exploding and landmines being triggered in the night. Duncan kicked in the back door and fired into the blackness as he entered the house. Ian crashed through the window on the rear bedroom, Jessica's room, hitting the bed and rolling to the floor, keeping low.

Pete pumped his shotgun and blasted his way closer to the house, the bullets clearing his path.

Then other shots could be heard firing inside the house and then silence. Stillness filled the air. Both men watched the windows and doorway in anticipation of another round of gunfire. Conrad looked over to Pete, who stood next to a tall tree, grinning. Conrad signaled him to wait.

They watched the front door for signs of movement. The house was silent. They quietly waited, ready and alert, assuming Duncan and Ian had entered the house from the rear and neutralized the enemy. But was the enemy dead, or were they waiting to shoot again. Were they waiting for a clear shot?

The seconds passed. The thunder cracked high above them as the clouds rolled across the sky and the wind blew hard off the ocean as the waves broke on the jagged rocks below the estate. The sound of the crashing waves, the rain pouring from the sky, and the distant thunder echoing off the mountains became deafening as the minutes passed.

"Dad!" Duncan yelled from inside the house. The lights went on. "We're secure. They're dead."

Conrad and Pete stood up and began walking to the house. It was over and they felt the calm come over them. They'd won and the enemy was dead. Was it just some thieves, caught in the act? Was it some past adversary coming back for revenge? Thoughts ran through Conrad's mind. They quietly walked to the house wondering what had happened.

Conrad turned and waved Thomas and the girls to drive up to the house. As he did, he could see them franticly moving inside the truck. Then the scream came. Jessica, screaming over and over, "Mommy, no, Mommy, no please, God…no! Mom!"

Conrad and Pete ran to the truck and opened the doors.

There, Jessica held her mother in her arms. Thomas sat with tears in his eyes, his hands bloodied and shaking. Mary's eyes were wide as she gasped for air. A stray bullet had pierced the windshield of the truck during the fighting and struck her in the chest. Her bloodstained shirt, the hole from the bullet, and her limp body told of the horror.

Conrad grabbed her body, putting pressure where the bullet struck her. "Mary! Mary! My God, no…please no!" he yelled, as he began to cry. Mary looked at him and closed her eyes. Franticly he tried to resuscitate her. His tears mixed with the rain as they trickled down his face.

"God! Please no!" were the only words he could say as he held her lifeless body. Then he pulled her from the truck and walked into the rain, looking into her face. He knelt down on the ground holding his wife's body tight in his arms, and he cried.

Pete watched his sister's dead body in Conrad's arms. He'd seen death many times before and knew she was gone. Grief filled his heart.

Conrad knew she was dead. He sat on the grass as the rain fell and cried, wiping the rainwater from his wife's face. Duncan and Ian stood at the front door with their heads lowered. Their mother was dead. Jara lay beaten and dead inside on the living room floor. The rain fell from the sky and death was in the air as the thunder roared and echoed, lightning flashing high above the Drakensberge. Ian walked to the back wall where the guard dogs lay dead in the grass. He hopped onto the wall and climbed over onto the other side. Revenge and hatred filled his mind as the rainwater ran down his cheeks.

Jessica sat crying, looking at the bloodstains on her clothing and hands. There were no words to be said as sadness overwhelmed them.

The storm clouds rolled overhead and the rain fell.

CHAPTER 10

The days passed quietly at the Sinclair house. Mary Sinclair was laid to rest on the hilltop next to her daughter, Sarah. The engraved headstone read: In loving memory of Mary Sinclair, Mother and Wife, she will be missed till we meet again. Fresh flowers, the King Protea, the national flower of South Africa, graced the headstone and the surrounding plot, circling both Mary's and Sarah's graves. After the funeral, Conrad and Jessica stood together for a while before she let her father mourn the loss of her mother alone at the grave. She walked down the path toward the house, the same path she had walked so many times before, turning back from time to time, only to see her father standing motionless, his head bowed. Hours later, she'd walk to the front porch of the house and look up at the hill. In the evening light of the setting sun, there stood Conrad, motionless, grieving for his lost love. His girl was gone, his friend and mate for forty years was gone. The only girl he'd ever loved was gone forever, and he didn't even know why.

Uncle Pete, Duncan, Thomas and Jessica were sitting near the fireplace talking as Conrad came into the room. The firelight made the room glow with a golden hue. The rain clouds had moved over the Drakensberge Mountain Range and off into the Great Karoo. Conrad knew that no rain fell from the clouds as they rolled over the Karoo and north into the Kalahari Desert. He stood quietly watching the firelight, transfixed and numb, mesmerized by the flickering flames. His eyes seemed distant and old. His heart felt old and he wanted to be with Mary.

Pete got up and went to him. He hesitated for a moment before talking. Conrad knew that Pete had lost his only sister and Mary had loved her brother. They'd been close over the years and had come from the same town that Conrad grew up. The De Kelders was a small Afrikaner fishing village located a few miles from Gansbaai and was known for its caves and beaches. As children, they had played and schooled in the De Kelders and worked the waters for their livelihood. It was there that Conrad had met Mary and he knew someday, she'd be his wife. Mary knew it too. They married at the De Kelders fishing club one bright sunny afternoon. It was hot and the summer winds crossed the Atlantic, bringing the smell of life to the day. It had been a charming wedding and, thirty-five years later, Conrad knew he and Mary were one soul. She was a Boer woman, he'd say, an Afrikaner girl who was tough as nails but had a heart of gold.

"How you doing?" Pete said, placing his hand on Conrad's shoulder. He knew his brother-in-law was hurting from Mary's death. He'd seen them grow up together and knew they shared a strong love.

Conrad stared at the fire, quietly sipping coffee, questioning why this had happened to Mary and what they had done to deserve this terrible misfortune. Tears built up in his eyes as the fire flickered.

"I can't believe she's gone, Pete."

"I know," Pete said as he rubbed Conrad's shoulder. "I know."

"Why, Pete, why?"

"I don't know, Conrad," Pete said softly. "Why don't you come have a seat? Jessica's worried about you...and so am I." Conrad and Pete went to the others and Conrad sat next to Jessica, who hugged her father. He hugged her back and again the tears could be seen building in his eyes. Thomas watched from the side and felt Conrad's pain, for he too remembered losing his first love and would never forget the feeling of loss in his heart. It was only after he had met Jessica that the pain had begun to dissipate but the anger he felt for the men who caused her death was still there. Now, with Jessica and him being sick with the virus and Mary and Jara's deaths, his anger was compounded. He hid it well from the others but both Conrad and Jessica knew he harbored this anger deep in his soul. He watched Jessica console her father and wanted to say something but could not find the words. Everyone sat quietly drinking coffee and wine as the fire burned.

"Where's Ian?" Conrad said suddenly, looking up. He remembered Ian walking off to the back wall in the rain the day of the attacks.

"He went off somewhere after mom's funeral," Duncan replied. "Said he had something to do and was gone before I could say anything. I think he's taking mom's death real hard, as well."

"Well, watch out for him, Duncan," Conrad said. "He's seen a lot of fighting and this sort of thing's not good for him."

"I know, Dad. I'm watching him, he'll be okay."

"Good, good." Conrad stumbled on his words. "How are you doing, Jess?" He placed his arm around her shoulders. "How's my little girl holding up?" She just hugged him and spoke no words. She knew if she answered, she'd begin crying again and wanted to be strong for her father.

"Conrad." Thomas finally spoke. "I'm sorry...I..." He could not finish. He lowered his head and began wiping the tears from his eyes. Conrad rubbed Jessica's back and nudged her to go to Thomas. She leaned over to him and kissed him on the side of his face and brushed her fingers through his dark hair.

He was embarrassed for not knowing what to say, and felt perhaps Conrad and the others blamed him for not protecting the girls as he'd been asked to.

"Thomas," Conrad said. Thomas looked up at Jessica and then Conrad. "It's not your fault," Conrad said, as if reading Thomas' mind. "It was a stray bullet and nobody could have known." Thomas nodded, but could not say a word. Jessica smiled warmly at her father as if to say, "Thank you."

It wasn't until days later that Ian returned to the estate. He had information about the perpetrators but did not let the others know what he'd found out. He would save it for another time.

***

As the weeks passed, Jessica and Thomas began preparing for their return to the United States. South Africa wasn't the same for Jessica and she wanted to go back with Thomas and see about the disease they had contracted. South Africa's new government, increased crime and her mother's death were enough to keep her away from the land she'd loved since her birth. She knew that she might never see her father and her brothers again and she knew she might die.

The weather began to change and the rainy season was ushered in with force. Gansbaai became cold and damp as the winter wind blew off the ocean. It was the great changing, as Conrad called it, and, as always, life continued around them and life would go on. Ian became aloof and distant, disappearing from time to time, not returning for days, and Duncan's witty, extroverted ways became withdrawn and introverted. Uncle Pete returned to his house, a Dutch Colonial located in Hermanus, to be with his son Jason. Pete's wife had passed away nine years earlier and it was just he and Jason now. Conrad's somber mood continued, and day after day he stood at Mary's grave, resisting the fact that she was gone, to never return to his side. He'd hoped they'd grow to a ripe old age together, feeling and experiencing life, loving and cherishing life's changes as they came. It was a sad time for the Sinclair family and the estate. Africa and the world did not seem the same after that horrible rainy day and without Mary.

Mobutu waited patiently for his men to return. The days passed and he knew that the plan had gone sour when word got back from Gansbaai that three security officers were killed breaking into a house. His disappointment turned to anger and he knew he had to silence the Sinclair family soon before word got out about his past military activities in Angola. "The white whore will die if I have to kill her myself," he mumbled as he called more of his men to survey the estate and investigate the murder of his men. He was an evil man with a callous regard for human life, a man who would do anything to survive and prosper.

131

Days turned into weeks and he received word that the girl was preparing to leave the country. His mind began to twist and bend as he thought about the girl and what she knew. She'll send word about me to the authorities and they'll remove me from office and throw me in prison, he told himself. Robert Island is no place for a general like me. I'll send men to ambush her on the road and I'll back them up by being at the airport. She'll never get out of the country alive.

***

As the day approached, Jessica and Thomas tried to spend as much time as possible with her family. Conrad cherished the time with his daughter and was saddened by the thought of their approaching departure. Duncan too enjoyed the time spent with his sister and began opening up about his military service in the Northern Transvaal. It had been a horrible time, especially during the night, as the guerilla fighters attacked with force. Hand-to-hand combat was common and death was everywhere. He also began to tell them of Ian and the company he'd been with on the front lines. They saw the worst fighting, he said, and Ian was the point man and scout for the company, the one-hundred-and-first renegades, who were known as the most ruthless fighters in the campaign against the terrorists. News came back from the front lines about Ian's accomplishments and his kills, most of which were hand-to-hand knife fighting behind enemy lines. The guerillas began to call him the Tokolosi, the devil and the white demon. News came back that guerilla fighters were found without heads, arms and legs. It was a horrible time and Ian would never be the same after returning from the war. Jessica had cried when she heard about the fighting and the news about her brother Ian. She knew, deep in her heart that Ian suffered from what had happened and she had always wanted to help him, but Ian came back quieter and spent most of his time alone and away. It wasn't until her rescue in Angola that she saw a change in his eyes but the look was, at times, deep and unfathomable, far off and silent; was he once again remembering the fighting and killing of his past?

***

Mobutu got word that the girl was preparing to leave and the trucks were being loaded for the drive to the airport. Off in the distance, his men watched the estate with binoculars and tapped the phone lines, gathering information, on direct orders from the General himself. "Find out anything you can about the girl," he commanded.

***

Jessica looked at her father. "Okay, Dad, its time to hit the road."

"Conrad, thanks for everything," Thomas said, with a firm handshake. Conrad shook his head and smiled, knowing that this was the day of their departure and he couldn't do anything about it. They were heading back to America and his girl would be leaving once again.

"I'm going to miss you kids." He smiled sadly. Duncan finished loading the truck and yelled to them as they stood on the front porch of the house. Bullet holes could still be seen in the stucco and brick and one window was still boarded up. It was a sunny day and Conrad looked out at the sky and ocean.

"It's a good day to fly," he said. "You two have a safe ride to the airport and a good flight. Call me when you get to the States, okay?

"Okay, Daddy," Jessica said as tears ran down her cheeks. "I'm going to miss you." She hugged her father. Conrad held his daughter tight and cherished the love they shared. She was so much like Mary, he thought, a true Boer and Afrikaans girl, strong and caring.

"Take care of yourself…okay." He grinned. "You two get out of here before I start to cry."

As they walked to the truck, Jessica looked for Ian. He was nowhere to be found and they'd not seen him for days. She wanted to see him before her departure and tell him of something she'd been thinking about. She was sad that she'd not had the chance to say goodbye and hoped he'd be at the airport to see them off.

They boarded the truck and headed down the road, through the gates and up toward the highway. Jessica looked back once more to see her father and the estate she loved so much. Conrad was not on the front porch but was slowly walking up the grassy hill toward her mother's and sister's gravesites.

***

Mobutu's men had set up the roadblock, a fake car accident blocking the highway on top of Blanks Pass. It was the perfect spot for an ambush, isolated and without escape, with a rock wall on one side and a steep cliff on the other. The road was narrow and curvy making it hard to speed and Mobutu's men waited like hunting lions of the Kalahari, cunning and hungry for death, they slowly maneuvered and stalked their prey for the kill. It would be more than fifteen minutes before their prey came up the road.

***

The air was hot as the truck made its way down the road. Jessica sat in the backseat smelling the air as it came through her open window. The warm wind and sunlight felt good on her face. Thomas smiled as he looked at her staring out the window. She quietly contemplated the moment and the warm scented air filled her mind with Africa. Her love for Gansbaai, the De Kelders and the African people was strong and she knew she would miss her home once again. Thoughts of her mother's death saddened her and she knew her father would be lost without his best friend and wife. It was a trying time for them but she and Thomas had to return and seek the proper medical treatment they needed before the disease took their lives. They were unsure as to what medical treatment they could get and what effects the disease would have on their bodies but they knew that in order to find out, they had to return to America.

"Something up ahead." Duncan spoke softly as the truck began to slow. "I think it is some kind of accident."

Jessica broke from her daydreaming and leaned forward between the seats. "Is it a bad one?" she asked, trying to make out the commotion on the road. The glare from the sun made it hard for them to see exactly what was taking place. There were a few cars and trucks before them that had already stopped and they were now stuck in traffic.

"Great!" Thomas fidgeted in his seat. "We're going to miss the plane now."

"Thomas!" Jessica pushed his shoulder. "There are probably people hurt." She grabbed the door. "Maybe I can help."

"Jessica!" Duncan's voice became loud. "You stay here."

"Just let me see."

"Jessica, no!" Duncan yelled. "Come on, we are going to be late and you'll miss your plane."

"Come on, Jess," Thomas said.

"You guys are something," she said. "Maybe I could have helped or something."

"There're some police up there already," Duncan said, looking around as the truck slowly moved forward. "Let them take care of this." He turned the wheel. "We are going to be late if we sit here."

Off in the grass, about twenty yards ahead, lay a policeman with a rifle. The crosshairs of his scope slowly glided across the windshield of the truck. On the other side of the road, two more policemen stalked around to the rear of the truck as it slowly edged up the road.

"Come on!" Duncan yelled out the window in Afrikaans. "What is going on here?"

"Duncan, have some respect." Jessica yelled at him. "Look, now the policeman is walking toward us."

"He doesn't look too happy." Thomas said as the policeman slowly neared the truck. Off in the grass, the assassin's crosshairs found their mark. Jessica was seated perfectly in the middle between the two seats. He placed his finger on the trigger of the rifle and breathed slowly waiting for the shot. The crosshairs were perfectly placed on her chest, an easy target. Thomas watched the policeman as he neared the cars ahead of them. The man slowly walked toward them and, as he did, slowly removed the safety from his revolver.

"Look at this guy." Duncan laughed. "He's got his hand on his gun as if he was going to shoot us."

"Well, after yelling out the window, I'd shoot you too." Jessica smiled. "Jerk, now we'll be late." She laughed.

Thomas looked into the truck side mirror and noticed a uniformed man climbing out of the grass behind and off to the right side of their truck. "What's this guy doing?" He shook his head. Jessica turned to see the man walking up to the rear of the truck.

"Duncan!" she yelled.

Duncan threw the truck in gear and slammed his foot on the accelerator. The truck jerked forward, just missing the policeman in front. The gunman in the grass fired, the bullet piercing the windshield and lodging into the front dashboard. Pieces of plastic and glass erupted into the front and back seats.

"Get down!" Duncan yelled. "It's a trap!" He turned the wheel, threw the truck in reverse, and slammed the car behind them. The assassin near the rear fell to the ground as the truck again jerked forward and off to the side of the road. Jessica fell to the floor as Thomas reached into the glove compartment and removed Conrad's Colt.

"What the fuck!" he shouted as the truck turned onto the grass shoulder and roared passed the stopped vehicles. Another shot shattered the windshield. The rifleman in the grass stood up to fire once more as the other policemen fired at the moving truck. Duncan crashed into one of the cars, sending it off the road and down the cliff. Thomas fired at the assassin in the grass but missed. Backing the truck up, Duncan rammed another car, making a path for their escape. The assassin in the grass placed his crosshairs on Duncan's chest and squeezed the trigger, ready to fire.

"There's one in the grass," Thomas shouted, pointing the Colt at the man. He squeezed the trigger and prepared to fire but the bouncing of the truck made it hard for him to aim. As he did, a bullet pierced the assassin's skull and blood shot from the front of his head. The man fell to the ground. Thomas aimed again but saw the man had been shot from behind. Ian was standing behind where the man had stood, his arm extended with gun in hand.

"It's Ian!" Thomas yelled as the truck rammed the hill and darted for the road to make their escape. He looked back to were Ian was standing but Ian had vanished into the grass.

"Did you say Ian?" Duncan yelled as the truck roared down the road to the other side of the mountain. Duncan's arm was bleeding from a bullet hole and Thomas had glass cuts on his face from the shattered windshield glass. Jessica sat up and looked into the rearview mirror.

"What the hell!" she yelled. "What the hell is this country coming to?"

Both Duncan and Thomas looked at her where she sat between them.

"Jesus, honey," Thomas, said laughing.

"What the fuck was that?" She said shaking her head.

"Thomas, did you say you saw Ian?" Duncan said.

"Yeah. There was a man in the grass shooting at us and I aimed at him and I saw his head get blown off."

"Were was Ian?"

"Behind the guy. Are you okay?" he said, turning to Jessica.

"Yeah, I'm not hit. Duncan! You're hit."

"I know." Duncan smiled. "It just nicked my arm."

"Let me look at it?"

"No, Jessica. It's okay. I've had worse." He laughed. "Thomas, you sure you saw Ian?"

"Yeah. I mean I think so...do you think we should maybe go back and help? I mean if he is there, then he's probably fighting those men."

"If Ian is fighting those men, they're probably dead already." Duncan grinned. "Don't worry about Ian, I'll see him once I get back to the estate. And I need to talk to Dad as well. There's something else going on here...I'm sure."

"Hey, Jess," Thomas said, wiping some of the glass from his face. "Next time you want to travel, we're going to Hawaii." He laughed. She smiled sarcastically, knowing he was right. But South Africa hadn't always been like this, she thought. There was something wrong and she knew what it was. Seeing General Mobutu at the airport and finding men with guns at her house wasn't a coincidence and she needed to let her father know the truth about what had happened in Angola. Her secret would tear him apart but he and her brothers now needed to know the whole truth about her being raped in the prison cell. She looked out the window, thinking of that rainy day in Angola when John Hanson was killed and she was beaten. Tears had filled her eyes as they pulled into Cape Town International airport. When would she find the nerve to tell them the truth?

"I'm heading in around the back," Duncan said as he circled around to the back of the airport.

"Why?" Jessica said coming out of a trance. "What's wrong with the front?"

"Nothing, but I have a friend who works at the loading dock in Departure and he'll get you through faster." Duncan knew he wasn't telling them the whole truth. "He'll get your tickets for you and I'll see you off."

"Thanks, Duncan." Jessica knew Duncan and knew he was just watching out for them.

"Considering we were almost killed by renegade policemen at the pass at high noon," Thomas griped, "I think the faster we get the hell out of here the better." He laughed. Jessica punched him in the shoulder as Duncan smiled. They would make their flight back to America and he was happy about that.

***

Mobutu paced back and forth at the Cape Town airport-security office. He had not received word about the ambush and he was anxious as to the outcome. He walked passed the camera monitors and looked out the window, down onto the departure floor. It was a busy day at the airport and this did not please him.

"Try and call them again!" he barked. "I'm heading down to the floor to use the bathroom." He shook his head and slammed the office door. The two security guards watched him walk toward the bathrooms. The security monitors were well placed throughout the airport, and covered most of the area. They felt relieved knowing their boss was gone for a while and they relaxed.

***

"Alright!" Duncan smiled as he walked toward Thomas and Jessica. "Bryan here has your tickets. Your plane leaves in twenty minutes."

"You guys should have told me you were under the same name," Bryan said in jest. "It was hard to find you in the computer."

"You're under the same name?" Duncan asked curiously. Jessica looked at Thomas and smiled. Thomas smiled and nodded his head, looking into her eyes.

"Duncan. I didn't want to tell Daddy and Mommy this, but Thomas and I are already married. Mr. *and* Mrs. Jennings now.

"No shit!" Duncan grinned.

"No shit, big brother. We got married in the States before we came out here. We were going to tell you guys but something came up and we decided not to tell you yet. That's why we went through that whole proposal thing in the Karoo."

"Wow, Jessica...my little sister is married, no shit!"

"No shit." Thomas smiled. "I'm your brother-in-law."

"Jessica," Duncan said, hugging her, "I'm happy for you." He swung her around in the air. "Thomas, well...welcome to the family. Mr. and Mrs. Jennings. I can't believe it!"

"I can't believe it myself." Thomas winked at Jessica, and then asked Bryan where the men's room was.

Thomas went into the main departure area of the airport, Jesus Christ; I've never seen so many black people in my life. *This place is a fuckin' madhouse,* he thought. It was noisy and crammed with people and luggage. He opened the men's room door and at a sink, looked into the mirror. Slowly, he began washing his face with soap and water, cleaning some of the small cuts. It was quiet in the bathroom, a sanctuary from the chaos and confusion outside in the departure lounge; he thought he was alone until a toilet flush broke the silence.

He continued to wash his face as footsteps approached from behind. Lather on his face, he looked up to see a large black man with sunglasses standing next to him. The man began washing his hands.

"Howzit." Thomas nodded his head in greeting the man. The man didn't reply, grabbed a paper towel and began drying his hands. Thomas finished rinsing off his face and walked over to the paper-towel dispenser, only to find it empty.

"Great." he mumbled, "This fuckin' country is something, I'll tell you." He dried his face with the sleeves of his shirt.

"You will tell me what?" the man replied in a deep voice. Thomas turned to look at him.

"Nothing." Thomas grinned. "Nothing."

"You settlers don't belong here," the man replied. "This is not your country." He took a step toward Thomas, who looked at the man curiously. The dark glasses hid his eyes and Thomas didn't like it. He started to feel uncomfortable as the man stared at him quietly. Thomas gave him a cocky smile, trying to break the tension.

"Hey, man, I'm only here on vacation." He smiled. "You people can have this place, for all I care."

'You people.' Mobutu said darkly.

"Yeah. It's your country. You guys should get better security or something. It's like the fuckin' Wild West out there." He turned and went to the door.

Like a bull, Mobutu's nostrils flared with anger as he watched Thomas walk out of the bathroom. Thomas turned and looked back at the bathroom door. Mobutu was now standing outside the door, watching. He grunted as Thomas disappeared into the crowd. As Mobutu walked back to the security office he began remembering the day he saw Jessica at the airport. He played the image over and over in his head. Grasping the doorknob, he stopped and suddenly turned, looking back at the crowd of people that filled the departure area. "That man," he mumbled, his nostrils flaring again, his teeth clenched in anger. "That man was with the girl. They're here!" He turned and ran up the stairway to the surveillance office. His men jumped in alarm as the door was thrown open and Mobutu rushed in. "They are here!" he shouted. "Turn your monitors to the departure area, let me find them." He pushed one of his men out of his way. The two security guards pointed the security cameras at the departure area and Mobutu studied the monitors for Jessica and Thomas.

"These are too blurred!" he said, hitting one of the monitors. "Search the departure lists for the name Sinclair. Call me on the radio when you find out what flight she is on." He grabbed one of the radios and a handgun from a locker. "I'm going down to the floor and search for this Sinclair girl. You, you come with me." Then pointed to one of his men. The man immediately stood from his chair.

"Okay, boss."

"Keep searching the monitors. If you see anything out of the ordinary, call me and let me know about it."

"Okay, boss," the other man said.

"This Sinclair girl will not get away! Understand me!" Mobutu yelled. Moments later, he erupted through the security-office door on the floor of the departure area; he walked amongst the people, searching franticly for Jessica.

"You go over there and search for a tall, dark-haired white man," he commanded the guard. "Quickly, go!" Mobutu headed into the crowd, toward where he'd last seen Thomas. He went through the throng of people like a hyena hunting its prey. His eyes searched the many faces as he walked. He felt his handgun, hidden and secure under his jacket, making sure it would be easy to withdraw when needed. He slithered between people, and then, like a raven perched on a treetop, he saw his victim, standing in a boarding line, her ticket in hand. Next to her, a tall, dark-haired white man stood, with a carry-on bag slung over his shoulder. Mobutu circled around a group of Japanese tourists who waited to board their flight home and slowly walked behind her, eased the handgun into his right hand and concealed it near his side as he made his way through the crowd. His eyes were fixed on the back of her head as he came closer and closer. Within seconds, like a hyena ready to make its kill, he was right behind her with the gun pointed to the small of her back. The gunshot was muffled but loud enough to cause people around them to start screaming, in the confusion. Mobutu backed away and watched the girl lying on the floor. Her body twitched as she began to die and the man next to her knelt by her side, confused as to what had happened, he looked around for help, screaming for someone to get a doctor. Over and over he yelled as he held her limp body in his arms. As the man brushed the hair from her face, Mobutu realized he'd shot the wrong girl.

***

"Wonder what's going on over there?" Jessica said as they walked from the loading dock onto the departure floor. The crowds of people at the far end of the departure area were moving franticly as Mobutu's security men arrived to the scene. Mobutu walked off in search of his prey, sensing she was near.

"Come on, Jessica," Thomas said. "Whatever it is, they have it under control."

"I know. I was just wondering. I want to get out of here as much as you."

They went to the boarding agent and handed him their boarding passes. The man quickly looked at their passports and handed them back. Thomas grinned at the man and the man gave him a wink as if to say, "Wish I was leaving too."

Duncan glanced around the departure area, wondering what all the noise was about and felt uncomfortable knowing that their near escape on the road wasn't just some thugs out to rob them but something deeper. Ian would find out what was happening and advise the family. Duncan knew South Africa was changing and knew there would be some troubles yet after Apartheid. With the reconciliation counsel in the works and the hordes of people flooding to the new South Africa, there would certainly be troubles in the future.

"You're all set, row 16, seats A and B at gate 13. You'll be boarding in around fifteen minutes. Have a nice flight and enjoy your trip." The ticket agent handed Thomas both tickets. Thomas turned to find Jessica and Duncan saying their goodbyes and at the same moment, saw Mobutu walk passed them. Funny, Thomas thought, as he watched Mobutu walk off into the crowd. That guy's looking for someone. I'd hide from him too…asshole. He shook his head. "Come on, honey," he said to Jess. They all headed toward the entrance door and said their goodbyes one last time while Jessica and Thomas waited for their seats to be called. It was hot and humid in the departure area and Jessica began to feel weak from the heat. The line was long and she stood as long as she could before feeling completely overwhelmed by the atmosphere of the busy airport.

"I need to use the bathroom, Thomas," she said, wiping the sweat from her forehead. "I'm feeling nauseous again."

"Okay, Jess," Thomas rubbed her back. "Want me to come with you?"

"No…I'll be fine once I wash my face," she said. "I'm feeling a little hot."

"Well, if you could, make it fast…I think we'll be boarding in a few moments."

Jessica walked off into the crowd, across the departure area, feeling worn, tired and hot. It had been an emotional day and with all the strange events, her mother and Jara's deaths and the attack on the road to the airport, it began to take its toll on her ailing body. She began to feel dizzy. Faces seemed to blur and her path seemed a maze of people and luggage. She squinted as she approached the restrooms trying to discern between the ladies and men's, feeling nauseous and weak and knowing she'd make the restroom just in time to vomit. Her stomach turned and she could feel the pain building deep inside of her. Her legs felt weak and shaky. Her mind raced and her stomach trembled as if an earthquake was erupting deep inside her. As she walked, she reached out to people close to her but kept walking for she knew there was safe haven, away from the crowds, in the restroom ahead. She reached for the door, pushed it open with the little strength she had and stumbled to the toilet, falling to the hard cool floor.

***

Mobutu searched the crowds like a predator on the Serengeti looking for food. His nostrils flared as if he could smell her presence in the crowd, just as a predator picks the sick and weak as its prey; he stalked silently among the people, searching their faces as they made their way to their flights. It was like picking out a springbok among the wildebeests on a grassy plain. Jessica was white and her petite frame made it easier for him to discern her from the rest of the herd and chaos of the airport. But still Mobutu could not find her and his temper became unsettling.

"Control!" he yelled into the radio. "Control!"

"Yes, boss," came a reply.

"Anything on the girl?"

"No, boss…we're still searching the computer log. Some flights are heading out in a few minutes to America, but nothing on the Sinclair name is coming up."

"Keep checking!" Mobutu yelled angrily into the microphone. "What gates are the American flights?"

"Gate 13 is boarding in five minutes and gate 16 is boarding in twenty minutes boss."

Mobutu looked across the floor at the gate numbers. There in the distance were gates 13 and 16. He looked down into the herd of people and saw his mark. There in the distance, thirty yards away was Thomas, the man in the bathroom and the man that was with the girl on the day she arrived. He slowly began making his way through the crowd toward Thomas and Duncan as they unknowingly talked of the past events.

"Where the hell is she?" Thomas asked Duncan nervously. "They're beginning to board."

"That's my sister, always late…just like a woman." Duncan laughed. "Want me to get checking on her?"

"No." Thomas smiled, shaking his head. "I'll head over…hey, if they call row 16 and I'm not here, come and get us, okay?"

Thomas walked off into the crowd, toward the restrooms. Duncan looked around at the chaos and shook his head. "The new South Africa. We have a long way to go."

Thomas made his way through the crowd, searching for Jessica returning to the gate. As he approached the ladies room he noticed that the door was open and some of the native African's were talking franticly in their native language. He quickened his pace, knowing something was wrong. His heart raced as he entered the ladies' room. There lay Jessica on the floor, tucked into the fetal position, her arms across her stomach.

"Jess!" he yelled as he hurried to her side. "Jess…can you hear me!" He felt helpless and didn't know what to do. She didn't answer him but just lay there on the hard, cold floor, holding her stomach. Thomas looked around the room. One lone native African woman stood watching them. She seemed aware that something was wrong and motioned that she'd get help. With tears building in his eyes, Thomas nodded at her. "Get help…please get a doctor."

The woman ran from the room and headed across the departure floor in search of help. Before her, just off to the right of the bathroom walked Mobutu.

"Jess…they're getting help…hold on," Thomas cried, looking down into her eyes. She opened them as if to say something but couldn't. In her eyes were fear, pain and confusion.

"They're getting help, baby. Don't die on me. Please, God, don't let her die."

"What the hell!" Duncan yelled as he walked into the room. "What's happening?"

"She's sick…Duncan, get help fast." Thomas turned, tears in his eyes.

"What's the matter?"

"She's been sick, Duncan…get a doctor," Thomas said, holding her head in his lap. Duncan ran from the room and headed for the security office for help.

"Mr. Security! Mr. Security man!" the African woman yelled to Mobutu in her native Bantu language. "There's a woman sick in the ladies' room…she needs a doctor." Mobutu's eyes kept focused on the area were he saw Thomas. He ignored her comments and steadied his gaze on gate 13.

"Sir…sir…there is a woman sick in the bathroom and she needs help," the woman yelled again as she went toward Mobutu.

"Go away, woman!" Mobutu barked at her in anger. She stopped and looked at him in shock. Stunned, she pleaded once more. "She needs help."

"Miss, did you say someone was sick?" a man standing near the ticketing agent asked.

"Yes," she said in alarm. She turned away from Mobutu as he walked off into the crowd.

"I'm a doctor," the man said. "Where is she?"

"In the ladies room."

"Take me to her," he said in the Bantu dialect. The two went towards the ladies' room and quickly made their way to Jessica. Minutes later, Jessica and Thomas were heading to the Cape Town Regional Trauma Center.

CHAPTER 11

Thomas looked on as Jessica was rushed into the emergency room. Within minutes, he was alone as nurses and doctors moved about the hallway. Twice he heard, "Code Blue" screeched over the intercom. He knew what that meant and preyed it wasn't for Jessica. The room felt cold and empty, and he was scared, scared about what was happening to his girl, scared about what he knew would eventually happen because of the disease. But this was too soon and he felt helpless and alone without her at his side. He'd sat in emergency rooms before—when his fiancée died—and he had hoped to never return to such anguish and pain again. Again death was close at hand and he knew he'd never recover if he lost Jessica to the disease. This was his love, his girl and his life and he just wanted to live it with her.

He placed his hands over his eyes and cried. The tears ran down his face but he didn't care if anyone saw. "God, please help us. Please take care of Jess. I beg you, Father, please help her." His shoulders began to shake as the tears fell to the floor and his heart sank with thoughts of her being sick and alone. Duncan walked into the waiting room and sat next to him. Duncan felt helpless as well, but the only thing he could do was be there for them in this time of trouble.

Seconds turned into minutes and minutes into hours before anything was heard. A nurse came through the emergency-room doors and asked Thomas if he was Mr. Jennings. He nodded. She smiled softly giving some relief to their fears.

"Doctor Simi wanted you to know that your wife seems to be stabilizing. She's breathing better and is conscious. She asked for you. We'll let you know what's happening in a little while." She disappeared through the emergency-room doors.

An hour later the emergency-room doors swung open again. The tall, thin African doctor walked toward Thomas and Duncan. The sunlight beamed through the windows, lighting up the cold waiting area but Thomas saw no light in this day. The doctor could tell that Thomas had been crying and was deeply compassionate, as he approached, extending his hand in greeting.

"Mr. Jennings? I'm Doctor Simi." Thomas looked up at the doctor who stood in front of him. He hesitated but then reached out and shook the doctor's hand.

"How is she?"

"Your wife is doing well."

"Thank God," Thomas closed his eyes. She was alive! "Can I see her?"

"Well, she's sleeping now, but if you want to take a peek...it'll be okay."

"What happened?"

"She had a pancreatic attack and we found that her white-blood-cell count is extremely low."

"Will she be okay?"

"For now...but we...we...need to talk about something."

"What do you mean? The HIV?"

"Yes, Mr. Jennings," the doctor said, seeing Duncan's expression change.

"What are you saying?" Duncan exclaimed. "My sister doesn't have AIDS!"

"Duncan sit down," Thomas said softly. "Doctor, did she tell you everything?"

"Yes." Dr. Simi said, nodding.

"What the hell man," Duncan said. "Thomas, what the hell's going on, man?"

"Duncan," Thomas said sadly, "we just found out."

"Tell me!" Duncan said, his eyes beginning to fill. "Tell me my sister isn't dying." His lips began to quiver and he shook with anger.

"She got the disease when she was raped in Angola."

"No...no, Thomas! Please tell me she's..." Duncan wiped the tears from his face. He began to remember back to the night he found Jessica in the jail cell, the bloodstains, the ripped clothing and her battered body. He knew she'd been assaulted but never imagined it would come to this, come to his little sister dying this horrible death. He remembered covering her up, the guard with the arrow in his chest and the stench of death and decay in the cell.

"That's why we were heading to the States...to get medical treatment," Thomas said, lowering his head. Nothing more could be said and the moments passed in silence.

***

Jessica dreamed that she was walking, walking down a sandy white beach. It was warm, the sun was high in the afternoon sky and she watched the soft, rolling waves of the ocean break on the shoreline. She smiled when she saw the Drakensberge Mountains and laughed as she watched the seabirds play in the clear blue African sky. "It's a beautiful day!" she yelled to the sky with outstretched arms. Off in the distance she could see a lion, a Cape Lion, walking near her mother's and sister's graves. She knew the Cape Lion had returned to South Africa and it was a time for healing, a time for renewal and a time of life once again in the African land and in the world. She continued down the beach. The sand was warm and inviting under her feet as the seawater washed over them.

She looked down to find the large Cape Lion walking alongside her. Silently it walked, as if protecting her; large and proud, it walked with confidence, knowing that change was once again in Africa. She smiled and looked up to the heavens. The sky was crystal blue, not a cloud in sight, seagulls danced on the unseen forces that carried them to the roof of the world. She began to run slowly down the beach, her white sundress moved in the wind. Like a bird, she ran with her arms outstretched. Her feet lifted off the sand and she began to fly, higher and higher, dancing in the air as the seagulls did. She was happy and at peace and she knew her life was good, that she was in the world for a purpose, and that she played a small part in time. As she moved through the air, dancing on the unseen forces, a warm and loving voice spoke to her. It told her the secret of Gansbaai. Someday she would know when to tell the secret to the world and the world would be good once again.

***

The following morning, Thomas sat next to Jessica's bedside waiting for her to awaken. He'd been there for the whole time and watched her as she dreamed and tossed and turned during the night. She looked so peaceful now, he thought, as he slowly rubbed his hands over hers. She slowly opened her eyes and smiled at him.

"Hi," he smiled.

"Hi, Thomas. I knew you were here."

"You did?"

"Yes. I had a dream that a lion was walking by my side and was protecting me." She placed her fingers over his and held him. "Thanks, Thomas."

"For what? I didn't do anything."

"Yes, you did. She looked into his eyes: "You found me on the beach that day in Avon."

"I think you found me."

"No, Thomas...you don't understand, I was giving up," She said, as a tear ran from her eye. "I was done and that was going to be my last day."

"Last day in the States?"

"No. I was giving up," She said, as tears increased like raindrops on a cloudy day.

"Hey, hey...what are these tears I see?" He wiped them from her cheek. "Giving up? What do you mean give up? You're the strongest person I know." He brushed a strand of hair.

"I was giving up." She sobbed now.

"Hey, hey...come on, Sunshine...you're with me now...everything will be okay."

"No, Thomas, you don't understand. I'm not sad now. I know now that this was all meant to be, that *we* were meant to be. If it wasn't for us meeting and our life together, all this would never have happened."

"All of what?"

"I had a dream, Thomas. Things happened that I can't explain but I know are true." She slowly reached up and held him in her arms, rubbing the back of his head and looked him in the eyes. He held her close and strong. Her eyes were wide as he looked into them and he kissed her softly on the lips three times.

"It was a dream, Jess. You get some sleep before you become weak again and we'll get you out of here and home to the States. You had a pancreatic attack. Doctor Simi said you'll be alright in a few days and we can get out of here and head home."

"Tom." A warm, soft smile seemed to say it all. It was a comforting smile, a knowing smile, a confident smile. She had seldom called him Tom. "My home is here in South Africa. Here is where I belong, but you will go on." Thomas looked at her and grabbed her hand.

"What do you mean, I'll go on?"

The sun was shining outside and it was a promising day. Tears came as he looked at his girl, lying in the bed, bright-eyed and full of life. He loved her for that. He loved her for the life she gave and the love she had for people; she was life to him and, to many people, she was hope. He would never leave her. He would never leave Africa if she wanted to stay.

"Jessica, what are you saying? I'm not going anywhere without you, kiddo."

"There's a secret."

"A secret? You must have had some dream." He softly laughed. "What's the secret?"

***

She leaned close to his ear and whispered the secret she'd been told in the dream. The bright sunlight filled the room and silence filled the air about them. Moments passed as the two held each other tightly. Jessica ran her hand over his face, feeling every inch, as she looked deeply into his eyes. It was comforting to him. There was a peace in her eyes that showed like a thousand suns. Somehow, he knew that what she had said was true but he denied his feelings. He would need to find the doctor and make sure, out of his own curiosity. Dream or no dream, he would be with her till the end, till the end of time.

"I can't leave you like this, Jessica."

"You have to. It's not just about us. There's a bigger picture happening here. You have to go and find out."

"But you're sick and I need to be here with you. I can't leave you now."

He remembered back two years ago when he had left a hospital room one cold winter night. When he had returned, his girl had died and he swore never to let that happen again. Now, conflict raced through his mind and he'd need proof before leaving Jessica's side.

"Maybe I can try to head home to Gansbaai," Jessica said, "and if I become sick again, we could stop at Doctor Vieter's office in Hermanus. I hope you understand that, I have to stay here and help the people."

"It's *because* of these people that you're in this hospital, Jess." He replied emotionally. "You don't understand these..."

"Stop, Thomas," She abruptly said. "It's not anyone's fault that I'm here or anyone's fault that your fiancée died years ago...yes, I know what happened." She could see the pain and the tears building, the pain that had been deeply rooted for years, and she knew he held pain in his heart for the loss of his girl and knew that he was angry about her death.

"How did you know?"

"I found news clippings in a box in the closet in Avon."

"But why didn't you say something."

"Because it was your business, Thomas. I found them by accident and knew you'd tell me someday...if you needed too. Thomas—-it's not anyone's fault—-not black or white—-and certainly not your fault. " She said brushing her hand on the side of his face. She looked deeply into his eyes.

"There *are* bad people in this world, Thomas...but they come in many shapes and colors."

He stirred in his seat. "I know...but these people have caused so much trouble, Jess."

"You mean like the doctor who saved me last night or the Mamzibi you met in the Karoo. You see, Thomas, I know what loss is...I know what it feels like to lose someone you love. Get rid of this anger that's in your heart. You have so much to live for and so much to give. I know because I fell in love with you. I wouldn't fall in love with an evil man. You have a good heart and soul. Help it heal. There are good people and bad people in all races."

"I know Jess, I know. There's just so much anger in me because of it all." He clenched his teeth, slowly lowered his head to her heart and silently lay in her arms.

"Why?" He said softly. "Why do bad things happen?"

She brushed his hair with her fingers and kissed his head as he trembled in her arms. But the anger stayed deeply embedded in his heart and would not let go of his soul. Jessica handed Thomas a small box.

"What's this?"

"Open it! I bought it at the market a few weeks back."

He hesitated for a moment, and then opened the box. He pulled out a thin leather necklace and gold pendant. The pendant was shaped like a lion's head. The sunlight made it sparkle.

"Put it on," she said, and watched him slip it over his head. "Well, do you like it?"

"I do." He smiled again. "It fits perfectly." He hugged her and brushed her hair with his hand and kissed her softly on the lips.

***

Mobutu swung open the door and stormed into the room. His anger could be felt in the dim light of the security office. Two of his men jumped to attention, knowing their boss was angry, while another sat sleeping in his chair and didn't hear the crash of the door as it hit the wall. Mobutu glanced around the room and saw the man. He pulled the revolver from his belt and walked over to the sleeping guard. With one powerful blow, the butt of the revolver smashed across the guard's head, bringing a cracking sound to the still air. Blood spattered onto the monitors and desktops as the man fell to the floor. The other men watched in horror as Mobutu placed his boot on the man's neck and crushed it. Blood trickled from the guard's mouth and nostrils as he died.

"They got away, didn't they?" Mobutu said softly clenching his teeth in anger. "They got away!" He smashed his foot into the dead guard's body. The other two men sat motionless, shaking, hoping they'd not end up like the dead guard, but they were too scared to speak. Speaking would draw attention to themselves. In fact, any motion at all would turn Mobutu's anger their way.

"What are we doing here?" Mobutu walked toward them. "I'm asking you a question!" he said, smacking one of the guards on the back of the head.

"General…we're doing as you told us to do." The man quivered nervously protecting his head.

"If you were doing what I asked you to do, then we'd have these two white people in our grips, wouldn't we?"

"Yes, General."

"General." The other guard nervously replied. "We had some things happen while you were on the floor. There was a shooting near gate 16 about a half hour ago and we sent men down to inspect the area, and…and we had a girl, a white girl get sick in the bathrooms and had to call an ambulance to take her to the trauma center."

"*What* white girl…*what* girl…do you have it on tape?"

"Yes, General."

"Let's see it…quickly!"

150

The guard rewound the security tape to the point when the African woman was asking Mobutu for help. Mobutu watched closely as the tape revealed the doctor and the arrival of the medics.

"Speed it up!" Mobutu ordered angrily. "There, there...*there* they are," he said as he viewed Thomas and Duncan walking alongside the medics carrying Jessica to the waiting ambulance.

"You let her slip out!" he yelled at the top of his voice, smacking the guard on the head with the butt of his revolver. "You idiot!" Like a predator in the night, his crackling, sinister laugh could be heard. The predator smelled the blood of a sick animal and made for the door. He would make his kill before morning.

"I've got them now," he howled. "I'll do this myself."

***

Duncan came to Jessica's room and quietly watched while Jessica and Thomas held each other, seeing the love they had for each other. He knew his little sister as a strong, independent girl who loved life to the fullest. She always was the one who ventured out, away from the family and into the unknown. He recalled the time of their childhood when they lost her in an outdoor market. Conrad, Mary and the boys had searched everywhere for her. Hours passed and they feared the worst but just as they were about to contact the authorities, there she was, sitting with an old blind man. A witchdoctor of the Bantu people, old and worn with time he sat talking with her as she sat on the ground in front of him. She was nine years old, innocent to the evils around her and naïve to the ways of survival. Conrad had been upset with her for disappearing, until she told him the man had just been robbed. She'd given him fifty rand, the rand she'd saved for a month for the day at the market. Conrad hugged her and tried to explain that running off was wrong and that she could have gotten hurt, but Jessica truly believed that what she did was right, and that the old man needed help. As time went on and she grew, helping people seemed to become a constant and everyone, both black and white, knew her as a person who cared.

Duncan recalled the old man turning to Conrad and Mary as they began to walk away and saying something in the Bantu dialect but Duncan didn't know the language. Years later, as they were on safari in the Great Karoo, Conrad told them the story of the old man and what he'd said as they walked away. He told them the old blind man had said, "This little one will save the world one day, the great spirit in the sky has chosen her to heal the people." Duncan remembered his father telling the story and always wondered if there was more.

"Hey, you two. Howzit," he said as he entered the room.

"Hey, big brother."

"Hey, Duncan. Glad you're here," Thomas said, "I need you to look after my girl for a while. I'm going to find the doctor. I need to talk to him about something."

"Okay Thomas." Duncan looked at Jessica, who winked at him.

"Look Duncan, there's more going on here than you know." Thomas said.

"Tell me something I don't know."

"Right...so please promise me you'll take good care of her and protect her while I'm gone. I'm going to talk to the doctor and see if she could be released so we could head home to the estate."

"Okay...do you need my help with anything?"

"No. You just guard my girl with your life," Thomas replied jokingly. "I'll be back in a bit and then we'll get the hell out of here."

"But I don't understand?"

"It's okay, Duncan," Jessica interrupted. "Tom needs to do a few things before we try to leave for the States again."

Duncan frowned. "But Dad and Ian need to know what's going on too."

"I got that covered," Thomas said as he leaned over and kissed Jessica. "I'll call Dad at the estate and let him know what's going on. Any word from Ian?"

"No. Nobody has seen or heard from him. I called Dad and told him we were going to the hospital. I told him about the attack on the road and you seeing Ian in the bush. Dad said he hasn't seen Ian either."

"I hope he's okay," Jessica said, worried.

"I'm sure he's fine. He sure knows how to fight."

What was happening and why the rush, Duncan didn't know, but Jessica was with the plan, whatever it was, and she seemed happy and at peace and doing well. Duncan knew that they shared a special love and bond. He'd seen that look before as his parents looked into each other's eyes.

Thomas left the room and headed down the hall in search of Dr. Simi and a phone. Conrad needed to know what was happening and what might take place. Preparations needed to be made for another trip to the Great Karoo.

The lion was on the move and nothing would stand in his way. He'd do what his girl asked and he'd make sure that she'd have everything she needed to heal.

Dr. Simi stood at the nurses' station as Thomas approached. Thomas looked at the tall thin black man in his white doctor's jacket, stethoscope around his neck and pen in hand. Simi was talking with the station nurse. Thomas could not help but think about being home in the States and the seemingly more stable hospital system America had, compared to other foreign countries. He wished he and Jessica were on their way home to better medical treatment and medicines, but here they were and here they'd stay until Jessica was ready for the sixteen-hour flight.

"Hello, Mr. Jennings," the doctor said, without looking up from his writing. "What can I do for you?"

"I wanted to thank you for helping Jessica."

"She seems to be coming along fine from what I see."

"Yeah...thanks, but I need to get her home and I need to do it soon." Dr. Simi looked at Thomas and removed his glasses. He saw the importance of the matter and the concerned look on Thomas' face.

"She shouldn't be moved now," He replied. "She could have a relapse. We just made it this time but the disease is destroying her immune system, Mr. Jennings."

"I know, but I was hoping we could monitor her from Gansbaai, where she lives."

"Oh Gansbaai. I thought you were talking about flying her to the United States. That would be too long of a flight for her now."

"No, no, just to Gansbaai." Thomas grinned with relief. "I just want her to be home for now. She has a family doctor called Vieter. Do you know him?"

"We've crossed paths." Dr. Simi's expression seemed to change. "I know you're an American so I can say this without upsetting you, those old-time-Afrikaner doctors don't like people like me, so I try to stay away, if you know what I mean."

"Yeah, I do, in more ways than you think," Thomas replied.

"Okay, but I need to do a few more tests...blood work and things."

"Yeah...about that...look, she's no drug addict or gay person or anything. I mean, I read up a little about this disease, and I just want you to know."

"Mr. Jennings, the disease is spreading to all peoples and sexes of the world. I didn't assume that she, or you, were drug users...or gay." Simi smiled and put on his glasses. "The disease is effecting all races, religions and sexual orientations now. At first they thought it was only effecting the gay population, but we know different now."

"So there's no cure whatsoever?"

"Sorry to say, but no. There's medication, but it's too expensive for the poor people here. That's why I assume you were heading to America."

Thomas nodded.

"When she's ready," Simi replied, "get her to the United States and maybe you could stabilize the disease for now."

"That's what I was hoping to do."

"But let me say this to you. The disease is breaking down her immune system and her organs are starting to be affected."

"What do you mean?"

"She's had the disease for a few years now, since her trip to Angola." Simi said. "Even if a cure or medication was produced, she may not survive."

Thomas stared into the doctor's eyes and then looked to the floor. He could feel the truth in what the doctor said but didn't want to believe it. "Does she know this?" Thomas asked.

"No."

"Just help me get her home then," he said, looking up at Simi. "I need to get her closer to the Great Karoo."

"The Karoo!" Simi hesitated. "Why the Karoo?"

"She seems to think the cure for this disease is there," Thomas said eagerly. "Also, I need to have blood work done too. I need to get retested for the disease."

"Sure, Mr. Jennings," Simi said, "Let's get that done now and I can have the results back to you in a few days."

"No. I need them sooner than that."

"Why, what's the rush?"

"Because I'm going to look for this cure in the Karoo and, if I don't find it there, if I still have the disease, then I'll take my chances in flying back to the States instead." Simi knew Thomas was serious and needed to know the results of the tests he wanted done, but why, he thought to himself, why the Great Karoo?

"Let's get those tests done then. The soonest I can have the results back to you is in a few hours or so."

"Fine. Could you relay the results to Doctor Vieter? We're heading out to Gansbaai and then the Karoo. Vieter has the original blood tests and results from both Jessica and me."

"Sure, Mr. Jennings, I could do that."

With that the two walked off to the testing room and Dr. Simi drew blood from Thomas' arm. Afterwards, Thomas headed for the door but then turned to the doctor.

"Thanks, Doc," he said quietly.

"You're welcome, Mr. Jennings." Simi said, nodding. "I don't know what you're up to, but good luck. She seems like a fine girl."

***

Mobutu walked through the emergency room and headed for the nurses' station. His presence could be felt like an approaching storm as he walked rapidly passed the door guard and pushed open the door to the nurses' station. Like a strong wind of evil omen, he entered the room.

"Can I help you?" the nurse asked, startled by Mobutu. She glanced out her window at the guard, who shrugged his shoulders, signaling uncertainty as to what was happening. Mobutu closed the door behind him and stared at the nurse, his dark glasses hiding his evil gaze, but she could smell the stench of the man.

"Sir, I know who you are...but I need to know what you are doing in my office." She could sense his anger, beating like a thousand, ominous war drums.

"There was a girl admitted a few hours ago." His deep voice shook her. "Jessica Sinclair...what room is she in?" Nervously, the nurse searched the computer for information. Her hands began to shake and her heart began to beat faster. Mobutu stood quietly knowing that he was close. The light above their heads began to flicker and the nurse looked up at it as it blinked on and off.

"Well?" Mobutu barked.

"I'm searching, sir, but I'm not seeing any Jessica Sinclair on our roster," she mumbled nervously. "Could she be under another name?"

Mobutu trembled with hatred and his anger could be felt throughout the room as he leaned on her desk. These incompetent people deserved to die, he thought. "She was brought in from Cape Town International." He snarled.

"Two people were brought in from the airport. One lady was shot in the back and has now died," she said shaking.

"Yes, yes...and the other?" Mobutu barked abruptly.

"A Mrs. Jennings...Jessica Jennings."

"That's her! What room is she in? Quickly!"

The nurse's hands trembled at his tone and she couldn't seem to find the right keys to punch. After a few seconds of fumbling with the keyboard she revealed the room Jessica was in.

"Room 413, East."

The door closed behind Mobutu and she was limp with relief. The guard came into the nurses' station office a few moments later.

"You okay?" he asked. "That was the head of security for Cape Town. He's a tough man I hear." The nurse sat at her desk, hands over her eyes, trying to regain her calm. She turned to the guard to say something and noticed that the light above her was no longer flickering. She wondered about the man and wondered why he searched for the girl.

"I'm going out for a smoke," she said nervously as she tried to pick up her pack of cigarettes. Three times she tried but each time dropping the pack to the desk.

CHAPTER 12

Mobutu climbed up the stairs to the fourth floor and opened the hallway door. He came out into the hallway like an approaching thunderstorm. With force and anger, he proceeded down the long hall to room 413. There he'd find Jessica lying in bed, an easy prey...he'd make her death fast and quietly slip away into the night.

***

Jessica and Dr. Simi stood in the room, talking. It was getting late and the sun would be setting in a few hours.

"Okay, Mrs. Jennings, we're all done here...you can go." Simi smiled. "Take the medication I gave you for now, and when you're back in the States, get checked again."

"Thanks, Doc."

"If you could, drop me a line and let me know how you are doing?"

"I will. Doctor...I'm curious...are you from Angola?" she asked as she studied him.

"Yes. I attended the university there and studied medicine, as well. How'd you know?"

"Your accent. I worked with the Red Cross there, near Cacolo. A relief worker...a few years back."

"I know it well." Simi looked at her curiously. "So you're a relief worker." He nodded, thinking back to Angola. "Did you know a Doctor Hanson?" he asked. Jessica's expression changed and Simi knew he'd brought up something from the past. "Oh, sorry." He hesitated. "I guess you knew him."

"It's okay," she said. "John was a good friend of mine." She paused. "He was murdered."

"He was...I didn't know?"

"He was murdered by so-called rebels," she said, grabbing her things. Looking out the window, remembering that rainy day in Angola when she was on the floor of the truck and seeing John shot and falling to the muddy ground. She could feel the tears building in her eyes as she remembered the blood trickling from his head as he lay in the mud. "John," she whispered.

***

Thomas and Duncan sat at the far end of the room, each with his eyes closed. Jessica smiled as she looked at her brother and husband resting. She knew they'd been up all night, with Thomas next to her bedside.

"Wake up, guys." She tried to smile.

"Doctor, can I ask you something?" She turned back to Dr. Simi, who still stood in the doorway. "Why aren't you in Angola helping your people?

Dr. Simi took his glasses off and looked at Duncan and Jessica. He seemed thrown and hesitated, thinking for a moment, putting down Jessica's chart on the bed.

"My whole family were doctors. They were all killed during the civil war a few years back. I escaped...barely...my wife, children, were all killed."

"I'm sorry." She went up to him and hugged him and then went to the door. Duncan stood silently, knowing that she and Simi now had a certain bond between them.

"We all lost someone there." She looked into the distant horizon of her mind, remembering her friends in Angola, the children she'd helped to feed and aid. "Let's help heal these people, here, now, doctor," she said. "It's people like you who give others hope. This country needs to heal, as well."

"Thank you, Mrs. Jennings." Simi looked at her, nodded, and went down the hallway.

***

Moments later, Mobutu listened for noise from within the room. The hallway was quiet and little movement could be seen on the floor. In fact, no nurses could be seen and no doctors walked from room to room as one would see in a busy hospital. He could hear talking from inside the room and knew he'd have to kill more than one. He slowly removed his revolver and readied it. His hand gripped the handle tightly and his finger was placed securely on the trigger. He looked down the hall and then at the door.

"Can I help you?" came a commanding tone from down the hall. Mobutu turned to find a nurse standing at the far end. He hid the revolver at his side.

"No," he shouted. "I'm new with security. I'm checking these rooms... making rounds."

"Okay. Just checking." She walked away down the stairwell.

Mobutu threw open the door. A lone nurse stood talking to herself. Startled, she screamed, looked at Mobutu for a moment, then saw the gun in his hand. She threw up her hands in fright.

Mobutu looked around the room. Nobody but the nurse was there. Lowering his revolver to his side, he looked, angry and confused, at the African woman. "Where are the people who were here?"

She hesitated, scared, and fumbled with her words. Mobutu quickly raised the revolver and pointed it at her. "Where are the people, bitch?" he yelled. "Why is there nobody here?"

She stuttered and began to cry. "They nobody here, sir." she said in broken English. "This section closed, sir."

"Closed!" Mobutu yelled, "What do you mean, closed?"

She looked out the window to the other tower, the east tower of the hospital. "This tower closed...west tower closed." She closed her eyes and began to pray.

Mobutu looked out the window to the adjoining tower. There, in room 413 East, stood Jessica.

***

Jessica felt the hair on the back of her neck rise. Funny, she thought. Slowly she looked up at the window. Twenty yards away, in the west tower, stood Mobutu, angrily looking across the open space between the buildings. Their eyes met in the coldness of the moment. She could tell he knew she'd recognized him and that she was terrified.

"Oh my God! It's him!" Her hands flew to her mouth. Her knees began to quiver and buckle beneath her. Thomas and Duncan jumped in alarm as she yelled.

"What's the matter?" Thomas said.

"Mobutu!"

"Mobutu?" Thomas looked out the window, across to the opposite room, looking closer at the man who stood in the window, knowing who he was.

"That's the man from the airport, the man in the bathroom."

"We have to run." Jessica cried. "Oh my God...it's him!"

"What do you mean?" Duncan went to her, knowing she wasn't one to cry wolf, but he didn't understand.

"General Mobutu!" she replied. "The man who killed all the people in Angola, the man whose men raped me." She turned fearfully and looked out the window again, Mobutu was gone.

"Mobutu!" Simi said nervously standing in the doorway. "He's an evil man. What's he doing here?"

"He's out to kill me," Jessica cried. "That's what's been going on. We have to run."

The three ran from the room and down the hall. Jessica felt danger in the air and death closing in on them. She jabbed at the elevator button several times, anxiously waiting for the door to open.

"Come on! Come on, damn it!" Frustrated, she repeatedly pressed the button.

"Jessica, it's coming. Give it a second," Thomas said. "We'll be okay. Duncan and I are here. We'll take care of you."

Jessica turned to Thomas and began to cry. Her body shook as the tears rolled down her face.

"We'll be alright, trust me." Thomas tried to smile as he watched the indicator light signal that the elevator was approaching the fourth floor. The elevator door slid open and they descended to the lobby and ran from the building to the truck.

***

Doctor Simi stood in room 413, finishing his charts as Mobutu swung open the door, his revolver in hand as he looked around the room. He went to Simi, grabbing him by the throat and pushing him to the wall. Mobutu was breathing heavily and had a crazed look about him. His anger dimmed the sunlight that came in through the window.

"Where's the white bitch?" he yelled angrily. Simi's thin, muscular frame was no match for Mobutu's size and strength. Mobutu slammed Simi into the wall again and he gasped for air as Mobutu's large hand choked him.

"She ran," Simi, replied slowly fighting for what little air he could. He looked into Mobutu's eyes in fright and knew death was upon him. With a powerful thrust, Mobutu threw Simi to the floor. Simi's glasses smashed to pieces on the hard surface floor and his head smashed into the side of the hospital bed. As if lifting a small child, Mobutu picked him up and pushed Simi to the bed. Leaning over him, choking the life out of him, Mobutu knew he'd get answers before he killed this weak man.

"Where's the bitch?" he yelled once again, enraged, smashing Simi in the head with the butt of the revolver. Blood trickled down the side of Simi's face. Simi saw death before him, knew he'd die if he didn't answer Mobutu's questions. Thoughts raced through his mind as his heart felt fear and beat faster and faster.

"They went to Gansbaai," he answered reluctantly. Mobutu lessened his grip and Simi could finally breathe without restriction. His heart pounded. Still Mobutu's hand was around Simi's throat and Simi knew it could tighten once again at any moment. Fear filled his mind and he thought about all the people in Angola who had died by this man's hands. He knew who he was and knew he was not a man, but Death. The hell he had caused the people of Angola was heart wrenching. Simi felt sick to his stomach, remembering seeing his family slain, murdered and mutilated by this man and his men. They were no better than a pack of criminals, no better than vultures, and no better than wild dogs that scavenged the land and used others to prosper. He could hear the crackling laughter in the darkness of the night and knew this man was no better.

"Who's the man she was with?" Mobutu yelled.

"Her husband."

"Her husband?"

"He was going to Gansbaai too and then the Karoo." He hesitated nervously shaking. "To see Doctor Vieter."

"Why was she here? How is she sick?" Mobutu shook Simi.

Simi didn't know what to say. He could feel Mobutu's breath on his face and see the anger in his eyes. Fear filled his mind and he wanted to run but knew he was no match for the bigger, stronger man.

"Tell me!" Mobutu's grip tightened around Simi's neck. Simi choked, he had to talk or die. He was scared. He knew he could call the police once Mobutu left and help Jessica this way.

"They have HIV." Mobutu's grip lessened and Simi could breathe again. "Her husband has it too but he thinks they've found a cure in the Great Karoo." Mobutu's eyes seemed to drift away to another time and place. He was remembering back to Angola, his men and the night they raped and beat Jessica.

"We'll see about that," Mobutu yelled. "I'll make sure they both die this time. And *I'll* have this cure." He laughed.

Suddenly, Mobutu grabbed a pillow from the bed, placed it over Simi's face and began to smother Simi. Muffled sounds came from Simi, pleading for his life; Mobutu placed the revolver to the pillow above Simi's face.

There was a muffled sound. The white pillowcase and bed sheets began turning red. Simi's body slid to the floor as Mobutu walked from the room.

***

The hours passed as Conrad sat on the front porch, deep in thought. The sun had set behind the western horizon and night once again came to the African land. His gaze was fixed on the now orangey-red, distant sky as he remembered back to better times to Mary, the boys and Jessica, and the land he loved so much. He knew there was no stopping the changes in Africa. The rocking chair felt good, he thought. He had hoped he'd be sharing his later years with Mary, but now she was gone and he only had memories of her. The pain was heavy on his heart. They'd had good times and she had always said how much she loved him.

He had anger in his heart for the men who had killed her and the man Mobutu who hurt his little girl as well. He had thought the pain and hurt was over with the end of Apartheid but now knew there was still healing and growing to be done for his country, for the people of the land.

He watched the seagulls fly in from the ocean for the night. The cliffs and caves of the De Kelders would be humming with life as the night unfolded.

He walked to the edge of the porch as the stars began to appear in the eastern sky; Orion, the hunter had his sword and shield ready for battle and the next few days would bring bloodshed to the land once again. He looked toward the hill that now held the graves of Mary, Sarah and Jara and slowly walked up the hill to their graves.

***

Mobutu's anger built at knowing Jessica had slipped away once again but now he was even more determined to kill the girl and her husband, for he now knew she recognized him and would tell the authorities. Jessica, Thomas and Duncan may have escaped but Mobutu was close behind them as they drove to Gansbaai. He knew of the strong Afrikaans presence in the area and that it would be harder to kill the girl if she made it to the Afrikaner stronghold. He knew that the Afrikaners were tough, well- disciplined fighters and that he'd have to do it alone. The quiet fishing village would see his anger, but for now, he would head for Hermanus.

An hour later, Mobutu's truck stopped and he phoned his men back in Cape Town, instructing them to grab whatever firepower they could and make their way to Hermanus.

"Stay near enough so, if I need you, you could be here in a minute's notice." He barked.

"Yes, General," his man replied. "How many men do you want?"

"Bring at least twenty...armed and ready to fight," he commanded and hung up the phone. Mobutu looked around the dark streets of Hermanus and decided he'd hold up there till morning. "She's not getting away this time."

CHAPTER 13

I called your father and explained everything to him." Thomas told Jessica who sat on the bed near a window.

"Thanks, Thomas." She tried to smile. "He'd want to know everything. How'd he take it?"

"Okay...I think. He's a strong man. Everything will be okay."

"Yeah, I know. It's just that all this has happened because of me." She lowered her head and began to cry. Thomas went up to her and sat down next to her.

"Hey, hey, what's this?" He cracked a smile and rubbed her back. "It's not your fault." He felt for his girl, knowing she was feeling sad and tired.

"Mommy's murder! Jara's murder! It was because of me." Her tears increased. "I should have told everyone."

"We'll take care of this thing."

"No, Thomas. It's done. This man killed Mommy, Jara and John Hanson. John was a good person." She wiped the tears from her eyes. "He wanted me to leave when the troubles started but I didn't listen. I saw the smoke in the village and ran to help the people. Mobutu killed him. Daddy wanted me to leave the camp. He and my brothers visited me before the troubles started. Dad said he heard that there were problems in the country and that I should leave."

"Is this man that evil?"

"He's evil, Thomas, *evil*. I should have listened to them. We have to find this cure, Thomas." She looked up at him. "Promise me you'll find the Mamzibi and the cure, Tom."

"I promise." he nodded. "But we'll do it together, right?"

"Yeah, we'll do it together."

The door opened and Duncan came into the room. "I hid the truck behind Vieter's office in a dark corner of the lot. He must be doing well, his office is bigger than I remembered." He shrugged.

Thomas shook his head. "What the hell's the name of this place, anyway?"

"Hermanus."

"No, no, the hotel name."

"The Lion's Inn," Duncan said, taking food out of a bag. "Perfect for the lion king." He cracked a wry smile. "Original Kentucky Fried Chicken, with a side of Yankee beans."

"Just beans, Duncan...they're not, Yankee beans...just barbequed beans. I can't believe they have a KFC here in Africa. That's American capitalism for you."

"You probably paid a fortune for that box of chicken, man," Jessica said, gingerly shaking her head. "How many rand did you spend on that?"

"Enough for a small house in Saweto."

"In the states, some families eat that every day for dinner."

"Really?" Duncan looked at the box of chicken. "Maybe we should let the lion king buy next time."

"Funny, real funny, now throw the lion king some KFC before I rip your leg off. What's next, towering billboards with neon lights?"

"Can't say much for that hospital food last night. And, breakfast, what the hell was that, man?" Jessica intervened. "If being sick doesn't kill you, the food will."

Thomas and Duncan both looked at her and laughed. It had been a long day and tomorrow's ride to Gansbaai would be dangerous as well.

***

After a peaceful and quiet night at the Lion's Inn, the morning light broke over the Drakensberge Mountains, promising a clear and sunny day in Hermanus. As the sun rose, songbirds began to accompany its arrival with a beautiful revelry of song. It was indeed a promising day and Hermanus, nestled along the cliffs of South Africa, awoke with life. The turquoise blue ocean sparkled like a million diamonds as seabirds swayed in the clear blue sky. Tourists, up early, gathered for whale watching, waiting for the giant mammals to surface the illuminated blue water. The water spout, just off the cliffs, gurgled and shot the sea water high into the air as spectators watched from the rocks. The morning outdoor market became alive with tourists making their way to the docks and fishing museum near the boat launch.

Duncan was first to wake and headed out for coffee and cake. The ride from Hermanus to Gansbaai was an hour, give or take, and it would be dangerous, with Mobutu in pursuit. Thomas wanted to see Dr. Vieter about the test results that Dr. Simi took and then head out to the estate and off to the Great Karoo to find the Mamzibi and the mosquitoes. He needed to know for sure if Jessica's dream had meaning and was not just some mirage in her mind, constructed from the pain and suffering she'd endured. But in his heart, he felt she was right, and he'd still go to the Karoo and find the Mamzibi if she wanted him to.

Thomas looked out the window at the market below. The ocean's turquoise-blue water sparkled and sailboats could be seen off in the distance. "I like it here—it has a Mediterranean look to it," he said. He thought of the Blue Heron back home and the sailing he and Jessica did back in the States. He missed Avon-by-the-Sea, the place of his birth, never thinking he'd be so far from home. But the ocean brought him comfort and he knew he'd be home again sometime soon. There he'd build Jessica the house she had always wanted, a Cape Dutch Colonial, with a barn for horses. The land he had purchased in Gladstone, New Jersey, with its rolling green hills and crystal clear streams, was just the spot.

He remembered the picnic they'd had under the old chestnut tree and the story he told her about the virus that killed most of the chestnut trees in the United States. He thought about the virus that was killing Jessica, and him, and many people in the world. *Could her dream be true*, he thought. Could the Mamzibi mosquitoes hold the cure for HIV?

"Morning." Jessica smiled and reached for him as he stood near the window. "You look worried. What about?"

"Just about everything." He leaned over and kissed her. "Sleep well?"

"Yeah. I had another dream."

"Please tell me that yesterday was a dream."

"Sorry, Tom. That really happened."

"You're in a good mood."

"Yeah, I feel good." She hugged him with all her might.

"Hey, you're going to crush me!"

"Good." She kissed him over and over.

"What was your dream about this time?"

"Same as before."

"You sure about this…I mean, you sure about this…thing?" He looked into her eyes, brushed her hair from her face, and kissed her softly on the forehead. "You know I'd do anything for you, Jess."

"I know."

"We could head to the airport, and go back to the States?"

"I know, Tom. We need to do this one thing first. It's times like this that set people apart. We could run, but what would that do."

"I guess I knew you'd say that." He frowned. "It's just that we could get the medication we need in the States." His expression changed. "I don't want to lose you Jess."

"I'll always be with you, Thomas, no matter what happens, you and I will always be one soul."

"You scare me when you talk like that."

"Let's just do this one thing and then we can return to the United States for treatment, okay?"

"I guess I have no choice. When we get back, I'll build you that Cape

Dutch Colonial you always wanted. This is why I'm doing all this. It's for you, sunshine."

"Deal!" She exclaimed. "You'll still have your job. You had a month's vacation time stored up."

The door opened and Duncan came with coffee and breakfast cakes. "Hey, what's all this yelling I hear?" he joked.

"Thomas just said he's going to build me a home," she said, pushing Thomas away. "It better be *big*."

"We'll call it Chestnut Estates, and it'll be the biggest house you ever saw."

"Well, before you get to building the African queen here a new house, let's eat and then see Doctor Vieter. I'll ready the truck for the ride to Gansbaai. I'm sure Dad has everything prepared for the ride to the Karoo. I hope he had a chance to talk to, Ian."

"I want to see the market before we leave," Jessica said excitedly.

"Yeah, like we have time for that!" Thomas said.

"But look how beautiful the day is. We have to go to the market to buy some Bolton for the ride."

Thomas laughed. "You mean that dried up who—knows—what—meat. It has flies all over it. And you said the hospital food was bad."

"Bolton's good," Duncan interrupted, "we should get a little for the ride."

"Well, come on, girl, it's already ten o'clock," Thomas said smacking her on the butt. "Get showered and let's get out of here."

The market buzzed with life as Jessica and Thomas searched for the Bolton. The merchants watched them as they passed, some beginning to haggle and others sitting quietly, knowing they had a long, hot day ahead of them. The makeshift tents, vibrant colors and noise of all sorts—trucks, birds, haggling merchants and children—filled the market with excitement. Thomas thought of places like Morocco and movies like "Casablanca." He smiled as Jessica haggled over African masks and carved wood animals that the merchants were selling. Sometimes she spoke Afrikaans and other times she spoke Xhosa, a native language of some South African people.

"Here's the Bolton," She said turning to him.

"Great. Hey, nice flies too," he said shaking his head. "They seem to be enjoying it." Jessica gave him an evil look.

"You'll like it, you liked the Boerewors."

"Yea, the sausage was pretty good."

"Boerewors...not sausage, Braai...not barbeque. When we get back to the States, then it's sausage and barbeque, Mr. Jennings."

"Oh, excuse me, Mrs. Jennings—Mrs. Sassy Ass!" Thomas laughed. He knew she was a proud South African and that she was true Boer blood. She was a true Afrikaner, and he loved her for it and would profess it to the world if he had to.

"It's getting hot," he said looking up at the sky. They should be heading toward Gansbaai but she was enjoying the day and he admired her for her love of life.

"There's Doctor Vieter's office," Thomas said. Jessica didn't answer but was staring at a crowd of people near the cliffs.

"Look, Thomas. There must be whales. Let's go have a look. Come on." She turned and walked toward the crowd. Thomas looked toward the cliffs and then toward Dr. Vieter's office, split between the two. He wanted to find out the results of the tests and head out to Gansbaai. He looked at Jessica as she began crossing the street.

"Jess!" he yelled. She turned and smiled. "I'm going to Vieter's office." He pointed to the building.

"I'll meet you there—-find Duncan, okay?" She shouted to him and trotted across the street to the cliffs as he headed to Dr. Vieter's office.

The congregation of Africans, tourists and local people were standing looking over the cliffs as Jessica approached. As she made her way through the crowd to the front, she overheard one of the African men say, "One less settler." Her heart sank, knowing what that meant and she instinctively felt fear in her heart. Slowly pushing the eager spectators to the side, she neared the wall.

***

Thomas went into Dr. Vieter's office and waited for the receptionist. "It figures!" He thought frowning. Always when you're in a rush. Then he said loudly, "Hello!" but nobody could be seen or heard. "Hello!" he said again a little louder. Where the hell are these people, he thought. This place would be out of business in a week back in the States. He reluctantly walked around the receptionist station and passed two examination rooms. From his previous visit, he knew Dr. Vieter's office was in the back and imagined he'd find Dr. Vieter sleeping on his lunch break.

The clock on the wall read one o'clock and he shook his head, knowing they needed to be on the road to Gansbaai.

"Hello?" he said, turning a corner. The door was ajar and light could be seen from inside the room.

"Hello, Dr. Vieter?" He knocked on the door. There was no reply. He slowly pushed the door open a little further.

"Oh my God!" he gasped. There on the floor was Dr. Vieter and Nurse Helen, dead, both with blood running from their heads, both faces with the look of horror, still on their faces; eyes opened, cold and lifeless. He turned to run but something caught his eye and he knew he had to stop.

167

He looked down at the floor. There, scattered on the rug, were sheets of paper. He saw his name on one. Under his name, just to the left of the sheet, were the results. He looked around the room. He looked behind him to the door and down the hall. He could feel the coldness in the air. He could smell the blood, the death and the horror about him. It was no longer a sunny day in his mind. The birds could not be heard and the ocean had become dark and cold. He leaned over and picked up the sheets of paper. On it was typed: Initial testing revealed patient tested positive for the HIV. Secondary testing revealed negative to having the virus. Patient believes that the cure for the HIV/AIDS can be found in the Great Karoo. Patient believes that a fluid transfer from a species of mosquito (only found in the Great Karoo) may hold the cure for the disease. Initial testing is yet to be done.

Thomas dropped the letter and ran for the door. Fear filled his mind, knowing Jessica was alone and unprotected.

***

Jessica could hear the sirens approaching in the distance. Someone, thank God, had called an ambulance.

She leaned over the wall and then screamed. Far below was Duncan, broken and mangled on the jagged rocks. The seawater washed over his body as it crashed on the rocks. Jessica looked at the surrounding people, who looked at her in shock. All the faces seemed the same. She looked around, confused and disorientated.

"Someone get help!" she cried. "Please...get help."

She searched the crowd of people for Thomas and saw, several feet away, Mobutu stalking her, moving in for the kill, not caring about who saw. He tried to force his way through the crowd, but was blocked. Again, she quickly searched the crowd for Thomas. She didn't see him and fear filled her mind. *Was he dead also,* she thought. She turned and ran for the museum, pushing people out of her way. She looked back and saw Mobutu was gone. She ran as fast as she could. Evil had found her and death was at her heels.

As the door museum closed behind her, she saw it was gloomy and dark, and realized that everyone must be at the cliff, or trying to retrieve Duncan's body from the water. She moved to the back of the museum and tried the back door. It was locked. She now knew she was trapped and that there was only one way out, the door she'd come in by.

She headed for the front of the museum and was coming around a corner when the front door squeaked. Seeing a flash of sunlight, she knew someone had entered the building and that she was no longer alone. She moved slowly to the darkest corner of the museum, creeping across the wooden floor in fear of making noise, and crouched down low near one of the exhibits. Surrounding her was the horror of man's brutality toward the great mammals of the sea. Pictures of past whale hunts hung on the walls, mighty whale jaws, dried and preserved, hung from the ceiling, and harpoons, instruments of the whales' death, lined the walls in the darkness. She could smell the years of decay in the rotting wood, the decomposing flesh of yesterday's living and the horror of man's past atrocities.

The sound of my heart beating, and the inhaling and exhaling of my breathing are making too much noise, she thought. She tried to close her mouth and breath through her nose, but still felt the danger of being in the small, dimly lit museum. She could hear the soft footsteps through the hallways, and the creaking of the wood floor, like the snapping of twigs. It helped her know where the man was in the darkness. She thought about the African night, sometimes so dark and forbidding, so silent and calm, it became deafening to her soul. Now *she* was the prey, and knew she'd made a mistake by running from the herd, now off on her own, caught in the darkness like a sickly antelope, to be slaughtered by her pursuer. She remembered the lion's roar that dark night in Angola, how silent the night became after the roar. She too would need to be silent, to hide in the overgrown grass, and hope that the killer would move on, thinking she'd found a way out. She listened in the shadows hoping someone would arrive to help.

Mobutu moved through the halls, searching every corner for Jessica. He knew she was in the building, and alone. His silver-plated-revolver could barely be seen. Only now and again, a display light caught its metal sending a razor like ray across the room. He knew the squeaking floorboards gave his position away, but the girl was no match for him. He felt no fear and wanted to kill the girl and find this cure he read about at the doctor's office. He would be a hero to his people and would establish a secure spot in this new country. With each step he could be closer to killing the white whore. He picked up an old harpoon with his other hand and waited for movement.

Jessica watched the darkness for signs; she would not be caught off guard by her attacker and would calculate her escape. She knew she needed to tell the authorities about this man Mobutu, and of what he had done to so many people in Angola and of the murders of her mother and Jara. She would make sure he was put in prison or expelled from her country. She looked around her, to the displays, the ceiling and the walls. There, two feet away, on the wall, was a small machete hanging loosely. She looked right, then left and reached for the machete. It was too far a reach and she knew she'd have to move from the darkness of her cover to get it. She could hear her own heart beating in the darkness. She looked about her. She tried to listen for the creaking of the wood under his feet but none could be heard.

Suddenly the door opened and a gush of sunlight flashed through the museum. Then the door closed. There was nothing but silence, no creaking of the floor and no people walking around. She tilted her head, leaning her ear to the front of the museum, listening to the darkness again. *He's left,* she said to herself, *he must have thought I got out, or didn't see me come in here.* She looked at the small machete and reached for it, knowing that she still needed to protect herself. Grabbing its handle, she slowly took it from the wall and pulled it to her. As she did, she looked around to listen for any noise. Just then, the tip of the machete hit a small ship's bell and the bell rang as the two metals collided.

Mobutu swiftly moved in the direction of the ringing bell. He'd found his prey and would make his kill. He fired into the corner where Jessica crouched. Her body tensed with the sound of the gunshot and fear suffused her mind. The bullet missed. Just off to her left, it lodged in the wall next to her head. She readied the cold steel and waited to attack. Mobutu quickly walked to the noise but stopped four feet in front of her. He seemed to search the darkness and she could just make out the outline of the man.

The front door swung open and Thomas rushed into the room. Mobutu quickly turned and looked at him. The light from the outside flashed into Mobutu's eyes, blinding him. He pointed the revolver at Thomas and fired. The bullet lodged in Thomas' right thigh.

"Tom, run!" Jessica shouted as Mobutu fired again but this time missed his target. Thomas jumped out of the doorway into the museum. The door slammed and darkness filled the room once again. Jessica stood up and swung the machete at Mobutu, hitting him in the arm. Mobutu fired again, but missed. She ran from the corner and headed for the door.

"Tom!" she shouted, as she neared the door.

"Jess!" Thomas stood up to meet her. "I'm hit!" They opened the door.

Mobutu angrily threw the harpoon at them, but it missed and pierced the wall of the museum. He fired again, hoping to hit his mark. The shots exploded as Thomas and Jessica ran from the darkness. The bullet missed Thomas but hit Jessica squarely in the middle back. She fell to the ground just outside the door, which slammed behind them.

"Jess, no...Jess," Thomas yelled, looking at the door and then to the watching crowd up near the wall. "Get help! Get help!" The blood began to soak the front and back of Jessica's shirt. He looked into her eyes. She was badly hurt and he needed to move. He picked her up in his arms and began limping toward the path to the wall. When he was ten feet away from the museum, the door opened and Mobutu stepped out.

A shot rang out once more. A bullet hit Thomas again, this time in the other thigh. Blood shot from the hole as he and Jessica fell to the ground.

Holding his arm, Mobutu began to walk toward them. Thomas tried to stand and protect Jessica but Mobutu fired yet again. The bullet hit Thomas in the shoulder and he fell to the ground next to Jessica. Their eyes met.

"I'm sorry," she whispered. "I love you." Her eyes closed.

"Jess!" Thomas gasped, in tears. He knew she was dying. Not a sound could be heard and he didn't care if he died too. Mobutu closed in on them as Thomas turned and looked into his evil stare. Mobutu drew closer and closer and raised his gun to fire.

"You fuckin' animal!" Thomas shouted in defiance. He saw Mobutu's arm was bleeding, blood drenching his shirt. "I hope you fuckin' die!"

Mobutu now stood above them.

"You will die first!" he said through his teeth.

"Fuck you! You fuckin' piece of shit!"

Mobutu raised the revolver higher, pointed it at Thomas' head and prepared to fire. Behind him Ian leaped forward, his arm crashing down on Mobutu's. The gun fell to the ground, spinning toward Thomas.

Mobutu swung around and attacked Ian with all the force he had. Ian quickly twisted his body as Mobutu swung at him, grasping Mobutu's arm and forcefully struck him in the neck with his hand.

Mobutu coughed as his head lowered, then suddenly kicked Ian in the side of the leg and Ian fell to the ground. Mobutu unsheathed a commando dagger and swung it at Ian, just missing Ian's face and neck. Ian kicked up at Mobutu, forcing him back to the museum wall where the harpoon lay waiting.

Shock filled Mobutu's eyes as he slowly looked down. Protruding from his chest was the harpoon he had so wanted to end Jessica's life with. The steel now dripped the blood of an evil man. Ian now stood in front of him. "Now you know the anger in my soul," he said as he slashed Mobutu's throat from left to right. Mobutu's head dropped to his chest. He was dead.

Ian turned and raced to Jessica and Thomas. Thomas held his dying girl in his arms. As she looked into Thomas' eyes, her lip quivered and her gaze became far-off. Darkness was overcoming her and she knew that her time had come, that her life here was over. She had lived and had made a difference.

"Thomas." She softly uttered, touching her stomach. "I'm pregnant," she said as a single stream of tear ran down her face.

"We're getting help. Hold on, Jess."

"Thomas, find the cure...find the cure and let the world know," she said with her last breath. Her eyes closed and her soul ascended.

CHAPTER 14

The soft ocean breeze blew warmer on the first day of spring. Two summers had come and gone since Jessica's death. The smell of life was in the air, and the bright blue sky showed the coming renewal of the land. It was a sunny day, with long, thin, streaking white clouds high above. Thomas watched the coastline as the truck made its way to Gansbaai and the deserted beach. He watched the seabirds dance high above in the unseen air currents and sadly remembered Jessica telling him that it was God's hand that held them so high. *Everything that happens, happens for a reason*, she'd say, and he now knew she was right. For better or for worse, there was a higher power to this world that he now tried to understand.

"We'll be there in about ten minutes," Conrad said.

"Okay, Dad."

"Hey, Tom," Pete said, placing his hand on Tom's shoulder from the back seat of the truck, "how'd you find the Mamzibi and the mosquitoes again?"

"Pete," Conrad interrupted, "we couldn't find them for three weeks. We searched everywhere but couldn't find any tracks, *or* the canyon."

"So what happened? How did you find the mosquitoes, on your own?"

Thomas looked out the window of the truck as it made its way down the road.

"Just before we were going to leave," he said, "I remembered the gold lion's head necklace Jessica gave me. I took it off and stuck it on a stick on top of the lion rock Jessica and I found when we were in the Karoo on safari. We called the rock, hope of the lion."

"So what happened?"

"The next morning, as the sun came over the eastern horizon, its light made the gold sparkle, making a beacon of sorts. Within hours, we were surrounded by the Mamzibi."

"So the cure for this HIV disease is in the mosquitoes?"

"Yeah," Conrad replied. "It seems that every time one of these mosquitoes bites, it injects a virus into its prey, but unlike many other viruses, it doesn't hurt humans; this virus completely destroys the HIV. It just kills it off."

"Why don't all other mosquitoes do it, as well?" Pete said.

"Probably because they're different, Pete," Conrad said. "There are about three thousand species of mosquitoes in the world, scientists say. I guess this species, being from an unpopulated and different place, evolved differently. It had to protect what little food supply it had, so it evolved in such a way that its bite was enough to keep other insects away from its food. Just like the animals and insects of Madagascar, and the Galapagos Islands, they just evolved in a different way."

"That's amazing!" Pete said. "Amazing...who knows what else is lying out there? I mean, the cure was right in our back yard."

"It could have been in anyone's back yard. I think it's a lesson from the Great Spirit," Conrad said, squinting as the setting sun beamed through the window of the truck. It was just above the western horizon and would be setting in an hour or two. "A lesson for mankind to watch out for other living things and respect all life. Who knows what other cures are out there, and who knows what other diseases may pop up in man's future. The world now knows of the cure, the name Great Karoo, Gansbaai and, Jessica Sinclair." He quietly remembered Jessica. Soon her ashes would be thrown to the wind and ocean on the deserted beach of Gansbaai. "Once again life comes out of Africa," he said in a distant voice.

Thomas sat looking out the window of the truck, remembering what Jessica had told him about the secret of Gansbaai, and that she was that secret. Her life was meant to be, and her soul was one with the spirit of nature. That whatever happened, it was a blessing of God, a gift for mankind.

The truck pulled up to the dunes. Thomas, Conrad and Pete got out of the truck and headed for the beach with Jessica's ashes. It was a sad day for them and they walked slowly over the dunes and rocks that lined their way. As they crossed over the last dune, Thomas suddenly stopped. There, standing on the dunes, were hundreds of people holding candles.

"What are these people doing here?" he said. Conrad and Pete looked out over the sand. Their ears were met with the soft humming of the people, singing a new African song; it rolled like the waves and moved with the air.

"I think they're here for Jessica," Conrad said, looking out over the sandy beach. "She gave the world a great gift. They are calling her the healing blood of Gansbaai."

"I had wanted to be alone." Thomas looked out over the dunes at the people. Candles flickered in the soft breeze and the ocean's crashing waves mixed with the sound of song.

"Go, Thomas." Conrad smiled. "This is for you and Jessica. Go and give her to the wind." He placed his hand on Thomas' arm and then touched the urn of ashes. He paused for a moment as he looked at the urn and Thomas could see the tears building in his eyes.

"Go on, Thomas."

Tom went toward the ocean as the sun lowered in the sky. The sound of life was about him and he began to cry. He stopped and looked out over the water, remembering holding Jessica in his arms and kissing her face. As he remembered, a small tribal boy came to his side. Thomas looked down at the boy who looked up at him.

"She was my friend." The small boy smiled. "Your lady was my friend." The boy reached and grabbed Thomas' hand and smiled broadly. There was innocence in his eyes. Tom looked down at him, and began to sob. He knelt in front of the boy, lowering his head. The boy hugged him.

"She is okay," the tribal boy said, "she is with the Great Spirit now." Tom hugged the boy, and as he did, he felt the years of hatred rush from his body. He once again could feel love for all mankind. He looked into the boy's eyes and smiled.

"You are my friend now?" the boy asked.

"Yes," Tom said, placing his hand on the boys shoulder. "I am your friend." He stood and saw, behind the boy, stood a Mamzibi warrior. The warrior was taller than the other Mamzibi.

"She was my friend," the warrior said, in a deep voice. "I saw her spirit when I was a boy, many years ago, in the land of thirst."

"The Karoo," Thomas said, looking at the man's bow and quiver of arrows. "She saw you too. She remembered you standing on the rock."

"I tried to protect her when I could," the man said, grabbing his bow, which was slung across his chest.

"Thank you." Thomas extended his hand. The Mamzibi warrior reached out and grasped it.

Thomas turned and slowly walked down the beach. As he did, the crowd parted and Ian came through, with other Mamzibi. Ian stopped. He silently nodded to Thomas. Thomas knew his silence, and respected him for it. Thomas knew the love Ian held for his sister and the pain he had in his heart. Thomas turned to the orangey glow of the setting sun. The turquoise-blue water and the darkening of the eastern sky were about him. Life was about him, and life would continue in the African land, and the world. He could feel the difference in the air and in his heart; it radiated life. He knew this was the moment to let her ashes to the winds. He undid the top of the urn and cast the ashes to the sky. As if by magic, they seemed to glide with the wind, down the beach, circling for a moment, and then lifting to the blue sky. The warm wind blew from across the ocean as the blue waves brought life to the African coast.

In front of him, as if in a different dimension, stood Jessica, Sarah and a small boy. He had wavy blond hair and big brown eyes. They stood there looking at Thomas as he looked down the beach, remembering his girl.

In the soft warm African breeze could be heard a whisper: "Look, there's Daddy."

"Daddy." The boy reached out to Thomas.

"He can't see us now, honey." She said sadly. "Soon, honey...soon, he'll be with us."

"Who are all these people, Sarah?" Jessica said looking to the dunes. "Why have they come?"

"They've come because of you, Jessica. These are the people of the world. They have been given a great gift of life, and you have helped bring them this gift."

"I understand now," she said, looking at her sister. "Look, there's Grandma." Jessica smiled at her son. He turned and saw Mary walking toward them.

"Grandma," he cried, running toward Mary's open arms.

"I'll miss him, Sarah."

"I know, Jessica. You'll be with him again someday. He will never forget you. Your two souls are one till the end of time. The great changing has happened, and now is the time for renewal of life."

The End.

Made in the USA